The Night the Dancing Stopped
The Nosy Chicks Mysteries Book 1
*The debut novel in a new young adult
mystery series*

Pat Meece Davis

Falling Waters Publishing

Falling Waters Publishing 2014
patmeecedavis.author@gmail.com
http://patmeecedavis.com

Dedicated to my six children,
the loves of my life,
Jeffrey, Matthew, Nathaniel,
Paige, Dominique, Kylie

Chapter One

"Hey, y'all, come here and take a look," I said, keeping my binoculars steady on my next door neighbor's window.

"What now, Amy?" Kristen said in a flat voice, eyes closed, body sprawled on her cot. "Vikki doing her pole dance again?"

"Uh-uh. Something different. She's practicing a new runway walk and rocking hot pink shorts and a matching top. Not only that, she's strung colored twinkling lights among the clear twinkling ones. Kind of dizzying but festive. I'd say Vikki got a major dose of inspiration. The new *Cosmo* must've hit the stands." At the mention of *Cosmo*, Kristen rolled off her cot, landed on all fours and, without bothering to stand up, baby-crawled the few feet to my cot.

Oblivious to what Kristen and I were talking about, Brit lay on the third cot, flipping pages on her Kindle and following her role model, fictional attorney Melissa Eagle, as she led yet another triumphant campaign for justice. Judging by the

1

cover, Melissa was not only brainy but blessed with a drop-dead body, something else she and Brit shared besides the love of law.

"Brit, come *on*," I said, throwing some barbs into my voice. She attempted Kristen's rolling maneuver and missed. With arms and legs askew and a black, curly ponytail bobbing up and down, she thudded when she hit the floor. Kristen and I laughed while Brit struggled to right herself.

When she got halfway vertical, I said, "Turn off the lamp, Brit, so I can open the curtains." Stretching to her full height of five feet, she flipped the switch and limped across the room.

Brit and Kristen piled onto my cot and, in my dark hideaway, we perched on our knees and propped our arms on the windowsill as we'd often done in the six months since newlyweds Vikki and Justin moved next door to me.

Best friends since kindergarten, Brit, Kristen and I were with pride and without equal, the three nosiest seventeen-year-olds in our small Great Smoky Mountains town of Sugar Liquor, North Carolina. Naturally, when I'd discovered Vikki's impromptu theatrics, I enthusiastically introduced Brit and Kristen to Peeping Tom-ism, our default entertainment on slow nights, which included most nights in our snoozing little burg.

Back when Vikki and Justin were in high school, I wasn't friends with them or anything even close because they were three years older than I was. The year they were seniors, I was a naïve freshman who eagerly and discreetly scoped out their on-again, off-again romance and developed an over-the-top interest in the couple.

Justin came across as laid-back and even-tempered, but Vikki's fickle mood swings, coming out of nowhere, generated a lot of spicy entries for my journal. After scrutinizing Vikki and Justin's high school quarrels, followed by makeup sessions in hallway corners, I couldn't believe my good luck when they moved next door to me. I could eyeball their racy adult lives from the privacy of my hideaway. A binocular focus away. How convenient was that?

Vikki and Justin lived on the third floor of a large, square house that had been converted into apartments. Oblivious that anyone could see in windows that high off the ground and their bedroom window being on the side of the building instead of the front, they never closed their blinds.

What Vikki and Justin failed to take into account was that my rambling Victorian house had a small, single room on the third floor, properly called a cupola by my parents and claimed as a hideaway by me. Windows wrapping around the cupola's four sides and my house set on a little knoll provided me with a commanding view of the neighborhood, my small town version of Alfred Hitchcock's film, *Rear Window*. Having been brainwashed into becoming a classic movie fan at an early age by my parents, I wove films and their characters into my everyday life, casting myself in the Jimmy Stewart binocular-wielding snooper role and Kristen as the cool Grace Kelly blonde. Brit got stuck with the leftover character, the wacky visiting nurse.

Cloaked in the darkness of night, we perched on our knees on my cot, noses pressed against the window screen, cheeks caressed by cool mountain breezes, and waited during a Vikki-initiated intermission while she fiddled with the lights. The twinkling rate zipped back and forth.

Settling on the max speed, Vikki moved to her usual starting spot at the far side of the room. "Show time, y'all," I said to Kristen and Brit.

Vikki unleashed a new runway persona, a ghoulish, non-blinking, super-model stare, maintaining a steady focus on a vague, distant object. High-stepping in measured strides, she allowed ample time for Justin to admire each shapely leg. As she pranced, Vikki rolled her hips from side to side in a seductive sway.

When she neared the window, Vikki turned and sashayed out of our line of vision, reappearing at her starting spot a few minutes later. Flipping a night gown over her head, a ripple of sheer, short and sizzling hot pink lace shimmied over her body.

Intrigued as I was by her costume upgrade, my life-long struggle with motion sickness brought on by most anything that moved kicked in. My vision blurred and my head spun faster than Vikki's dancing. I saw doubles of her. Double scary. No way was this world ready for two Vikkis. I closed my eyes to shut out the twinkling lights and grasped the window sill to slow me down.

Having seen all of Vikki I could take at one sitting, I closed the cupola's blackout curtains. Curtains personally selected by me at Big Lots based on minimum cost and maximum thickness to protect the secret location of my hideaway.

Brit got up and switched the lamp on. "You look weird, Amy. You aren't going to puke, are you?"

"I'll be okay now that the lights stopped twinkling," I said, feeling more woozy than I admitted. "You know something? I'm getting tired of Vikki and Justin. Same old, same old."

"Me too, but Vikki's pink nightgown is hot," Kristen said. "Is it in that *Victoria's Secret* catalog you just got?"

"I don't remember." Endless pages of sexy garments ran together.

Settling down on her cot, Kristen prepared, as I'd seen her do many times, to drift into her private cyberspace to unravel the glitches of her latest computer challenge. "Watching Vikki wasn't worth the effort of scooting over to the window," she said, scrunching her eyes and closing them. With her thinking face on, she wiggled the rest of her body into a comfy position, head lolling to one side, toes digging their way under the blanket.

"Ditto," Brit said, standing in the middle of the room, rubbing her arm. "I banged up my knee and nearly broke my wrist for nothing. Except the pink nightgown. I like it." In need of comfort after her clumsy mishap, Brit took her time choosing one of my DVR-ed episodes of *Pretty Little Liars*. She turned up the sound and flopped onto her cot.

I lay down on my cot with my sweet Hildy cuddled beside me. I named my gray and white cat after a bright, ambitious newspaper reporter in an old Cary Grant movie filmed before women were making it as reporters. Hildy was way ahead of her time, my kind of girl, and Cary Grant's *My Girl Friday*.

Ready to put Vikki and Justin out of my mind, I picked up my journal to enter the day's happenings, beginning with Vikki's runway prance and dance show. I stared at the waiting page, pen poised in the air, my brain blank. Although the scene I'd been watching next door looked typical for Vikki and Justin, something was amiss in Newlywed-ville.

Something too vague to jump out at me. Closing my eyes tightly, I willed the oddity to materialize. Crap. Nothing.

"Turn off the light again," I said to Brit, who was nearest the switch.

"You just said you were tired of snooping on Vikki and Justin," Brit said with a snort.

"Never mind what I said. I want to take another look."

"Damn, Amy, make up your mind," Kristen said, turning her head and forcing her eyes open enough to drill a hole through me. I glared back but I couldn't muster up Kristen's intensity. Kristen owned the intensity in any room she occupied.

Brit switched off the light. "Come on, y'all. Something's out of whack," I said, using one of my grandma's favorite expressions. "Help me figure out what it is." To exaggerate their annoyance, Brit and Kristen stood, exchanged their best bored looks and moseyed back to my cot.

Balanced on our knees again, we watched the couple's bedroom window. When that didn't resolve my angst, I said, "Get your binoculars." I'd installed wall hooks above our cots to keep our binocs handy. Without having to move, I reached for mine. "Get with it, girls."

Brit sighed, noisy and drawn-out. Kristen yawned, mouth hanging open. Their not-so-subtle responses made sure I knew they weren't interested in a Vikki encore.

It was back to the same old dirty dancing but with a twist. Vikki added a hot pink negligee that matched her gown.

"Wow," Brit said. "Awesome."

Kristen laughed and clapped her hands. "Rock

it, Vikki."

After seeing more than enough hot pink lace for one evening, my friends drifted into boredom. I was thinking of joining them when it whacked me over the head. "Oh, my gosh. Y'all see what I see?"

Kristen didn't because she wasn't even looking. Believing the darkness hid her from my observation, she'd put her thinking face back on and was freewheeling through cyberspace. I gave her a hefty elbow in the ribs. Ticked off at being plucked out of orbit, she made a big deal of turning her head slowly toward Vikki's bedroom window.

Standing buck-naked, except for strings of Mardi Gras beads around his neck, and with his back to the window and to us, Justin waved his arms wildly, encouraging Vikki to put more pizzazz into her dancing.

Kristen's face leaped from blank to super-animated in one second. The wicked gleam in her eye signaled me she got it. "Way to go, Amy," she said, giving me a high-five.

Brit's puzzled frown said she didn't get it. "Don't you see?" I said. "That's not Justin. Justin's hair is medium brown, this dude has dark hair. Justin's shorter and his butt's not nearly that tight. Lord knows I've seen his butt from enough angles to recognize it anywhere."

"You're right, Amy," Brit said. "That's not Justin. I thought I could've picked him out of a sea of asses."

"Unique metaphor, Brit," I said laughing. Kristen's vacant look told me *metaphor* wasn't in her cyberspace dictionary, and she didn't care anyway.

"Do you realize what this means?" My friends didn't answer, keeping their mouths shut and their binocs fixed on the anonymous, unidentified butt that we unanimously agreed didn't belong to Justin. Forced to answer my own question, I said. "This means that Sugar Liquor's sexiest bride is screwing around after only being married six months." Who would've guessed? Not me, for sure. Vikki excelled in off-the-wall behavior but this was out there, even for her.

"The reason we didn't notice that the man in the bedroom wasn't Justin is because we're always focusing on Vikki's cute little outfits and sexy moves," Kristen said. "Vikki's the star of her Vegas show. Justin's like us, part of the audience watching Vikki cavort around the bedroom." Not that we'd ignored eye-popping views of Justin in his birthday suit, but Vikki was the designated headliner.

"Do y'all think this is the first time Vikki's messed around?" Brit asked.

"I doubt it," I said, having converted to being a major cynic when it came to matters of Vikki's virtue. "Just the first time I caught her."

I waited and watched through my binoculars, hoping the Justin impostor would turn around so I could see who he was. He didn't. Show time ended without seeing his face. Vikki turned off the lights.

I closed my curtains and Brit turned the lamp on. One by one, in slow motion, we flopped down on our cots. Disillusioned and deflated, I summed up my disappointment. "This is so pathetic. Vikki the Vixen, undisputed winner of the hottest bride of the year, is just another two-timing wife."

Brit channel-surfed the TV, found nothing and clicked to a DVR-ed episode of *Glee*. This choice suited Kristen so she settled down to watch it too. As for me, I had some writing to do. My discovery of

Vikki having a boyfriend was worthy of a new chapter in my journal.

For a dull Monday night, this was looking like a page turner.

***

Red and blue lights rotating across Kristen's and Brit's sleeping faces woke me. On second thought, maybe I'd been caught up in a bizarre nightmare brought on by too much triple chocolate ice cream followed by too many nacho chips and spicy salsa. But real shouting voices, sirens winding down, and car doors slamming came through the window screen.

Leaping up and craning my neck to see outside, I jumped to the floor, yelling at Kristen and Brit. "Get up. There's a police car and ambulance at the apartment building. Put on your flip-flops. Let's go." With my untied sneaker laces clinking on the wooden treads, I took the stairs two at a time. Kristen followed, right on my tail. I heard a thump behind Kristen. Brit tripped on the first step, I guessed. A single flip-flop gliding silently past me to the bottom of the stairs proved me right.

"Shhh," I said, holding up my hand for them to slow down when we reached the second floor where my parents slept. Their room was on the opposite side of the house from the police uproar. "I hope the commotion doesn't wake them, at least not until I've had a chance to get the low-down on what's going on," I said in a whisper. My folks would put the stops to my middle of the night investigation in a hurry. Intruding into a neighbor's misery didn't exist in their respectable, mannerly world. I, on the other hand, thrived on meddling in other people's business. I was real-life proof that two negatives make a positive. Or, depending on the perspective, two positives make a negative.

As soon as I hit the first floor, I picked up the pace and rushed out the back door. Brit and Kristen raced behind me. My mother's lush flower garden between our house and the apartment building forced me to hit the brakes. Brit and Kristen followed my lead as I zig-zagged along a stone path, dodging Mom's plentiful plantings of leg-ripping, arm-slashing thorny rose bushes.

"Be on the look out for Mike," I told my friends. My well-established and proudly earned reputation for showing up immediately at the scene of local calamities with Brit and Kristen in tow, not to mention my recent crime-solving success, would have Mike Kilpatrick, chief of police, on the alert for me. He hadn't taken it well, not well at all, when I beat his officers to identifying and catching a group of teen hoodlum burglars.

Getting credit for bagging those low lifes fueled my longing for adventure and intensified my ambition to be a news reporter. I wasn't particular what kind. I liked magazines, online, newspapers, television, especially CNN International or BBC. I wanted to travel the globe, thread my way into the middle of cataclysmic events and report on topics of international magnitude. While a camera live-streamed my face and breaking news to the citizens of the world, I'd stand serene and speak in a calm, confident voice as bombs dropped around me. My vision of my future was so vivid, I could almost hear the explosions and smell the smoke.

The police chief wasn't into my career plans at

all. With his hyper-intolerance for nosy spectators in general and me in particular, he'd relish sending me and my little detecting force scurrying for home.

I put the chief out of my mind for the time being. Mom's arbors and trellises, overgrown with roses and blossoming vines, provided cover, allowing me and my friends to get close to the action next door without being discovered. Brit, Kristen and I had a prime viewing spot from my mother's garden with our feet firmly and legally planted on my own property.

Lights shining through the apartment building windows, stark outdoor security lights and flashing emergency vehicle lights gave the driveway the look of a carnival without any music or laughter. In addition to the police car and ambulance I'd seen from the cupola, I spotted a second police car. Did it arrive while the three of us were hustling down the steps or did I miss seeing it in my half-asleep stupor? The ambulance was backed up close to the building, ready to receive a patient for a short but guaranteed speedy ride to the hospital. With Ron Bryant at the wheel, the town ambulance only had two speeds-- idling and flat-out.

The apartments in the building opened off a stairway leading from the central front door. The ambulance parked in front of it didn't offer a hint which of the building's occupants was in peril. Mostly I worried about Georgia and Clyde Ashworth, my sweet elderly neighbors. I feared one of them was at the unfortunate center of this commotion.

"Uh-oh," Brit said, ducking her head even though she was already hidden by darkness and foliage. "Uncle Mike's here." She grabbed my arm with a bruising grip. Brit's uncle and my nemesis,

11

Chief Mike Kilpatrick, sprinted out the front door of the apartment building. Yeah, Mike wouldn't be here in the middle of the night if this wasn't a big case. Cut-off jeans, a *Grateful Dead* t-shirt and flip-flops confirmed he'd been hastily summoned to the scene. I'd never seen our impeccable chief not properly decked out while on duty. Mike was a stickler for protocol, a by-the-book kind of guy.

Mike stopped beside the open rear of the ambulance, huddling with serious-faced, sober-minded Ron who'd been driving the ambulance as fast as it could whiz through the streets of Sugar Liquor all my life. An oncoming white blur topped by flashing lights, accompanied by a deafening siren was all the warning residents got that Ron was on a call. Locals knew to get out of his way or risk ending up as a hood ornament on the ambulance.

Ron did the talking. Mike listened, standing slightly stooped, eyes staring at the ground, one hand fiddling with the door handle. I couldn't hear what Ron was saying but Mike, who usually peppered people with impatient questions, didn't say a word. For once, his mouth stayed closed.

As for Ron, there could only be one of two reasons he was standing out here talking to Mike instead of being inside the building helping his partner administer emergency care. Either the patient recovered or was beyond needing help. When Ron stopped talking, Mike looked up, his face defined by gloom. He slapped his palm hard against the door of the ambulance and disappeared inside the building.

Chapter Two

One look at her Uncle Mike's reaction and Brit's eyes filled with tears. "Miss Georgia or Mr. Clyde's dead," she said.

My eyes watered too but I wasn't ready to accept Brit's dire conclusion. "As far as I know, they don't have any life-threatening issues other than a little hazardous forgetfulness."

Everybody in town sympathized with the old couple when their son forced them to move into a first floor apartment next door to me. Their escalating difficulties managing their large home down the street came to a head one morning when Mr. Clyde struck up a philosophical conversation with a telemarketer and left a pan of bacon sizzling on the hot stove. When Miss Georgia came to Mr. Clyde's rescue to help put out the grease fire, the two of them succeeded in igniting the kitchen curtains which Miss Georgia heroically yanked down and doused in the sink.

Of course, when Miss Georgia and Mr. Clyde consented to move into the apartment building, their son had to do some fast-talking to convince the other tenants that their lives, pets and possessions were safe from geriatric torching. To cinch the deal, Mr. Clyde was permanently banned from all cooking activities. Miss Georgia, still allowed kitchen privileges, turned up at neighbors' houses on a frequent schedule with a plate of freshly baked chocolate chip cookies. Other than Miss Georgia and Mr. Clyde's one unfortunate experience with pyrotechnics, they were a sweet and thoughtful couple and my eyes stung at the thought either of them might be in jeopardy.

"Y'all are such dorks," Kristen said bluntly.

"Kristen, you don't have any feelings. I happen to like Mr. Clyde and Miss Georgia." I flung the words at her.

"For God's sake, nothing's wrong with them. Both of them are sitting on a garden bench on the other side of the driveway. Clear as day. If y'all stopped bawling and opened your eyes, you'd see. And, FYI, I like them too."

Sure enough, through my teary eyes, I focused on the couple huddled together, seriously rattled-looking but definitely alive. "Maybe they started another fire," Brit said.

"Oh, right. At two o'clock in the morning? Do you honestly think Mr. Clyde sneaked in the kitchen and started frying bacon at this hour? Besides, the fire truck's not over there." Its absence sealed Kristen's argument.

Relieved that Mr. Clyde hadn't started another fire, I let out the breath I'd been holding. If he repeated that fiasco, his neighbors in the other apartments would have his skinny ass evicted, and I didn't want the couple to move.

I dearly loved Miss Georgia and Mr. Clyde, as

little southern girls are taught to address special members of the older generation. "Let's go talk to them. They'll know what's happening," I said to my fellow snoopers.

"Don't let Uncle Mike see us," Brit whispered. Kristen rolled her eyes at me, a sure sign she was pissed at Brit for pointing out the obvious. I let it pass. We had a big enough problem with Mike and his fellow officers crawling all over the place without squabbling among ourselves. Getting from my mother's garden to the other side of the driveway where Miss Georgia and Mr. Clyde sat challenged my planning skills. Police officers and medical personnel swarmed everywhere, making official faces, giving orders to each other, exchanging documents, talking on their radios, going back and forth to their vehicles, opening and closing car doors, carrying mysterious cases into the building.

"This sucks," I said. "We can't make it across the driveway. There's too much open space between vehicles. Somebody'll spot us, for sure." A minute later, the deal was on. The three of us went at each other about how to get to Miss Georgia and Mr. Clyde's bench. As usual, each of us had an opinion on how to handle whatever situation we faced. Generally, we ending up taking bits and pieces of each plan and hoped they'd mesh into a workable strategy which rarely happened.

"Hush and follow me." I ignored Kristen's and Brit's open mouths, tongues primed to object. Hunched down, I crept through Mom's garden toward the street, staying parallel with the apartment house's driveway.

"Hold on a minute," Brit said before I'd made three steps. "One of your mother's frigging rose bushes is stuck to my pajama leg." Standing on opposite sides of Brit, Kristen and I bent over to look at the same time and cracked heads. We staggered backwards, moaning in pain. "I swear, y'all are no help," Brit said, grumbling. "I can't even move and y'all are screwing around."

"Shut up, Brit, or we'll leave you here." I cringed. Kristen wasn't good at subtlety. Brit was on the losing end of this fight so she buttoned it but Kristen wasn't about to give it a rest. "You're so self-centered. Amy and I were trying to help you, you fool. Our heads really whacked each other. Man, I got a goose egg coming up already." Kristen touched her forehead and grimaced. I hugged her, apologizing repeatedly. She got the worst of the collision.

Brit, who was too caught up in her own predicament to sympathize with Kristen, had good reason to be worried although she didn't know how much. Her initial squirming to free herself from the rose bush had stretched the knit fabric of her pajama bottoms so that a sizeable piece was twisted over and around the thorns. Kristen and I took turns trying to tease the fabric loose but no way was it going to give. So without consulting Brit and keeping my fingers clear of the thorns, I gave the fabric a yank, and it came loose with a noisy rip. It was either that or leave Brit grafted to the rose bush as Kristen threatened.

With Brit free, I headed for the street and crossed to the far side where I darted down the sidewalk in the shadows of trees and bushes. Brit and Kristen, sniping at each other in whispers, followed. Hurrying past the driveway abuzz with police and medical personnel, we re-crossed the street and walked along the edge of a neighboring yard until we could approach Mr. Clyde and Miss Georgia from behind.

"Miss Georgia," I said, squatting behind her so I couldn't be seen by the police in the driveway. Miss Georgia jerked her head in my direction so quickly, I worried my abrupt appearance might bring on a heart attack.

A tough old bird, she recovered quickly. "What are you young'uns doin' out here in the middle of the night?" Before I could answer, she nudged Mr. Clyde. "Look, Honey, Amy and Brit and Kristen are here."

Mr. Clyde turned around and nodded somberly at us. "Awful, ain't it?" was all he said.

"What happened?" I asked. "I was having a sleepover in my cupola. Sirens and flashing lights woke me up. The three of us came over here as fast as we could."

"Oh, girls. Clyde's tellin' the truth. It's awful bad. I don't think I'm able to talk about it." She turned to Mr. Clyde. "Tell the girls what happened, Honey."

He shook his head. Mr. Clyde's eyes, brilliant blue and usually sparkling with mischief at the anticipation of passing on a silly joke or funny story had lost their joy. I'd never seen him so down.

"Miss Georgia," Brit said brusquely, "Uncle Mike's liable to catch us here any minute. For God's sake, tell us what's going on before he throws us headfirst back into Amy's mother's briar patch. You know how Mike feels about Amy. And me and Kristen, by association."

Brit's no-nonsense tone took Miss Georgia by surprise. She ran her fingers though her *Sunrise*

Copper hair, stopped sputtering, straightened her plump, rounded shoulders and swallowed in a loud gulp. Although no one else was near, Miss Georgia's voice was soft as if to keep this a secret between her and Mr. Clyde and the three of us. I scooted closer to the couple with my head resting against Mr. Clyde's back. Touching him comforted me. Plus, I could hear Miss Georgia above the clamor in the driveway. I motioned Brit and Kristen closer and they huddled against Miss Georgia.

"Well, you see, girls, I was sound asleep but something woke me up. A crashin' racket. Clyde wasn't in the bed so I figured he was in the bathroom and dropped something. I listened but I didn't hear him or the noise again so I decided I must've been dreamin'. I went back to sleep before Clyde came back to bed. I don't know how much later it was, but, Lord have mercy, I woke up again and there was no mistakin' this time that someone, a man, was yellin' at the top of his lungs. Even Clyde, as sound as he sleeps, popped wide awake, didn't you, Honey?"

"You betcha. I threw my bathrobe on and went a-runnin' out in the hall. It didn't take me but a minute to figure out it was somebody upstairs who was a-doin' all the yellin'."

"Who?" I asked while he caught his breath.

"Young Justin Wilson. I reckon y'all know him and little Vikki." I nodded without mentioning how well we knew the couple.

"What was Justin yelling about?" Kristin asked.

"He wanted somebody to call an ambulance for Vikki. By this time, everybody in the buildin' could hear Justin and they all come out in the hallway. Ethan Matos, that young fellow who lives on the second floor came out of his apartment with his cellphone in his hand and called *911*."

"Did Justin say what was wrong with Vikki?" I asked.

"I couldn't hear him 'cause everybody was in a uproar, me and Georgia included. We were a-yellin' up to him and a-askin' if Vikki was sick or hurt or what. I offered to bring her aspirin, Pepto-Bismol, Band-Aids. Anything I could think of to he'p her feel better. God, what a noise. I doubt Justin could make sense of a word a-bein' said to him. Nobody else made a move to he'p the poor boy so me and Georgia started toward the steps. Ethan must've had the same idea 'cause he passed us and beat us upstairs.

"By the time me and Georgia got to the third floor, Justin was in the bedroom a-kneelin' over poor Vikki. She was a-layin' on the floor, still as could be. Justin kept a-talkin' to her but it didn't look to me like she heard him. Ethan was a-kneelin' on the other side of Vikki a-doin' that CPR stuff. Justin was beside hisself with worry. He kept a-beggin' Ethan to he'p her. Me and Georgia didn't know what to do so we just stood there like fools.

"Barbara Allison, who lives across the hall from Justin and Vikki, came a-hurryin' over too. She sleeps with the TV on for company so she didn't hear Justin when he first started a-screamin'. Barbara don't know nothin' about CPR so she wasn't no he'p either.

"Ethan kept on a-tryin' to bring Vikki around. Justin couldn't get hisself together to do nothing besides cry like a baby. Poor fellow. I know Ethan was wore out because he was a-havin' to do all the work by hisself. I felt terrible bad I didn't know how to he'p him.

"Thank the Good Lord, Ron and Buddy came a-flyin' up the steps and took over. With them there, me and Georgia was in the way so we come back downstairs and set down out here on this bench. Barbara came down the stairs with us."

"Where is she?" I asked, looking around the yard. "I don't see her."

"She wanted to be by herself. She's a-settin' in the garden. I know 'cause I keep a-seein' her cigarette light up when she takes a draw. Chain smokin' to calm her nerves, I reckon. She's awful upset 'cause she liked Vikki. Them two was pretty friendly." Mr. Clyde paused and added, "Poor little Vikki didn't look good. She didn't look a bit good."

"So what happened to her? Is she going to be okay?" I asked.

"We ain't heard nothin'. There's a lot of a-comin' and a-goin' but no news." When he finished speaking, Mr. Clyde's mouth twitched. I thought he was going to cry. If he started, we'd all start and never stop bawling.

Brit, Kristen and I stayed put in our hiding place behind Miss Georgia and Mr. Clyde. I murmured soothing words to the couple and to my friends. "Vikki was young, healthy and vivacious. Nothing serious could've happened to her." I was trying to convince myself too.

I poked my head between Miss Georgia and Mr. Clyde far enough that I could see what was happening. The police had emptied the building of its residents. Poor Myra McJunkin who lived on the first floor across from Miss Georgia and Mr. Clyde and partially handicapped from arthritis sat in her wheel chair in the driveway. Gigi, Myra's little white curly-haired, yappy dog, perched on her lap. Her perky little dog face drooped in bewilderment. For once in her life, Gigi clammed up. Sandy, Myra's caretaker and Gigi's walker, leaned against a nearby wall sending messages on her cellphone.

Tommy and Rachel Miller, a middle-aged, overweight, truck-driving couple, who made long cross-country runs and lived on the second floor, spoke softly to each other as they sat on the steps leading to the garden.

Where was this Ethan person? The one who performed CPR on Vikki. I didn't see anybody who could be him.

I asked Miss Georgia if she wanted to go to my house to lie down and rest. "No, I have to wait until I know how Vikki is," she said. I understood. I couldn't leave either. Brit and Kristen said they were staying too.

Suddenly a hush fell over the crowd of officials standing in the driveway. I knew something big was about to happen so I raised myself to my knees for a better view. Miss Georgia and Mr. Clyde seemed unaware that I'd wedged my head between them. Brit and Kristen scooted away from me toward the ends of the bench so they could see around the couple's shoulders. We didn't have to worry about being seen. Nobody looked our way. All eyes were on the front door of the building.

Ron came down the stairs slowly and deliberately, guiding the front end of a gurney. Buddy handled the back part. A sliver of hot pink lace, caught in the zipper of the body bag, dangled wispily as the gurney moved along.

Inside that grotesque bag, wearing her hot pink night gown, was Vikki.

Chapter Three

Those of us who were seated rose to our feet and watched in stunned silence while Ron and Buddy loaded Vikki's body into the back of the ambulance. Brit and Kristen stood beside me, shoulders sagging, faces as forlorn as Gigi's. Ron climbed behind the wheel and, for the first time in my memory, he didn't turn on the flashing lights and siren and roar off at full speed. Instead, he pulled gently down the driveway as if he were hauling fragile crystal. In southern small town fashion, the police officers and medical personnel stopped what they were doing, faced the ambulance, removed their hats and stood still as a show of respect to the deceased.

Vikki's neighbors, steeped in mountain tradition, stood in courteous silence, looking more in control than I imagined they felt. Even Myra forced her hunched frame to a half-standing position, braced herself against her wheelchair with one hand and clutched bewildered Gigi in the other.

Tears ran down Miss Georgia's wrinkled old cheeks. In an effort to comfort her, I gave her a sympathetic hug. "I'm ready to go inside now, girls. Little Vikki didn't make it," she said in a quivering voice. Mr. Clyde left Miss Georgia for a moment and spoke to a policeman who nodded at him. Mr. Clyde returned to where we waited and mumbled a hoarse good-night to us. He took Georgia by the arm and led her slowly toward the front door.

Myra's meager strength gave way and she slumped into her wheelchair, her face twisted in physical and emotional pain. Her valiant effort to stand up to say good-bye to her young neighbor drained her strength. Sandy signed off her cellphone and pushed the wheelchair carrying Myra and Gigi behind Mr. Clyde and Miss Georgia. Nearby neighbors, awakened by blaring sirens on their quiet street, milled around the driveway, whispering, wiping tears, wondering what happened.

Kristen, Brit and I sat down, leaning against Miss Georgia and Mr. Clyde's vacated bench, backs to the driveway, out of sight of the police, huddled together, not knowing what to make of Vikki's death. Too dazed to think, I followed Gigi's example and kept quiet.

Although the night air was unseasonably warm, a shiver ran through my body, prompting me to snuggle closer to Brit and Kristen. Vikki's death rattled me. Badly. How could a twenty-one year old woman who'd been dancing like Miley Cyrus a few hours ago die so quickly? The causes of sudden death scrolled through my head. Heart attack? Stroke? Blood clot? Those sounded like old folks' diseases. Not something that could happen to Vikki.

Accident? I had a horrible thought. Maybe Vikki

got electrocuted by her rigged-up light system. But that didn't add up. She used wonky combinations of lights all the time and nothing happened.

I'd never known anyone in my age group who'd died in an accident except a girl younger than I who was killed in a car crash several years ago. I'd barely known her. Of course, I didn't know Vikki very well either except from observing her in high school and watching her prance and dance around her bedroom night after night showing off for Justin or, as I'd discovered this evening, for some other guy. Strange as it was, my binocular intrusion into Vikki's nightly activities had made her part of my life.

Huddled close to Brit and Kristen, I began to warm up. In fact, I shot right past warm to hot. Brit's and Kristen's foreheads *glistened*. That refined word for sweating came from Kristen's great-aunt during a visit from Savannah. 'Southern ladies don't perspire, they glisten,' she told us. Figuring I too was beginning to glisten, I scooted away to give myself a little cooling-off space.

The police raced back and forth from their patrol cars to Vikki and Justin's apartment but their scurrying didn't tell me anything about what happened to Vikki. With all the lights on in her apartment, I could see the officers moving about but, because they were on the third floor, all I could see was heads bobbing past the windows.

Enough waiting. I had to do something. If I didn't, I'd end up sitting on the ground behind this dumb bench, glistening the rest of the night. I asked my friends for suggestions, knowingly initiating another raucous decision-making session. Kristen, a quick thinker, came up with an idea to pitch to us. "Why don't we sneak to the other side of the building so we can see in Vikki's bedroom window? Mr. Clyde said she was lying on her bedroom floor."

"*Un problema*," I said. "From down here on the ground, we can't see anything on the third floor except heads, regardless of which room it is. Heads don't tell us anything."

"Why don't we go back to the cupola where we'll have a straight shot right into Vikki's bedroom?" Brit said. "With our binocs, it'll be like when we're watching her dance." Kristen shook her head. "What's wrong with my idea?" Brit asked, bristling for a fight.

I answered before she and Kristen had a chance to get going at each other. "If we go back to the cupola, we'll miss what's happening here in the driveway," I told them. "At least, here we can see what the officers are doing."

An idea came to me. "Hey, get up and be ready to make a move."

Kristen gave me the eye squinch, digging in her heels, waiting for details before she decided if she wanted to go along with me. Brit, face screwed up in annoyance, was shooting Kristen cold stares for nixing her idea.

Dude, it strained my patience to keep them apart. Of the three of us, I was the one who should be lacking *gets along well with others* skills since I was an only child but it was Brit and Kristen with multiple siblings who blew up our riffs and then kept them aloft with plenty of hot air. My twelve years' experience keeping them separated would pay off some day. I might never win a Pulitzer for journalism but I was shoo-in for the Nobel Peace Prize.

Without saying anything more to Brit and

Kristen, I got up, stretched my muscles and joints that had become stiff from sitting.

It wasn't long until Mike came out of the building. Time to act. I strode briskly across the driveway and intercepted him before he reached his vehicle. Kristen followed me but Brit didn't budge. Leery of getting Mike riled up, I understood her reluctance to cause a family row. I didn't blame her for not joining my chat with the chief.

"Well, well, I was getting worried about y'all," Mike drawled, sarcasm flowing.

In spite of his negative greeting, I couldn't stop myself from sighing in silence and taking a few well-spent seconds admiring how movie-star gorgeous Mike Kilpatrick was. Medium height and super-muscular from working out at the gym, Mike had dark curly hair, big brown observant eyes, a perfect tan from his outdoorsy lifestyle and a cheerful word and friendly smile for everyone except lawbreakers and me. Mike was as perfect as if he'd been sculpted by Michelangelo on his best day.

Almost every female in Sugar Liquor had a thing for our hunk of a police chief at one time or another. Mine happened when I was fourteen and he was twenty-two. He'd just graduated from college and returned home to join the police force. The uniform did it for me and a lot of other girls and women too.

Fortunately, my short-lived infatuation wore off in a few weeks. With Brit being one of my two best friends, she and I ran into Mike all the time, and I felt so uncomfortable in his presence. Like, he knew. No way did I ever tell Brit or Kristen. It would've grossed Brit out. Kristen would've blurted it during one of her snits. That secret stayed with me.

"Well, well. All this commotion next door to the

girl wonder detective," Mike said, looking directly at me without flashing his public relations smile, "and you nowhere in sight. I was about ready to issue a missing persons alert. Looks like it won't be necessary since you're here as I expected, trying to stick your nose where it doesn't belong."

"Mike, please tell me what happened to Vikki." I said, ignoring his insult. "I saw Ron bring her down."

"How'd you know it was Vikki?" Mike asked, scowling at me.

Brit wouldn't want her uncle to know about us spying on Vikki so Kristen spoke up. "Miss Georgia and Mr. Clyde told us about going up to the apartment. They said Vikki was lying on the floor, unresponsive, unconscious."

"Y'all happen to know anything about what happened up there tonight?" he asked, nodding toward Vikki's apartment on the top floor of the building. Donning his hard-ass cop face to intimidate us, he drilled both of us with his piercing eyes. His lips were clamped tight by his aggravation at seeing us and a hunch that we knew something he didn't and should. I wondered if Mike was born suspicious or if the combination of majoring in criminal justice and working on the police force had stripped him of his trust in his fellow man. And teenage girls.

"We don't know anything." I said. "We were asleep." I wasn't about to tell him what we'd seen through Vikki's window. I could imagine his reaction to my confession that we were voyeurs, snooping on my half-naked, sometimes fully naked, neighbors with binoculars. Wouldn't that just make his day? But it wasn't going to happen because he wasn't going to find out. Ever. Besides, I came looking for information from the police, not volunteering what I'd ferreted out on my own.

"Come on, Mike," I begged. "What happened?"

"What was wrong with Vikki?" Kristen joined my pleading.

Brit stayed crouched in the shadows, keeping out of Mike's sight.

"Get out of here and go home," he said. "You'll get your answer when everybody else does. I'll release information through proper channels in due time." With that quote straight out of the public relations chapter of one of his criminal justice textbooks, Mike made an abrupt turn and walked away.

"A hell of a lot of good that did," Kristen said.

"Ah, he never tells anybody anything. I don't know why I bothered to ask him. Dumb idea," I said.

Mike was gorgeous to look it but he was a pain in the butt otherwise.

While Kristen and Brit argued about what to do next, Mike stood beside his car talking to his chief investigator, Drew Moore. Drew was older than Mike, thicker around the middle and nowhere near as gorgeous as his boss. This looked like the opportunity I'd been hoping for. If Mike wasn't going to tell me, I'd find out what happened to Vikki by myself.

This little open air police conference was my chance, and I was going to take it. Before Brit and Kristen had a chance to object, I ducked down and took off between police cars toward the two officers. Kristen and Brit stood with open mouths, ready to argue, then changed their minds and fell in behind me.

My sneaky trek between cars worked and I

made it within hearing distance of Mike and Drew. I whispered to Kristen and Brit to breathe quietly so Mike's suspicious nature wouldn't sense our presence. I knew he'd be madder than hell if he caught us, especially since he'd told us to butt out. And there was no way on this planet we could explain why we were crouching behind a parked police car.

Although Mike and Drew showed no awareness we were in the vicinity, an eerie feeling swept over me that someone else was watching us. I scanned trees, bushes, benches, parked vehicles but there was no sign of anyone other than policemen going about their jobs. Usually when I got these feelings, there was something to it but I saw no one suspicious. Deciding it was bad vibes in the air brought on by Vikki's death, I tuned back to what the chief was saying.

"So exactly what was it?" Mike asked Drew.

"They're called negligees. Like a fancy housecoat. Lace. Bright pink."

Negligees? They were talking about Vikki's negligee? I shot Brit a *what the hell* look. Too bad I didn't hear the beginning of this conversation. "There's no mystery about where it came from. It belonged to Vikki. Matched the night gown she was wearing," Drew said.

"No clues there," Mike said. "The killer found it in her apartment." Clues? Killer? Were they saying Vikki was murdered? I almost gasped so loud it could've been heard all over Sugar Liquor and certainly by Mike and Drew a few feet away. I kept my cool, barely. Vikki the Vixen was murdered? No way.

"Whoever killed her twirled the negligee around

and around until it was tight like a rope. Strong too. It didn't stretch when it was twisted around Vikki's neck."

Mike ran his hand through his hair. "Do we know about when this took place?"

"Not yet but we're getting there," Drew replied. "Gene's Diner is closed at this hour so I called him at home and woke him up to see when Vikki finished her waitress shift. He said she quit work at nine o'clock but sat and chatted with some high school girlfriends before leaving the diner. She didn't mention to him if she had plans to go out or if she was going straight home. He said they're not that friendly. How could anybody be friends with Gene? He never comes out of the kitchen or talks to anybody except to go to the bank.

"I'm sure when word gets out about Vikki's death, we'll hear if anyone saw her around town. A couple of her neighbors were out for the evening, but I've talked to those who were home and nobody saw Vikki come home except Barbara Allison who said she talked to her in the hallway. She told me if I wanted to know exactly when she saw Vikki, she'd check her notes, whatever that means."

Mike rolled his big brown eyes. "Barbara's so senile she can't remember what happened five minutes ago. She could've seen Vikki tonight or a month ago and not known the difference. Not reliable. Too bad.

"New topic. I couldn't get much out of Justin. He keeps repeating Vikki was lying on the floor, asleep or unconscious, when he got home from work. When he couldn't wake her up, he ran out in the hall and started yelling for help."

Drew said, "He doesn't usually come home from

31

his construction job during the week. Why was he here tonight and what time did he get home?"

"I don't know yet. His mind was all messed up. Not coherent. I'm going to try again when he calms down. You talk to the residents again. Except Barbara. See if they know when Justin got home. By the way, who else lives in the building?"

Drew flipped through his notepad and ran down the list. "Six apartments in all. Barbara Allison lives on the third floor across from Vikki and Justin. Ethan Matos, new in town and single, lives on the second floor. Tommy and Rachel Miller across the hall from Ethan. Georgia and Clyde on the first floor. Myra McJunkin and her full-time caregiver, Sandy, live across the hall from Georgia and Clyde." Drew closed his notebook with a snap.

Mike said, "Keep Vikki's apartment sealed off and a guard posted. If you see Barbara, tell her that she can go back to her apartment. The guys didn't find anything relating to Vikki's murder in the other apartments either.

"Vikki was killed in her own apartment. No sign of forced entry tells me she knew her killer and let him or her in. Or, the killer had a key. Do you know who has keys to her apartment?"

"Justin, of course. And Clyde. He's the handyman and caretaker," Drew replied.

"Clyde--" Mike said, drawling the name.

"Whoa, Mike, you don't consider Clyde a suspect. He's over eighty years old."

"I'm not ruling anybody out. Clyde's in good physical condition. You watched him work in the yard? He's tough. Probe into what he was doing tonight. Didn't Georgia say she heard a crashing noise?" Drew nodded. "I didn't see any mention of

Clyde saying anything about it. Ask him."

"Will do," Drew said.

"You're sure there was nothing in Clyde's apartment?" Mike asked. He wasn't ready to let Mr. Clyde off the hook.

"Yeah, I searched it myself with Breedlove doing a separate search. There's nothing."

"Okay, that's all for now."

Drew nodded and returned to his work. Mike opened the trunk of his car, rummaging for something.

While he was busy, I seized the chance to escape from our hiding spot. "Miss Georgia and Mr. Clyde's lights are still on," I whispered. "Let's go talk to them. Maybe they can tell us more now that we know Vikki was murdered. You know, I just had a thought. Since Mike was talking about Vikki's negligee being used like a rope, is it possible Vikki used it to commit suicide?"

"No way," answered Brit without hesitating. "She was having too much fun to check out. She wouldn't have wanted to miss anything."

"Absolutely. I can't see Vikki packing it in. She hadn't had time to try all the tips in her new *Cosmo*," Kristen said. Callous sounding but it summed up Vikki. She had way too much going on in her life to bail.

As I led my friends across the driveway, Mike spotted us and bellowed, "What're y'all still doing here? I told y'all to go home."

"We're on our way," I said, "as soon as we check on Miss Georgia and Mr. Clyde. They've had an upsetting evening." Mike frowned.

Uh-oh, Mike came stomping toward us. He bent over and got right in my face. In his attempt to threaten us, he did the same to Brit and then to Kristen.

"I'm going to tell y'all this much about what happened tonight." His voice was so low, I had to strain to hear him. "Vikki was murdered, viciously murdered. Somebody went up to her apartment and killed her in cold blood. Now, listen to me, this is a warning. Y'all stay out of this investigation. Amy, you think you're a hot shot detective because you solved that string of break-ins but this is different. It's not about a gang of punk kids. This is dangerous business.

"You start nosing around looking for a killer and you're liable to find one and end up dead. Any part of that you don't understand?" One by one, each of us looked him straight in the eyes and shook our heads. "Now, go check on Georgia and Clyde. Make it quick and get the hell home." We stood still until Mike entered the building.

"Whew. He sounded like he meant that," Kristen said. Yeah, he meant it all right but I had no intention of backing off. By solving the dumbass burglaries, I'd established myself as a good detective and I planned to enhance my new reputation. Plus, I had something to prove, something big. Borrowing a current buzzword, I had my own agenda. I needed to solve Vikki's murder and prove I was a dynamic, aggressive reporter who could go out and get to the bottom of a story. I needed to solve this murder and do the reporting too. My first case got me some good newspaper coverage but I didn't get to tell the story. This time I was going to solve the case *and* write the story.

I didn't feel guilty about lying to Mike that I'd stop investigating Vikki's murder but I did feel a little shady telling him I was going to check on Miss Georgia and Mr. Clyde. Although they should've been my number one concern, I was selfishly going to them for information. I soothed my conscience that, in the process of gathering info, I'd make sure they were alright.

"Lord, young'uns, what are y'all still a-doin' up?" Mr. Clyde asked when he opened the door.

"We've got some news. At the sound of our voices, Miss Georgia came out of the bedroom wearing a lavender chenille robe decorated with pink and yellow flowers and fuzzy purple slippers. She and Mr. Clyde looked older than usual. Puffy, red eyes from lack of sleep. Backs slumped from exhaustion.

The three of us crowding into their apartment always felt like a bit of a squeeze. The couple's furniture from their original home was too big for the apartment plus Miss Georgia had never gotten around to arranging the furniture for function or aesthetics. The movers had sort of put the pieces where they thought they should go and two years later, they were still in the same place. Miss Georgia and Mr. Clyde's apartment needed an extreme makeover.

"Have a seat, girls," Miss Georgia said.

"That's okay, we won't be here but a minute." Taking a deep breath, I said, "Mike told us Vikki was murdered." Miss Georgia murmured and grabbed onto a chair for support. I'm going to end up scaring her to death before this night ends.

Mr. Clyde didn't say anything. He punched his open palm with his other fist in a soft, slow, steady rhythm. He nodded his head in the same strange rhythm. Even his words came out in time to his motions. "Yep--I--knew--some--body--killed--her."

"What? For God's sake, Clyde Ashworth, you knew and you didn't say a word to me. Why didn't you tell me?" Miss Georgia asked angrily, big-time pissed-off at Mr. Clyde. In spite of the circumstances, I wanted to laugh. I'd never seen her get mad at him.

He forced a weak smile. "I was a-savin' you from the truth as long as I could, Sweetheart. I knew it was a-goin' to be ugly when the whole story came out." Mr. Clyde turned to me. "Did Mike say anything about a piece of pink cloth? That's what somebody used to kill her, ain't it?"

"Mike and Drew mentioned a cloth twisted into a rope," I said.

"I saw that twisted up piece of cloth a-layin' on the floor close to Vikki's head and ugly marks on her neck. I knew that rope had been pulled tight around that poor girl's neck. Somebody strangled little Vikki."

I didn't know who showed more shock. Brit, Kristen, Miss Georgia or me. Mr. Clyde had known all along that Vikki was strangled? Why hadn't he said anything during that agonizing period we waited for news? Why keep it to himself when he was certain Vikki was dead?

With no more ideas to pursue for the time being, Kristen, Brit and I left Miss Georgia and Mr. Clyde and slipped back into my house, undetected by my parents who'd apparently slept through the entire drama next door. Recordings of frogs, crickets, birds and other noisy little creatures enveloped my parents in an eight-hour loop that could've been lifted from *The Jungle Book*. That nature stuff weirded me out. I couldn't have slept a wink.

Unlike my parents, if something happened on the other side of town, within minutes I knew from my network of sources that something was up. First, I texted Brit and Kristen to alert them where to meet me and then busted my butt getting to the scene. I loved being in the middle of the action and wouldn't have it any other way. I thrived on excitement. Maybe that's what pushed me toward a college major in journalism.

Chapter Four

Exhausted, I dropped on my cot expecting to fall asleep. It didn't happen. Mike's hostility irked me. Sometimes, when I was in a magnanimous mood, I kind of understood why he held such strong feelings against me. My butting into the bad boys' crime spree riled him. My solving it embarrassed him. In all fairness, he was entitled to some resentment. I'd set out to prove I could succeed at news investigating and reporting, not to make him look bad. That was never in my head. I liked Mike sort of okay as a person and respected him as a police chief.

He couldn't get over being showed up by a seventeen-year-old.

***

I got hooked on the burglaries' story because the *Sugar Liquor Times*, the world's crappiest newspaper, uncharacteristically provided halfway decent coverage of the ongoing break-ins. My passion to break into journalism coupled with unsolved burglaries on my turf was too much to resist. I plotted the sequence of the break-ins on my free Sugar Liquor Chamber of Commerce Visitors' Map. "Check out this pattern," I told Brit and Kristen while we were hanging out in the cupola. "No surprises here. Look who lives in the part of town where most of the burglaries have taken place. Some of Sugar Liquor's *numero uno* jerks. Help me think of their loser friends."

Kristen took notes while Brit and I came up with names. When we ran out of ideas, Kristen said, "Twelve names."

As far as I knew, this band of bad boys hadn't been in trouble with the law yet, but there was talk about them around town. None of it good. After creating chaos at school as far back as I could remember, they were flexing their delinquency muscles now that they were driving age. "Looks like they've found their calling in life. Burglary and vandalism."

By the time I finishing circling the houses of the jerks and their friends on my map, I'd come up with some solid ideas about which businesses they were likely to hit next. Figuring out their next likely hits wasn't hard. They were too lazy to put out much effort, even to steal something, and definitely not smart enough to be cunning. This bunch of mini-goons hadn't changed since kindergarten.

I planned a stake out and recruited the reluctant duo of Brit and Kristen as my assistant lookouts since I couldn't stake out multiple sites by myself. Kristen balked. "Put a lid on it, Amy. Investigating isn't my thing." She might've been more into my plan if she could've worked it out on her computer instead of the reality of sitting slumped in a dark car on a cold night. Engine off. Heater not running.

"Come on, Kristen. You'll be really good at this," I said, bombarding her with flattery. I wasn't worried though. She couldn't bear to miss the excitement.

Brit went along with the deal because it involved lawbreakers, the makings of her future livelihood. "Just keep in mind, Amy, my goal is to defend the accused not set traps to catch them."

A bag of Cheetos for each of us, my leftover Easter candy divided into three Ziploc bags, a supply of cold Pepsis along with our cellphones and photocopies of my town map were our only crime-detecting tools. *CSI*, we were not.

On the second night of our stake-out, Brit and Kristen headed for their undercover assignments. I backed my mom's Buick inconspicuously into an open slot in a row of cars left for early morning appointments at Jimmy's Tire World. I was slouched down behind the steering wheel licking melted Kit-Kat chocolate off my fingers when a streak of light darted behind the building. I didn't move a muscle. I barely breathed. I didn't even pull my tongue back into my mouth. I looked like my cat, Hildy, interrupted in mid-grooming.

A few minutes later, a flashlight beam swept erratically across Jimmy's grimy plate glass windows. The gang was inside, ready to haul off what they could and trash what they couldn't.

I texted Brit and Kristen:

Me: *hurry to jimmy's be quiet*

Kristen: *DUH!!!*

Brit: *on my way*

With trembling, sticky fingers, I pressed *911* and

41

spoke in a soft voice even though I was in a closed car, and the thieves were inside a closed building. "This is Amy Jackson. A burglary is in progress at Jimmy's Tire World." I didn't have to give the address. Everybody knew where Jimmy's was.

Although I felt like I was going to explode from the excitement, I delivered my report to Molly, the night dispatcher, in what sounded to me like a clear, rational voice. "The thieves are inside the building so tell the police to arrive quietly. No sirens or screeching tires." Molly ignored the last bit, her way of letting me know the police could figure that out without the advice of a smart-ass seventeen-year-old. She knew everybody's life story, even parts they tried to hide. Not only was collecting and storing info her nature, it saved her having to ask for a lot of details and speeded up the wheels of justice.

Minutes later, dark-clothed figures crept past the clutter of rusted barrels and discarded tires slung alongside Jimmy's unpainted cement block building. Blocking all exits, the police trapped the clueless punks in the act.

Brit and Kristen tapped on my car window. I slipped out, and we hunched behind Mom's car watching the police line up nine boneheads against the side of the building. With their wide-eyed, pimply faces bleached white under police lights, this was the crew I'd fingered. I'd hit these low life nails on the head.

One big question got answered for me on the spot. Two dumpy pick-up trucks and an old, rusted mini-van. That's how the thieves were able to haul off so much merchandise from their heists.

By morning, my reputation as a hot shot detective had spread all over town. Brit and Kristen got high praise as my back-up unit. I ignored phone calls from the *Sugar Liquor Times*. I didn't want my name in that loser tabloid. On the other hand, I welcomed a female reporter from the *Asheville Citizen-Times* and poured out all the blow-by-blow details of how my sleuthing led to nabbing the culprits.

The interview process was backwards since I was supposed to investigate and write the story, not create the story and star in it. But the reporter gave me meritorious credit for my role in halting a crime spree plus she spelled my name right. All in all, not a bad career start for a seventeen-year-old.

Since I didn't do anything dangerous, my parents were okay about my crime busting exploit and got caught up in my fleeting foray into fame.

But I was hurt and disappointed when rumors reached me that the upstaged police chief's supersized hostility was aimed at me. Basking in the glow of my new celebrity status, I hadn't counted on making an enemy. I wanted to be a hero.

Chapter Five

After a short night's sleep which left me feeling wobbly, I crawled out of bed. Oh, no, it was seven o'clock. I wanted to be at Gene's Diner at six-thirty when the regulars started showing up for breakfast. Since Vikki waitressed at the diner, it would be, as Mr. Clyde would say, a-buzzin' with talk of her death. Not only gossip but real news maybe.

"Hey, sleeping beauties," I yelled at Brit and Kristen. "We're late. Move it."

Kristen hopped up, took off her pj bottoms and stood beside her cot in her tank top and bikini underwear. She was trying to turn her shorts right side out and having trouble getting both legs going the same direction. Kristen in her underwear wasn't a sight I wanted to see first thing in the morning. "Spare me, Kristen, cover it up."

She snapped back. "Why didn't you wake up on time? You had the alarm clock." That was true. I didn't tell her I accidentally set it for six PM, not AM. It wouldn't go off for eleven hours.

Kristen turned her wrath from me to Brit who was still in bed. "If you aren't ready in two minutes, we're leaving without you." Brit was a slow riser who insisted it made her queasy to spring out of bed like Kristen and I did. She sat on the edge of her cot, slipped on shorts and a t-shirt and finished by bundling her big mass of curls into a ponytail.

Slipping on flip-flops with one hand and snagging my small backpack with the other, I ran out the door. I didn't go anywhere without my backpack stuffed with skinny spiral notebooks, my journal and a supply of pens. Kristen fell in behind me. Hopping on one foot, Brit put on flip-flops and caught up with Kristen.

"Do we have enough cash to get something to eat?" Kristen asked, still in a snippy mood. Brit and I pulled some crumpled dollar bills out of our shorts' pockets. Without bothering to count them, I assured Kristen we were in good shape for breakfast at Gene's and bolted down the hall.

Spoons and bowls clattered from my parents' kitchen, so I stuck my head in the door. Mom and Dad were early risers. Both of them taught science at Sugar Crossing College and always had eight o'clock classes, summer session included. In my opinion, their schedule sucked, but it worked well for me. Mom rode to work with Dad, freeing up her car for me to drive.

Seated at the counter, my parents were eating their usual morning bowl of Special K, my mother's scaled down version of a Southern breakfast. Actually, it was the pits as Southern breakfasts go. "Hey, y'all, we're going to grab a bite to eat at the diner." Chomping on his cereal, Dad smiled and waved at me. Mom, who wasn't one to chatter in the morning, nodded indicating she got it. She didn't question me about eating out or the early hour, because I loved the diner's cooked breakfasts, and the food was cheap and the portions so large they had to be served on platters. Those breakfasts held me all day.

Neither Brit, Kristen nor I were early risers during the summer, but we all had jobs so Mom probably figured one of us had to get to work. She didn't mention Vikki, which meant she didn't know yet. My family's next door neighbor gets murdered and, hours later, my mother's still clueless. I didn't have time to tell her the story now and shook my head hopelessly as I scrambled outside where Brit and Kristen waited.

My house was only two blocks from the main part of town, which was only three blocks long, so my friends and I took off on foot for Gene's, racing along at a half-trot to make up for lost time. Kristen kept grousing because we got a late start. Her car was at my house, and she could've driven us, but it was faster to walk than to spend time looking for a parking place near the diner during the breakfast rush. As we sprinted past Vikki's apartment building, several police cars were parked in the driveway but no officers in sight. Still investigating.

"I guaran-damn-tee y'all that the diner will be packed," Kristen said, grumbling as she hustled along. "There won't be a single booth open." A waste of time to argue. She was probably right.

Gene's Diner used to be a locals-only hang-out until the multitudes of tourists flocking to our mountains discovered it. What we saw as cheap and filling food served in grungy surroundings, the tourists saw as quaint and rustic. I didn't like tourists overrunning our town, but their money kept Sugar Liquor afloat since most of the county's industries had closed their doors, never to reopen. Now, we were the peddlers of antiques, collectibles and local color.

The newcomers deserved credit for saving our town's colorful name though. A hundred years ago when making moonshine liquor was the only way to earn a living in the county, the moonshiners drove their vehicles to our crossroads of a town to buy sugar to make their liquor. As time passed, the words smooshed together and the town ended up being called Sugar Liquor. From time to time, prudish town council members tried to change the town's name to something sounding more respectable to their pious ears. But most citizens stood steadfast against a name change. It was all settled by our affluent newcomers who loved telling people they lived in *Sugar Liquor*. For the time being, our town's historic and apt name seemed safe from meddling do-gooders. Another snippet of local color we could sell.

As we walked toward the diner, Kristen kept bitching and squinching her eyes into little slits to remind me it was my fault we overslept. I hated it when she made that face. Kristen blamed Brit, too, although she didn't specify what she thought Brit had done to throw us behind schedule. Before long, Brit's patience snapped. "Well, ex-cuse me for liv-ing, Kris-ten. I only slept three hours so I had a little trouble waking up."

"Listen, dork, for your information, I only slept three hours too. And thinking back, I didn't hear the alarm go off. Did you even set it, Amy?"

I didn't answer because I'd never hear the end

of it if Kristen found out I set the alarm wrong. "Actually, Kristen, you could've set the alarm on your cellphone as a back-up." That shut her up. She was too tired to press the point, and I was glad because I was too tired to argue with her or referee her and Brit. I had more important business than squabbling about setting alarms.

As Kristen accurately predicted and ground into our heads, the diner was full, so we had no choice but to wait for seats. Our usual blissfully temperate mountain area was locked in an intense heat wave. Even the early morning was already hot and muggy. We crowded inside the air-conditioned doorway instead of waiting on the benches outside. Waitresses scurried back and forth, bumping into us and each other in their good-humored haste to feed their customers and refill coffee cups. While standing there, I had a chance to look over the crowd.

Rhonda, the eyes, ears and mouth of Sugar Liquor, who'd been waitressing at the diner since before I was born, squeezed past, carrying a tray of platters overflowing with eggs, home fries, grits, sausage gravy and biscuits. I hadn't expected to run into her at breakfast because she worked the evening shift, the same as Vikki. Rhonda was always an overflowing fountain of gossipy tidbits. I'd never needed to tap into her vast reservoir of secrets more than I did right now.

"Hey, girls, what're y'all doing up so early this morning?" Rhonda greeted us. Without waiting for an answer, she whispered, "Keep your eyes on Art and Earl. They're done so be ready to grab their stools. One of y'all get that vacant stool beside Earl before somebody else does."

I shoved Kristen forward, getting rid of her and her cranky attitude in one swift push. A line was forming behind me as more customers arrived, so when Art and Earl reached in their back pockets for their wallets, Brit and I pounced and staked our claim for their seats.

Kristen was laughing and having a great time. A few minutes of listening to Art and Earl's good-natured foolishness had that effect on people. I was grateful the two old brothers had improved Kristen's mood, since she could be a while getting over a mad spell. Friends again, Brit and I settled onto our stools with me, the buffer, between her and Kristen.

Sitting at the counter provided a better chance to chat with Rhonda while she rushed around taking and delivering orders. Generally I preferred a booth so Brit, Kristen and I could discuss our love lives in private but today was different. I was working on a case, the biggest of my two-case investigative career and my ticket, I hoped, to the big world of journalism.

In a few minutes, Rhonda handed us Gene's limp, greasy, first-edition menus. She bent over the counter toward me, her instant-tanned, pushed-up boobs ballooning out of her pink uniform top. Rhonda was aging noticeably and trying too hard to disguise it with too much make-up, brassy blonde hair and way too much cleavage assaulting the diner's patrons in the face. "Can y'all believe 'bout Vikki?" she asked in a low voice so the other customers couldn't hear. "Mike and Drew were in here earlier this morning for breakfast. I tried but I couldn't get much out of them. Mike was pretty hush-mouthed talking to Drew since everybody was trying to eavesdrop. He mentioned your name, Amy.

Frankly, he sounded pretty pissed off. He was saying he's sure you're holding out on him, something you're not telling him. So what'd you see last night?" Rhonda perched in front of me, waxed eyebrows arched, expectantly waiting for an answer. In return, she got my carefully practiced innocent look.

I might as well get a spot on the local radio station as tell Rhonda anything. But I needed information that only she could provide so I was going to have to negotiate it out of her. She'd never cooperate if she didn't get something juicy in return.

"Did Mike tell you how Vikki was killed?" I asked although I was certain straight-as-an-arrow Mike hadn't revealed any of the details. Rhonda looked at me, open-mouthed, shaking her head. I had her attention but I wasn't about to reveal what I knew to the people sitting near us. They could do their own snooping if they wanted to know anything. In a slow voice at a slow, deliberate pace, I said, "Mr. Clyde and Miss Georgia went up to Vikki and Justin's apartment and saw Vikki lying on the floor, still and motionless." Brit and Kristen breathed hoarsely, eyes glued to my face, hanging on every word like they were hearing the story for the first time. I must've been laying on the melodrama pretty good.

"Mr. Clyde said he was sure Vikki'd been strangled because he saw marks on her neck and a piece of pink cloth twisted like a rope laying on the floor near her head. But the weird thing is Mr. Clyde didn't tell any of this stuff to Miss Georgia or to me until after Brit and Kristen and I found out that Vikki was murdered. Pretty dodgy he kept all that to himself for so long."

"Yeah. Strange," Kristen added.

I didn't feel guilty revealing how Vikki was killed, even knowing Rhonda would tell everybody who came in the diner. Leaking that part wouldn't compromise Mike's investigation because as soon as Miss Georgia got out of bed and on the phone, she'd tell every gruesome detail to everybody she knew. By noon, Miss Georgia would reach all Sugar Liquor natives with or without Rhonda's assistance.

Rhonda stared straight through me while I described Vikki's murder, rubbing her own throat as if it somebody had tried to strangle her. "That's freaking awful. Vikki must've been so scared and helpless. The poor girl knew she was gonna die." Rhonda fixed her gaze beyond Gene's streaked plate glass windows, her facial expressions alternating between sadness and anger. My plan to feed Rhonda enough info to satisfy her had backfired. Instead of getting her to start talking freely, she'd slid into some kind of introspective, morose zone.

"Yeah, it sure is sad." I said, "You know, Rhonda, I'm kind of looking into Vikki's murder with Brit and Kristen's help. I know some things about Vikki that Mike doesn't know and I think you know some stuff that can help."

"Me? You were there. You know a lot more than I do."

"Tell me about the guys who hung around Vikki here at the diner."

Rhonda's mascara-clumped lashes flickered. "Mike's right. You are on to something. Oh-h-h, I see what you're getting at. You think Vikki had a boyfriend and he killed her."

"Now, Rhonda, I didn't say that. But let's face it, Vikki was cute and sexy and she liked to show it off. It makes a lot of sense that some guy hanging around the diner might've gotten interested in her and Vikki played along with him. Right?"

Rhonda agreed that a boyfriend killing Vikki made more sense than pointing the finger at Justin. "Why, that boy was crazy about her," Rhonda said.

A little sarcastically, Kristen asked, "And was Vikki likewise crazy about Justin?"

"Who knows? But something's been bugging Vikki pretty bad 'cause she hasn't acted like herself lately."

I asked if it was trouble with Justin. "Could be. Lately, when Justin came in the diner, Vikki acted like she didn't want him anywhere near her. And when he left, she'd watch him go out the door like she couldn't stand the sight of him. I didn't know what was going on between them but the honeymoon was definitely over."

Yeah. Rhonda got that right. After six short months, that honeymoon was history.

"I'm warning y'all," she said, pointing at Brit, then at Kristen to make sure they knew she included them. "If y'all breathe a word of this to Mike, I'll deny saying it," Rhonda said. "What I'm telling you is my gut feeling. What I think about what I've seen. I don't have anything to back it up and I sure don't want to point my finger at Justin. Being married to Vikki and being in the apartment make him a suspect. These days, it's usually the husband, isn't it?" From watching the news, it seemed to be.

"To tell you the truth," Rhonda said and lowered her voice to the point that I had to stretch toward her to hear. "I'm not surprised Vikki had had it with Justin. Back when she told us she was getting married, I couldn't see her settling down with one guy especially as flirty as she was. Justin's a sweet boy but he's no match for Vikki's need for constant attention. You know how she liked for guys to make a big fuss over her. The more guys and the bigger the fuss, the more she played up to them. She got a lot of that here at the diner and she ate it up. The customers who come in during the supper shift are a young, lively crowd for the most part. These early morning coots are too old to flirt," she said, casting a bored glance over the diner's predominantly white-haired patrons. Brit, Kristen and I giggled. I couldn't picture the likes of Art and Earl coming on to Vikki or anybody else.

"I tried to talk to Vikki a couple of times about what was wrong but I didn't get nothing out of her. When it was just us waitresses here, she was quiet and moody. She only laughed when customers came in." That definitely didn't sound like the Vikki I'd watched through her bedroom window. "I'm sure something was bothering her. She was awful jumpy. Like she was scared or something."

"Jumpy? How?" Brit asked.

"Oh, if somebody walked up on her and she didn't hear them, she'd jump off the floor. And boy, if there was a loud noise, she'd jump higher than the rest of us. I asked her about being so nervous and she told me to mind my own business and in words not anywhere near that nice. So, after a time or two of being told to go to hell, I took her at her word and left her alone. I figured she was old enough to work out her own frigging problems. But, damn, if I'd known she was in danger, I would've tried harder."

I assured Rhonda she did what she could. "You can't help somebody who doesn't want to be helped." Been there. Done that.

Attention-craving Vikki was the one I'd

observed in high school and watched through her bedroom window. Jumpy, nervous Vikki, whatever that was about, wasn't known to me.

I was about to ask Rhonda if she knew who the mystery boyfriend was when she grabbed the coffee pot to make a round of refills. While Rhonda was gone, I motioned Brit and Kristen close for a mini-conference. We put our heads together and I laid out what I knew so far. "Vikki's marriage was on the skids and if Justin knew about Vikki's boyfriend, he had a strong motive to kill her. He was alone in the apartment with her so he had the opportunity. He admitted she was lying on the floor. Question is if he's the one who put her there." I wasn't ready to accept him as a suspect. He didn't strike me as being aggressive enough to kill anybody, plus I felt sorry for him.

Back in the early days of Vikki and Justin's romance, when I was a freshman and first started paying attention to them, she didn't treat him right. She made fun of him in front of his friends, followed by a lame attempt to smooth over her harsh words with a pat on the arm, a wink, a teasing smile.

And so went their romance. Vikki flirted openly with other guys, hugging them a little too tight and a little too long, rubbing against them a little too close and a little too much. I didn't understand why Justin didn't dump her but he kept tagging along, taking her crap. Nothing had changed.

Ironically, as much as I'd spied on Vikki's personal life, I'd been completely unaware that she was living a secret life or maybe several secret lives right under my nose, right at the end of my Bushnell binoculars. Of course, I hadn't expected a newlywed to start straying so soon after her wedding vows.

Vikki must've set some kind of Sugar Liquor infidelity record.

"You know, all these times we've watched Justin playing up to Vikki, before we figured out last night it wasn't really him, I was surprised he was so animated. It didn't fit Justin's personality," Kristen said. "He's not that outgoing."

"I know. Sometimes, I thought his actions seemed out of character. I need to get in closer touch with my intuition," Brit said.

The mention of intuition reminded me of the funny feeling I'd had in the driveway of the apartment building last night, the feeling that someone was watching me eavesdrop on Mike and Drew. I was going to pay attention to funny feelings too. Who was spying on three teenage girls and why?

Still chewing on the same bone, Brit said, "Remember that time Justin was wearing cowboy boots and a hat and nothing else?"

"Yup," Kristen replied like the sheriff of Dodge City, unaware how hokey she sounded. "That was way beyond normal for him."

"Yeah," I said. "Justin's hair looked funny those nights when Vikki rigged up that funky revolving light. His hair turned every color on the wheel. Remember? It would've been hard to tell the difference between light brown and dark brown when his hair was changing from green to blue to red." We all laughed.

"It reminded me of my grandma's old silver Christmas tree with the color wheel. Remember, Amy? Grandma's tree always made you queasy," Kristen said. The reminder made me queasy.

"From what I've learned since last night, the

only times I'm certain it was Justin with Vikki was when they first got married, back when I actually got a good look at him."

"We don't get more than a few glimpses of the male now that Vikki's moved up to big productions. Justin or the boyfriend usually stays off to the side. Last night was an exception," Kristen said.

Rhonda brought our breakfasts. As I launched into a double order of steaming hot, buttered grits, my all-time favorite breakfast, I asked, "So, who had a thing for Vikki?"

"Look, Amy, I know you want to be a detective or something like that and it was really cool the way you caught those little dead beats breaking into all those stores and stealing everything they could haul off. And I know Mike was bent out of shape because you beat the police at catching the thieves and I know you want to do it again.

"This is different though. Vikki was murdered. It's dangerous stuff." Rhonda wiped a tear escaping down her cheek. "I'm afraid to tell you anything because you might get hurt. Or, worse."

"Rhonda," I said, patting her hand. "I'm not going to do anything risky. Just asking a few questions, trying to find out who Vikki was fooling around with and who might've been mad enough at her to kill her. But you're right, I desperately want to solve Vikki's murder and write the news story. It happened next door to me. This is my chance of a lifetime. Please help me, Rhonda. I promise, promise to be careful. Tell me who Vikki's boyfriend was."

Rhonda leaned forward, her advancing boobs forcing me to retreat from my propped position on the counter. Sounding like an overprotective parent laying down she rules, she said, "Okay, I'll tell you what I know but don't do anything that might get you in trouble. And don't tell Mike I fed you information."

"That's the last thing you have to worry about. I don't tell Mike anything. Besides, anything you pass along to us, Mike would dismiss as town gossip," I said.

"Yeah, Uncle Mike's only interested in hard facts. He needs evidence to build a case to turn over to the prosecutor," Brit said. I wondered if she was speaking from her serious legal reading or quoting the invincible, fictional Melissa Eagle, who didn't have to make things work in real life.

"Okay, but you have to promise that if you uncover anything that points to Vikki's murderer, you'll report it to Mike and let the police handle it." Rhonda made it clear the deal applied to all of us.

"All right, that's settled. I don't want to have to worry about y'all blundering into danger," Rhonda said, satisfied we wouldn't be taking any chances. "About them guys who were hitting on Vikki. Several who knew her in high school come in together pretty often to eat their supper and kid around with her. They had their crushes on her years ago and got over them. The guys who were serious about her are newcomers in town, like that fellow who lives in her building."

"What guy?" I asked.

"Ethan. I don't know his last name. Vikki said he has some kind of computer business. You live next door to him, Amy, you ought to know him. He's tall, tan, dark hair, well-built. Dreamy looking but no personality."

"Actually, I don't know him. Mr. Clyde said a neighbor named Ethan gave CPR to Vikki last night."

"What? You didn't mention anything about Ethan giving Vikki CPR." Rhonda puckered her Viva Scarlet red lips, annoyed that I'd left out a vital piece of information.

"Sorry, I didn't realize you knew him, Rhonda," I said in a soothing voice, an attempt to chill her indignation. "Are you saying Ethan liked Vikki?"`

"No. No. Not Ethan. These guys who come in here with him. One is called Eric. Thick blond hair, bluest eyes I ever saw. Like being face to face with the sky. Snazzy dresser too. He's a sweet eyeful. Vikki sure piled it on but I don't think he fell for it. Then, this other guy started coming with Ethan and Eric. Right away, Vikki turned her ammunition on him. The new fella, Colton, is Ethan's younger brother. Vikki said they're from Chicago or someplace up north." Rhonda bolted away to deliver an order.

I scanned the other diners to make sure nobody was eavesdropping on us. No problem. They were too busy speculating about Vikki. I could hear her name echoing off the diner's chipped, fake wood paneling.

"Some investigator I am. Vikki's chasing my next door neighbor's brother and I don't know anything about it," I said to Brit and Kristen. "I knew some guy moved into the building a couple months ago but I've never seen him. If he runs a computer business, he must stay inside all the time."

"The further we go, the more tangled Vikki's life gets," Brit said. When Rhonda returned, Brit asked her, "Any more boyfriends?"

"I don't know but I don't think so. Vikki's been crazy about Colton from day one and I don't blame her. If I was a little younger, I would've gone for him myself. He's a hottie. He looks like Ethan but more outgoing and loads more fun, always dressed up too. You know, even wears a tie. No wonder Vikki fell for him.

"Uh-oh, y'all, I can't talk any more. Gene's back from depositing his millions in the bank," she said, laughing. "I gotta clear tables." Before she got away, I asked if she thought Colton would keep coming to the diner now that Vikki was gone. Rhonda shrugged. "There's no other place in town to get home cooking, as Gene fondly calls it, so who knows. Maybe." She whispered over her shoulder as she headed to a table. "Colton sometimes eats around five o'clock so come early if you want to see him."

I finished nibbling my last piece of toast. I handed my wadded-up dollars to Brit to pay our bill.

All this business about Ethan, Eric and especially Colton was news to me but come five o'clock, I'd be at the diner to find out if any members of Vikki's fan club, past or present, showed up.

Chapter Six

"What now?" Brit asked. Most of the early customers had cleared out. The near empty diner cued Rhonda to get busy clearing tables. She loaded dishes into a plastic bin with her left hand and wiped tables with her right.

Gene, bald head shining and white apron dingier than Rhonda's dishrag, moved around in the kitchen. With regularity, he poked his head out the pass-through window to make sure his waitresses hadn't slacked off.

Kristen checked her watch. "Uh-oh, time for me to get ready for work." Of the three of us, Kristen had the most grown-up summer job. Her repertoire of computer skills landed her a part-time position with a local start-up company. Kristen loved everything about computers and was born to sit at a keyboard.

The three of us walked back to my house so Kristen could get ready for work and pick up her car. Since it took a while for the hot water to work its way from the water heater in the basement to my bedroom-bath combo on the second floor, I turned on the water for Kristen right away. She walked upstairs to the cupola with Brit and me to get her work clothes. Wrinkle-free and on hangers.

While Kristen showered and dressed, Brit and I checked email on our phones. Mine was mostly junk as usual, the never-ending offers to check my credit score although I was pretty certain I didn't have one and, for the third day this week, a chance to win millions in some dodgy lottery. With that, I could buy my way into journalism. If all else failed, I could cleanse my colon.

Transformed from school girl to career woman, Kristen came up to the cupola wearing her business attire--black pencil skirt, silky ivory blouse and yellow heels--subtle make-up and hair falling straight and shiny. All glammed up, Kristen could go from looking seventeen-years-old to twenty-one in minutes. Her natural blond hair, blue eyes and delicate features reminded me of a teenage Nicole Kidman.

When I dressed up, I looked the same except for having on different clothes. No younger, no older, and I certainly didn't look like a movie star. With Kristen it was synergistic, the parts came together better. Her resemblance to the elegant Nicole ended when Kristen cranked up the attitude. Boy, she could make a football player cringe.

"So what are y'all going to do this morning?" Kristen asked. Half of her inquiry was genuine interest and the other half was hoping Brit and I didn't find out anything important about Vikki's murder while she was at work. Although crime investigating had been my brainchild to further my journalism ambitions, Kristen couldn't bear to miss a minute of action. Brit told her we were going to spend the morning thinking. That was usually code for taking a nap but today Brit and I really were going to think. Looking relieved that nothing exciting was likely to happen, Kristen bid us *adieu* and set off for her well-paid shift in cyberspace.

Brit and I lay down on our respective cots. Some years ago when Brit, Kristen and I were deemed old enough to sleep on the third floor, my mother had furnished the cupola with three cots outfitted with *Hello Kitty* sheets and comforters from Target. As a result, Brit and Kristen slept over often because they loved spending time in my private penthouse.

It was a magical place, unlike Brit's and Kristen's houses. At Kristen's we had to sleep on the living room floor because she shared a small bedroom with her younger sister leaving no space for overnight guests. Brit's house was even worse because her mother was paranoid we were going to drop crumbs or spill something. I felt so clumsy and nervous in that house. Even Brit, her kid brother and dad were on pins and needles at home.

My mother didn't mind mess, and she didn't care how often my friends slept over as long as she didn't have to cook for them. Mom excelled in her academic endeavors and career, but she sucked at household chores. Pouring extra bowls of cereal or microwaving extra frozen dinners challenged her domestic skills.

When I turned sixteen, Mom offered me funds to update the decor in the cupola but I opted to keep my cherished kitty motif. I'd spent countless weekends and summer days and nights with my best friends in my treetop kitty-themed hideaway, so for sentimental reasons, I nixed any suggestions of redecorating. The only additions to my mother's original cots and linens were a banged up chest of drawers which I spray painted pink enamel and covered with kitty decals, a flat-screen TV with cable, DVR and wireless internet. Although Mom bought the TV and gave me permission for the electronic connections, she freaked out when she got the bill. When I called to arrange installation, I didn't think to ask about the cost. After all, it was only a couple of boxes and cables. Who knew the wiring would take all day and be so expensive? Mom recovered and I got inducted into reality.

Brit and I got down to current business. "First of all," I said, "we've got to find out more about Ethan, Eric and Colton. And whether this was public flirtation because Vikki was cute and sexy and fun or if it traveled outside the diner."

"Well, let's go ask Miss Georgia," Brit suggested. "She can probably give us the low-down on Ethan. She lives in the same building and you know how nosy she is."

Brit and I hopped off our cots, ran down the stairs and through Mom's rose garden to the apartment building next door. "By the way, y'all tore a big hole in my pj bottoms last night." Brit groused as we walked. "They were my favorite. You're going to have to fix them."

"No problem," I said in agreement. Unlike my mother, I enjoyed sewing and was pretty decent at it. Mom even bought me a sewing machine.

Mr. Clyde was deadheading roses in the flower garden on the side of his building nearest to my house. A tall, wiry bundle of energy, Mr. Clyde had been hired as his building's handyman and gardener shortly after he and Miss Georgia moved into their apartment. He liked to brag that he was eighty years old and still bringing home a weekly paycheck. He waved us over to where he was standing. In a loud voice, I said, "Got to see Miss Georgia." He grinned and we kept going.

The apartment door was standing partially open, and I could hear Miss Georgia talking on the phone in the kitchen. "That poor girl layin' on that floor ... " How many times had Miss Georgia told that story today? She was going to have to cut this version short though. I didn't have time to wait while she went through all the details.

"Miss Georgia," I yelled.

"Ooops," she said, "somebody's at my door." She abruptly hung up.

"It's my girls," she said, smiling and giving Brit and me hugs. She always made us feel like it'd been ages since she'd seen us, and she seemed so joyful we'd returned.

"Lord have mercy," she said, "I thought I'd never drag my weary old bones out of bed this morning." She was still wearing her housecoat instead of getting dressed in one of her colorful jogging suits, her year-round daily outfit. "Even Clyde slept late. Have a seat, girls." Flopping down in a chair, I felt myself being swallowed by the cushion. Grinning while she watched me disappear into the stuffing, Brit wisely chose a wooden chair. "How are y'all today?" Miss Georgia asked.

"Not enough sleep but hanging in there. Just got back from breakfast at the diner," I said. "Boy, you wouldn't believe how word's spread about Vikki's murder. Everybody's talking about it."

"I don't doubt that," Miss Georgia said. "Things

like that don't happen here."

What she meant was that kind of murder didn't happen. In fact, we have a fair number of killings but they usually involve two people who know each other and get into a squabble over the usual--a woman, property, money, booze, drugs. Tempers flare, threats escalate, and, with a rifle hanging in every pick-up in the county, sooner or later someone reaches for a gun, shots are fired and somebody ends up dead. Everybody knows how it happened and who did it. The shooter, who is firmly convinced his actions were justified, stays on the scene so he can be first to tell the police his side of the story.

A young woman mysteriously murdered in her own home, like Vikki, was not typical of mountain town killings, making this one all the more sensational.

"Miss Georgia, we want to ask you something but you have to promise not to tell anybody we asked you, especially Mike," Brit said, shifting from her hard chair to the padded sofa arm beside Miss Georgia. "It's okay if you tell Mr. Clyde but he can't tell anyone, okay?"

"Me and Clyde would never tell anything my girls told me. It must be about Vikki," she said. "What is it?"

"What do you know about the man named Ethan who lives on the second floor?" I asked her. "The one who gave Vikki CPR."

Miss Georgia sat back, her little wispy hair net serving as a makeshift thinking cap. "My goodness. That's the last thing I expected you to ask. What does he have to do with anything?" she said. "If you don't tell me why you want to know, I won't tell you anything." Miss Georgia was like Rhonda. She didn't give without getting.

"Before I make a deal," I said, challenging her, "do you actually know anything about him?"

"Maybe," she teased. Sometimes she could be way too coquettish and coy for my straight-forward way of thinking. Miss Georgia must've been tutored at Scarlett O'Hara's knee. Sensing my exasperation, she relented. "Okay, Amy. I know a little about Ethan, but why do you want to know about him?"

"I'm pretty certain Vikki was cheating on Justin. Ethan's brother and his friend might've been kind of hot for her. What's the deal?"

"Well, Ethan Matos has lived on the second floor about five or six months. He moved in right after Vikki and Justin. Quiet, close-mouthed. Clyde's tried to talk to him," she said, "but he can't get much more than hello or good-bye out of him." I asked if Mr. Clyde ever got anything out of him.

"No, not really, except Ethan told Clyde he runs a business out of his apartment. He does it with a computer. Clyde doesn't know what kind of business though. When Clyde passes in the hallway, he tries to peep in the apartment when Ethan's goin' in or out but he can't see anything. Clyde says there's a lot of computer stuff in the livin' room but since Clyde don't know nothin' about them, he don't know what he's lookin' at. Clyde claims Ethan shuts the door fast so he can't see inside."

Ethan's apartment had to be located directly below Vikki's because I knew the layout of the building and where the other occupants lived. That meant I could see his bedroom window from my cupola, but, thinking back, those drapes stayed closed all the time, never a glint of light showing. Maybe Mr. Clyde was right and Ethan was secretive, careful to cover windows and close doors quickly. Or maybe Mr. Clyde was getting paranoid in his old days, and it was all in his imagination. Maybe Ethan kept the drapes closed because he was too lazy to pull the cord or liked being in the dark. Maybe he resented nosy old men who tried to look inside his apartment. Perhaps, he was evading the nosy chick next door who trained her binoculars toward his building.

But on the chance Mr. Clyde was right, was Ethan hiding something or simply fending off invasion of his privacy? And why was Mr. Clyde so interested in what Ethan had in his apartment? He sounded a little over the top about Ethan.

Brit asked Miss Georgia if she'd ever seen Ethan go up to Vikki's apartment. My neighbor shook her head and reckoned that Ethan was so quiet nobody would know if he did. "I don't think Ethan was interested in Vikki. He's not her type. Not exciting enough."

Brit asked, "What about Ethan's friend and his brother?"

"I don't know if either one of them was Vikki's boyfriend but I do know she had gentlemen callers when Justin was away at his construction job," Miss Georgia said. She leaned forward and lowered her voice although we were the only people in the room. "I don't know if y'all know but Justin's been workin' on the other side of Asheville since before him and Vikki got married. He told Clyde he stays in a motel with the other construction workers over there during the week and comes home on weekends."

Miss Georgia lowered her voice. News was coming. "I see a young man park his car in the back lot almost every night, except weekends, and use the back stairs to go up to Vikki's apartment."

Brit's eyebrows shot up. "Who?"

"I don't know. It's always too dark to see him but I'm sure he's young because he walks and acts like a young person."

I asked, "What does that mean?"

"Let's just say he's got a spring in his step," Miss Georgia said with a giggle.

The back staircase of the apartment building was originally built for servants in the old days when the houses on our street were owned by rich families who could afford household help but didn't want them in their faces. One time, Mr. Clyde showed Brit, Kristen and me the back staircase. It was narrow, steep, poorly lit and doubled back on itself. Utilitarian at best.

According to Mr. Clyde, no one parked in the small, unlit back lot or used the gloomy back staircase any more. The building's residents and guests parked in the large, paved, well-lit lot on the far side of the building and used the front entrance with its wider, more accessible entry and staircase. It was easier to negotiate with groceries or packages, plus the front door was unlocked during the day unlike the back door, which had a self-locking mechanism for security.

"Do the residents have keys to the back door?" I asked Miss Georgia.

"Oh, sure."

"So, if Vikki's companion entered the back door, he had to have a key, which meant someone, as in Vikki, gave it to him. Or, she went down to let him inside. Are you sure the young man went to Vikki's apartment?"

"The first time I saw him park and head toward

the back of the building, I got scared he was up to no good. I sneaked out into the hallway and heard the back door close with its usual clang. The fellow didn't come down this hall so he had to have gone upstairs. A few minutes later, I heard Vikki out in the hallway talking and laughing to a man and then they went inside and closed the door."

Interesting. This was a significant revelation considering I didn't know until last night that Vikki had a boyfriend. If I'd known Justin worked out of town, I might've figured out the boyfriend situation earlier. I needed to revamp my information-gathering sources. I wasn't as well-informed as I thought.

"Miss Georgia, I have a really important question. Did you see Vikki's boyfriend arrive or leave last night? Especially leave?" I asked.

"Oh, I wish. Like I told Drew last night, our son took us out to eat and play bingo at the senior center. We didn't get home until after eleven o'clock. A late night for us," she said. "I was so weary, I didn't look out the back window. I don't know if the boyfriend's car was there or not. Of all nights for me not to be home."

Brit asked if she saw Justin's truck in either parking lot when she came home. "We got out of the car in the front driveway and walked straight in. Clyde locked the front door when we got home, and we went straight to bed."

Miss Georgia insisted Brit and I take some oatmeal-raisin cookies. Although I was stuffed full of grits, I never turned down free food, especially homemade cookies. Brit and I took a handful for a later snack. "Thanks for the cookies and your help, Miss Georgia," I said. "Mr. Clyde's out in the yard, so

I think we'll ask him about Ethan."

"We're going to the diner tonight and see if Ethan or his friend or brother shows up," Brit said. I gave her a *shut-up* stare. She should know better than to say anything in front of Miss Georgia. She was nosy enough to show up at the diner too. I didn't want the whole freaking town there.

Mr. Clyde was resting on a bench in the shade, a half-empty bottle of water in his hand. Sweat dampened his shirt, and his few wispy hairs were plastered to the top of his bald head. "You young'uns found Georgia, I reckon," he said.

"Yeah, we wanted to ask her some questions about Vikki's personal life," Brit said.

Mr. Clyde took a deep breath. "Vikki was a-playin' with fire."

"Did you hear that crashing sound Miss Georgia told us about? The one that woke her up?"

Mr. Clyde looked surprised at the question. He opened his mouth to answer but closed it, licked his lips and opened his mouth again. He paused before he spoke. "Well--uh--no. I didn't hear it." Did he hesitate to answer?

"Can you describe Ethan Matos?" I asked. "I've never seen him."

"Well, let's see. Ethan must be about thirty. About my height. Say six feet. A little heavier. More muscular too. Of course, I'm muscular but I don't flaunt it around a-wearin' them tight shirts with the sleeves cut out," he said with a wink and a hearty laugh, sounding a whole lot more like my joking friend than he had last night.

Mr. Clyde was strong and could work all day, but he was tall, skinny and scrawny. Everybody was more muscular looking than he was. Mr. Clyde

71

narrowed his eyes and I figured he was trying to conjure up a picture of Ethan. "Let's see. He's got dark hair and he's tan. He looks Greek. Name sounds Greek too." Mr. Clyde was stationed on a ship off the coast of Greece when he was a young man in the Navy and tended to think anybody with a tan was Greek. "He's a nice-lookin' fellow, but he sure don't have much to say, although he's kind of friendly with Justin, more so than to the rest of us anyhow. When Justin comes outside to smoke, I see him and Ethan a-talkin'. Personally, I think there's something fishy about him."

"Fishy, like how?" Brit asked.

"Too quiet. He acts like he's a-hidin' something." Back to the *Ethan's hiding something* conspiracy theory.

I thanked Mr. Clyde for his description and observations. I was careful not to mention I was going to the diner tonight. If we were lucky, Miss Georgia would get busy on the phone talking about Vikki's murder and forget about it. I didn't need Mr. Clyde reminding her.

"One more thing, Mr. Clyde," Brit said. "Do you know Ethan's friends?"

"Well, I don't really know 'em, but when I see 'em, I say hello. Friendly types. They're nice lookin', clean-cut fellows. One of 'em is Ethan's younger brother. He looks a lot like Ethan. He's Greek too. Dresses awful nice. The other fellow's real fair. He ain't Greek."

Brit and I had to get ready to go to our jobs, so she walked home after we finished talking to Mr. Clyde. I tromped through Mom's garden to my house, but I felt fairly satisfied with my expedition. Miss Georgia and Mr. Clyde were good sources of information. Not much got past them and it was a real shame they chose last night to play Bingo.

What I wouldn't give to know when the boyfriend left and Justin arrived. Or was it the other way around?

Chapter Seven

Due to bad timing and fast traffic, I arrived at work five minutes early. Man, it really pissed me to get there even one minute ahead of starting time. One extra minute in hell was one too many. Five were unbearable.

My summer job wasn't grown-up or responsible like Kristen's. I was Cart Return Girl at Doubleman's Supermarket, located in what passed for a shopping center in Sugar Liquor. Meaning it had a grocery store and a handful of half-assed stores.

The temperature was in the mid-nineties and *mighty hot* for the mountains as several hundred people had remarked to me in the last few days. After seeing my blaze red face, frizzy, dripping strawberry blonde ponytail and half-soaked shirt, they seemed to feel obligated to mention the weather. I was but a few sweat beads away from qualifying as an entrant in a wet t-shirt contest. Way beyond genteel glistening.

Swearing to myself, I crisscrossed back and

forth across the parking lot gathering stray carts and forcing them back to the store. The wheels on half of the stupid-ass carts didn't line up straight so I had to scrape the wheels side-ways along the pavement rather than rolling them, defeating the purpose of someone having gone to the trouble to invent the wheel. As bad as the wheels not rolling was my hike to the far ends of the lot where the fitness nuts parked. They liked to get in a little cardio-vascular speed-walk on their way to and from the store. I despised them for leaving their carts so far away. If they wanted more exercise, why not bring the empty carts back to the store, jog back to their cars and cut me out of their fitness routines?

I hated my job although it was my own fault I'd ended up having to work in the hot sun baking my brains out. Back in the spring, I applied for a summer internship at our local newspaper, the *Sugar Liquor Times*, and made it through several cuts. As pathetic as that newspaper was, I wanted the internship.

A great believer in the power of positive thinking, I bombarded the Universe with good vibes. I'd already decided on my first day of work outfit. Professional, of course. With a touch of Katie Couric cuteness for balance.

It didn't matter how lowly my internship duties were. Writing anything for a newspaper, obituaries or classifieds for garage sales, was a step toward my goal. I was desperate and this internship was my chance.

In the final round of the newspaper competition, a girl two years older than I was and finishing her first year at UNC got *my* internship. That's when my feud with the *Sugar Liquor Times* began and why I dissed them when they called to get my story on how I caught the brat-pack delinquents. The Asheville newspaper article about my exploits reached a lot more readers and lauded my intuitive investigative skills. Awesome coverage. The article should earn me some points when I applied to college. The *Sugar Liquor Times* had muffed their chance at Amy Jackson. They wouldn't get another one. When I was in the right, I excelled at grudge-bearing.

By the time I found out I didn't get the internship and in spite of my mother's multiple warnings not to put all my eggs in the newspaper basket, only crap jobs were left and I was hurled into shopping-cart hell. This summer was never going to end, trapping me in the mindless cycle of rounding up shopping carts forever. I even had nightmares about shopping carts. The scariest was when the carts pulled me through the parking lot onto the highway, and sneering drivers in speeding vehicles tried to run me over.

I gritted my teeth preparing for the worst part of my day. During my shift, I had to make a lap behind the grocery store which creeped me out. It was deserted, shadowy and ghoulish with rows of rusty dumpsters parked helter-skelter and hidden out of the sight of decent, clean, God-fearing shoppers.

The nasty carnage nauseated me. Squishy tomatoes, slimy green vegetables and other unidentifiable remains decomposed on the hot summer pavement. Discarded plastic jugs of milk, their caps jarred loose when they thudded on the pavement instead of landing in the dumpster, oozed grimy lumps of curdled milk. The ever-present local village of rats darted around snatching bits of the putrid feast enjoyed only by rodents. It was enough to gag me. And usually did.

The stock boys were supposed to pick up trash when they carted flattened cardboard boxes and garbage to the dumpsters. From the looks of things and in my opinion, they never picked up anything and, instead of bringing the carts back into the store, they left them for me. Slacker bastards.

Taking a deep breath and checking that no rats hovered nearby, positioned to pounce on my sneakers and climb my legs, I rounded the corner of the store to see what new hell was splattered or spilled for me to zig-zag my way around.

Stopping abruptly, I ducked back behind the building.

Several cars were parked beyond the dumpsters. Near them, about a half dozen people stood in a circle talking. I'd never seen anybody back here other than the lazy stock boys sneaking a cigarette when they were supposed to be working. Although I wasn't close enough to hear what these people were talking about, I recognized serious faces when I saw them. Heads turned in unison when a different speaker joined the discussion. No telling jokes or sharing funny stories in this crowd. A social get-together? No way.

Curious about this out-of-place group, I edged forward and hid between two stinking dumpsters to get a better look. Three of the men and the sole woman wore quality-looking business suits and the other two men wore pressed khakis and *Ralph Lauren* shirts. I could identify polo ponies from any distance.

From my hiding place, I checked out the

individuals. The two guys in casual dress were in their late twenties or early thirties. The other three men and woman ranged from their thirties to their sixties. Old people look pretty much the same to me so I'm not good at guessing people's ages after they hit thirty. The six people passed papers back and forth, studied them with alert eyes and discussed them with other members of the group. As they shifted positions, I got good looks at their faces, but I didn't recognize any of them. Not locals, for sure.

Being a clever detective, I came up with a clever idea. I eased my cellphone out of my shorts pocket, turned off the flash and took close-ups of the individuals and a few group shots. Satisfied with the quality of those, I took photos of their randomly parked cars. Fronts of some, backs of others. Whatever faced my position.

Why were these people gathered back here? This had to be the grossest meeting place of all time. Didn't businesses have conference rooms for this sort of thing or provide expense accounts for long lunches in nice restaurants with Mediterranean menus or to linger over cocktails in trendy bars? What kind of operation holds meetings behind nauseating dumpsters?

Not a real business, that's what kind. Maybe these guys were gangsters. Mafia guys in the movies always dressed nice. I thought the Mafia always met in Italian restaurants. Sugar Liquor didn't have much to offer them other than a couple take-out pizza parlors. As I watched the men and woman in their chosen meeting place, it made more sense that they were fashionable common criminals. Mafia seemed a little far-fetched for Sugar Liquor. There wasn't enough money in the whole town to attract them.

The attendees made motions of heading for their cars so I hunkered in my hiding place, out of sight. They drove right past me without a glance my way. What idiot would look at garbage dumpsters anyway?

Three of the cars were so generic in style and color, I had no idea what makes they were but the fourth car was clearly a black BMW. I could read the letters on the emblem, and the last one was a little red sports car convertible. Probably a Miata.

After the cars left, I continued standing between the dumpsters for a couple minutes trying to make sense of what I'd seen. Part of the answer was clear. These people didn't want to be seen.

By the time I got the carts gathered up from the back of the store and returned to their corral, it was time for my afternoon break. Hallelujah. This was the only part of my work day I enjoyed. I didn't like to take my break at lunch, so depending on my shift, I took it during mid-morning or mid-afternoon. I bought a couple Kit-Kat bars and a cold Pepsi at the store and headed for my mom's car. I was so grateful for the luxury of a car to get away from my job.

The mini-strip mall where I worked was near an entrance to Pisgah National Forest. It only took a couple short minutes for me to get to Rocky River, the closest recreation area. It was popular with locals, but the tourists didn't stop. Thank goodness. They whizzed past, following the winding highway to higher elevations where they could experience more spectacular vistas and dramatic waterfalls.

I was glad the out-of-towners didn't stop, because I liked my break spot just the way it was. Shade trees, sunny areas, a cold, shallow river with lots of rocks and ripples, picnic tables, pavilions and a clean, modern, tiled bathroom with flush toilets and good-smelling foamy hand soap. Mother Nature with the comforts of home. My kind of roughing it.

Unless it was raining, I sat on top of one of two riverside picnic tables. Sometimes I sat and read on my shady picnic table, and sometimes I vegged out and lay on my ratty beach towel atop the sunny picnic table to catch some rays. Today, because of the heat, I slouched on the shaded table and let my mind drift as I watched the water jump over rocks in the riverbed.

I wasn't the rustic type who wanted to flee civilization and live off the land, so my little piece of semi-wilderness, close to town with plenty of picnickers and walkers and joggers passing by my table, but not too closely, suited me fine. I always saw somebody I knew, but I avoided getting entangled in conversations with them during my break. This was quality time with myself.

The weird incident behind the store kept interrupting my efforts to zone-out so I got my journal and pen out of my backpack. I was stumped what to write about the episode. With a slew of questions swirling around in my head, I had trouble deciding where to start. I looked at the photos on my phone to jog my memory. I wrote down everything I could remember--the male-female composition of the group, what their clothes and cars looked like, how they passed papers around, facial expressions and the time of the rendezvous.

The big questions, I couldn't answer. Who were these people and why were they taking a meeting behind the store?

I scarfed down a Kit-Kat bar and sipped my

Pepsi, but no answers came to me. The one thing I was certain about was that these people, however nicely dressed, were up to no good. They might not be bona fide Sicilian Mafia, but they were involved in something so shady, they weren't willing to be seen in the huge, public parking lot in front of the shopping center.

***

At five o'clock, the beginning of supper time, I met Kristen and Brit at Gene's Diner. The line was out the door, so we grabbed seats on the outdoor benches to wait. The seats were so hot, we had to sit on the edge so our bare legs didn't touch the metal.

"What'd y'all find out after I left this morning? Anything interesting?" Kristen whispered.

"Yeah, we went to see Miss Georgia." I related the news about Vikki's boyfriend coming through the back door.

"Oh my gosh, so that's how Vikki sneaked boyfriends up to her apartment. Pretty clever."

"Not clever enough to keep from getting killed," I said.

"True," said Kristen. "So who is the mystery boyfriend?"

Brit replied, "Miss Georgia doesn't know. She couldn't see him because the back parking lot's too dark at night."

· Kristen's excitement faded. "So he could be Ethan's friend or brother?"

"He could be anybody," I said. Who knew how far Vikki's fan club membership reached?

Brit and Kristen didn't ask about my afternoon. I made a rule that my summer job was off limits as a topic of discussion, so they knew better than to mention it.

While we waited for a table, Kristen rattled on non-stop about her exciting new computer project. I was ready to kill her. "I came up with a programming solution that even my boss didn't think of. She was so impressed she bought my lunch." I dearly loved Kristen but right now, she was getting on my overheated nerves.

Show-and-tell time wasn't finished. I still had to hear Brit's daily report. She worked part-time for the county government as a clerk. She and another high school girl had been hired to transfer data from old disintegrating paper records to the computer system. It was a boring job but the way my luck was going, Brit had probably been appointed acting governor of North Carolina for the day. "I love the people I work with," she said. "They're so sweet and they're talking about giving me more responsibility. But let me tell you, they're going to have to do something about adjusting the air-conditioning. That courthouse is freezing. I had to wear a jacket all afternoon." My sweaty heart and mildewed hair ached for poor frozen Brit, and I wanted to kill her along with Kristen, but I was too hot to dwell on the mechanics of how I could take out both of them at the same time without having to expend any energy.

As diners trickled out, Dusty Rose, a waitress a couple years older than I, signaled for us to come inside. A shy, thin, pale, stooped girl with little to say, who kept her eyes fixed on the cracked, checkerboard linoleum floor, halfheartedly pointed to an empty booth and thrust menus in our direction. I was used to dealing with Dusty Rose's minimalist approach to hostessing but I wondered what the tourists thought. Spooky probably covered it. I'd resolved several times to try to muster up some sympathy for her, but after I'd been around her for a few minutes, I ending up wanting to throttle her for being so mousy. On the other hand, if my parents had named me Dusty Rose, I might have some hang-ups too.

Of course, who were the first people I saw in the diner? Who else but Miss Georgia and Mr. Clyde? They waved enthusiastically so Brit, Kristen and I had no choice but to stop and say a quick hello. Miss Georgia stood to give us a group hug and whispered, "Ethan's sitting at the counter. That's Eric with him." Sporting blue-shadowed eyes and heavily-blushed cheeks, she gave us an innocent smile. I was developing respect for Miss Georgia as an undercover agent. She was pretty cool.

Only one booth was open at the far end of the diner so I assumed it was the one Dusty Rose half-way pointed at. Navigating the diner under her directorship required reading her mind with no feedback. The table provided a good view of nearly everybody including Miss Georgia and Mr. Clyde and Ethan and Eric. Brit and I sat on one side of the table and Kristen on the other. Kristen and I turned sideways and rested our backs against the wall, the way we always sat at the *Chatterbox*, our teen hang-out, and the better position to see who was coming and going which was why we went there in the first place.

I studied Ethan from the back. Mr. Clyde's description of him was right-on. He looked Mediterranean, but he could've been Italian or Spanish as easily as Greek. Although I could only see him from the back, he embodied at least two traits of the trilogy of tall, dark and handsome. I needed to see his face to decide if he was handsome. Eric was tall, well-built and as Nordic as his name.

The two were immersed in conversation, paying no attention to the other diners. I took the chance to observe the duo. I asked Brit and Kristen if they thought we'd ever seen Ethan in Vikki's bedroom. "No," Kristen replied emphatically. "He's really distinctive looking with his coloring and size. We would've remembered him." Of course, with Vikki's funky lighting, who could be sure what anybody looked like in normal surroundings?

Eric was surfer boy blond, tall, ruggedly good-looking and about Ethan's age. "Well, what about Eric? Rhonda said Vikki liked him before Colton. Did we see Eric at Vikki's?" I asked.

"Only one way to find out," Brit said. "Amy, go over and tell him to drop his pants so we can get a good look at his ass." I laughed out loud picturing Eric standing bare-butt in Gene's Diner. That'd bring Gene out of the kitchen.

"Seriously, do y'all think we've seen Eric with Vikki?"

"Maybe he's the one who was wearing the cowboy boots. He had light-ish hair," Kristen said.

Yeah. Eric was a definite maybe for the naked cowboy.

Even now, I was still pretty much stuffed from my big breakfast and afternoon snack in the forest, so I ordered a Pepsi and a plate of nachos with melted cheese. Brit and Kristen both had dinner plans, so they didn't order anything except drinks. I couldn't eat all my nachos so I kept pushing them at Brit and Kristen.

Brit looked around and said, "Where's Dusty

Rose? These nachos make me thirsty. I need a drink refill." Not seeing our reluctant waitress anywhere, she said, "Oh, I'll go get it myself." Before she got the last word out of her mouth, she was out of the booth and halfway to the counter. I shot Kristen an annoyed look. I didn't want Brit drawing attention to us in front of Ethan and Eric. Too late now. Brit, oblivious to blowing our cover, casually propped her elbow on the counter and waited for one of the waitresses to see her. She was standing only a few feet from Ethan but he and Eric were deep in conversation and didn't seem to notice her.

"Hurry up, Brit," I said under my breath.

Gene spotted Brit and made one of his rare ventures from the kitchen, forehead wrinkled, hawk-like eyes peeled to see where Dusty Rose had gotten to. Lucky for her, she was busy on the far side of the diner taking an order from a large, boisterous family all talking at once. Gene's scowl lines softened, satisfied his waitress wasn't goofing off. He took Brit's glass, returned with a refill, said nothing and retreated to his lair in the kitchen.

Ethan and Eric turned momentarily as Brit passed behind them on her way back to our booth. I got a good look at Ethan's profile and the trilogy was complete. He was handsome. But nothing about his face told me anything about the person. Maybe I was swayed by Clyde's claims that Ethan was secretive, but I was inclined to agree that he didn't reveal anything about himself. Was it deliberate? Was he hiding something as Mr. Clyde thought? Or just shy?

Brit slid into our booth and without looking back at the counter, she said, "They've finished eating. When they leave, let's see what kind of cars they're driving. Try to get license plate numbers, too."

"Little Miss Attorney. This law stuff runs in your family, doesn't it? You must have CSI in your DNA," Kristen snapped.

"Zip it, Kristen. It's a good idea, Brit." We argued about how we were going to pull this off. While we were disagreeing, Ethan and Eric paid their checks and started out the door.

We scrambled over each other trying to get out of our booth and crashed into Dusty Rose. "Y'all have to pay before you leave," she said in her meek little girl voice.

"Chill, Dusty Rose. We're going to the bathroom," Kristen said, snapping harshly. Dusty Rose murmured apologies before slinking behind the counter.

As soon as Ethan and Eric were outside, both reached in their shorts pockets for keys, so I figured they'd driven separate cars. I grabbed Kristen's arm and pulled her across the diner to peer out the window with me in the direction Ethan went and told Brit to follow Eric and get a description of his car. A minute later, Brit tapped me on the shoulder. "Get back over there and watch Eric like I told you," I said. God, why couldn't she do anything right?

"Lay off, Amy. Eric stopped outside the door to answer his phone, and he's walking and talking his way toward this side of the parking lot. Don't worry. I've been hot on his trail all the way over here though," she said, sarcasm coating her words. As if timing it to prove Brit right, Eric rounded the corner of the diner and strode across the lot to where Ethan was parked. Brit flashed me a smug smile but I let it pass. The three of us crowded into an empty booth and watched Ethan get into a black BMW with a

Chicago Bears license plate on the front. Eric unlocked the door of a snazzy red Miata.

"I know those cars," I said, feeling giddy. "Earlier this afternoon, they were parked behind the dumpsters at work."

Leading Brit and Kristen back to our booth, I yanked them toward the center of the table. "You won't believe this but I saw Ethan and Eric at the grocery store today," I whispered. "Until I saw the BMW and Miata just now, I had no idea it was them."

"Big deal. They were shopping. Doesn't everybody go to the grocery store?" Brit said, still miffed.

"But they weren't shopping. That's the problem. They were parked behind the store talking to some other people."

"Not back where they keep the garbage?" Kristen asked, her nose wrinkling in disgust.

"Yeah. That's why it was so weird. I saw people when I went around back looking for shopping carts. So, seeing cars and people where they shouldn't be and being the super investigator that I am, I hid behind some dumpsters and watched. Hey, I even took photos," I told them. "Look. That's Ethan. There's Eric," I said as I flipped through the series of shots. "And you can even see the *Chicago Bears* license plate on the front of Ethan's BMW."

Brit and Kristen looked closely at the photos of Ethan and Eric. "Damn," Kristen said, "it's them. And they were behind the store?"

"What about the others?" I said. "Recognize them?"

"Never saw them," Brit said. Kristen shook her head.

"Well," I said, "Mr. Clyde said Ethan was fishy. These photos prove it."

"Amen," said Kristen.

"Forgetting the dumpsters, they look like regular business people," Brit said, scrolling through the photos again.

"I'd say business people who meet behind dumpsters sound like crooked business people," Kristen said.

"I agree," I said, "I'm sure neither I nor anybody else was meant to see that meeting."

"Could it have been a drug deal?" Brit asked.

"Maybe but I didn't see them exchange packages or cash or anything. Of course, I don't know how long they'd been back there or what happened before I came across them. During the time I watched, they passed around papers and talked and made serious faces." Then I added, "Well, whatever they were doing isn't my problem. I'm focused on Vikki's murder. No time for sideshows."

The three of us stopped to say good-bye to Miss Georgia and Mr. Clyde. "Did you find out anything about Ethan and Eric at the counter, Brit?" Miss Georgia asked.

"Not really," Brit said. "They were talking about playing poker. Guy talk." Miss Georgia looked disappointed that the information wasn't sensational. Mr. Clyde nodded approvingly. He understood guys talking about playing cards.

As soon as we got outside and didn't have to worry about eavesdroppers, Kristen and I both jumped on Brit for drawing attention to us. "Lighten up," she said. "They barely looked at me. What difference does it make anyway? Ethan's probably seen us around your neighborhood," she said to me.

I didn't like it. Good journalists and good investigators didn't call attention to themselves. Except, of course, when they ended up being the subject of a big spread in the *Asheville Citizen-Times*.

Chapter Eight

We walked past Vikki's apartment building on the way to my house. Barbara Allison sat on a garden bench, puffing away on a cigarette. She was going to smoke herself to death. She gave us a limp wave. I said to Brit and Kristen, "You know, I'm going to ask Barbara what she was going to tell the police about Vikki last night." My friends rolled their eyes at me, making it clear how stupid they thought that was. "Oh, stop with the eyes, y'all. This might be one of Barbara's good days."

"From what I hear, she doesn't have many so your chances of randomly hitting one are like, zero," Kristen said.

"Not only that," Brit chimed in, "but whatever it is, she'll tell you five times in a row in the exact same words before you can escape. On this one, I have to agree with Uncle Mike. Barbara is la-la. You're wasting your time, Amy."

I didn't need Brit to tell me Barbara was pretty far gone. I knew that from living next door to her.

Repeating herself over and over drove me crazy but she'd told Drew, the police investigator, she talked to Vikki last night and could check her notes what time it was. Being a note taker myself, I identified with people who wrote things down. It seemed unlikely that Barbara was a totally reliable note-taker but who knew? Granted Mike and Brit and Kristen were probably right that Barbara imagined she talked to Vikki but I couldn't rest unless I asked her myself.

"You go talk to her if you want to, but count me out," Kristen said. "I've got to call my mom. See you in the cupola." Brit sided with Kristen saying she'd rather go to my house than listen to Barbara rattle on. Annoyed at both of them, I abruptly turned and walked up the driveway to the garden alone. I didn't need their tag-along company, thank you.

"Hello, Barbara," I said. Everybody called her by her first name. Her ancestors were astounding reproducers making the family related by blood or marriage to about everybody in Sugar Liquor including me. Our grandparents were cousins or kin folks in some way. "I'm sorry about Vikki. She was your good friend." Barbara nodded. "You told Drew you talked to Vikki last night when she got home."

"Yeah, I did talk to her. I guess I'm the last person who saw her alive, except for whoever killed her." With tears starting to flow, she said, "Vikki was a sweet girl." Sweet? I'd heard Vikki called lots of things but sweet wasn't one of them. Actually I was glad Barbara had warm feelings toward Vikki. Not many people felt kindly toward her.

"What did you and Vikki talk about last night?"

"I heard you're playing detective," she said. I was surprised she knew about my investigation and wondered if Miss Georgia told her. If she did, Miss Georgia needed to zip her lips.

Barbara seemed to lose track of where we were in the conversation so I tried again. "What did you and Vikki talk about?" She still didn't speak so I more or less repeated what I'd just said and added, "Barbara, you may be the only person who has information that can help catch Vikki's murderer. You don't want that person to get away with killing her, do you?"

"No. Whoever killed her has to be caught and punished," she said in a firm voice. Barbara hesitated before she spoke, looking at my face. Was she trying to decide if I really wanted to hear her story? I felt sorry for her, not aggravated by her confusion.

"Well," she said after taking a long drag on her cigarette, "I tried to tell Drew last night but he wouldn't listen to me." Barbara scooted over so I had space to sit beside her. Her face was flushed.

I patted Barbara's bony knee which her denim Capri pants didn't quite cover. "I'm not Drew," I told her. "I want to hear what you have to say." She rubbed the hem of her blouse between her fingers while her dark eyes darted anxiously. I began to think I'd been wrong. Maybe this conversation Barbara thought she had with Vikki was a product of Barbara's muddled mind.

She stopped fiddling with her blouse. I hoped she was pulling her thoughts together. When she began speaking in a clear strong voice, she caught me off guard. "Amy, this is what I know that Mike doesn't. What I was going to tell Drew. Vikki had a boyfriend. His name is Colton Matos and he's Ethan's younger brother. You know Ethan? He lives on the second floor below Vikki and Justin. Anyway,

Colton's awful cute and a whole lot friendlier than Ethan."

I straightened up and perked up. Barbara knew about Vikki and Colton? Maybe she wasn't so far gone after all. "Since I live across the hall from Vikki, I hear and see a lot. I'm getting awful forgetful about things so I started making notes of stuff. You know what I mean? I write down dates and times and people's names. That's so if somebody asks me something, I can check my notebook and answer without sounding like a damn fool."

The more Barbara talked, the less agitated she became. The nervousness that caused her to act so herky-jerky faded. "Colton hasn't been in Sugar Liquor but a couple of months. He stayed with Ethan when he first got here until he bought one of those fancy new condos on Riley Street. Anyway, Colton came to visit Vikki at her apartment almost every night."

Rhonda said Vikki had a thing for Colton and it looked like she was right. He was likely the boyfriend Miss Georgia saw park in the back lot and heard climbing the steps to Vikki's apartment. "I wrote down the details about Colton in my little notebook. I was going to give it to the police but after I heard Mike and Drew talking about me last night, I'd sooner burn it than let them have it. In fact, I was thinking about burning it anyway. Maybe that's what I should do."

"No, no. Don't burn it. If it has anything that'll help track down Vikki's murderer, please let me see it."

Barbara eyes looked vague and I thought I was losing touch with her. I almost panicked but she turned to me and smiled. "I want Vikki's killer found, and if this is a way I can help, I'll let you read it. Vikki was a friendly girl who came over to my apartment all the time for coffee or a beer. I know she was kind of trashy but I liked her. She was funny and fun to be around. She never confided in me about her personal life, and I never let on that I knew about her boyfriend. I figured she was over eighteen and could live her own life.

"Last night after Ron left with Vikki's body, I hung around outside for a while to calm myself, plus the police wouldn't let me go inside until they'd finished my apartment.

"I was sitting in the garden when I saw you hiding behind a police car listening to Mike and Drew talk about Vikki's case. I was eavesdropping on them, too, although I didn't plan it like you did," she said with a smile. "Mike and Drew just happened to do their talking near where I was sitting so I heard everything they said, including Mike telling Drew not to pay any attention to what I say because I'm senile. Mike can go to hell. That really hurt my feelings. You know, when you get old, people ignore you and don't listen to you." She looked like she was going to cry.

I'd solved another mystery. Barbara was the *somebody* watching Kristen, Brit and me hiding behind the police car last night. My intuition had been right. Thank goodness it was a friend.

Following Barbara's lead I climbed the steps behind her and waited while she unlocked her door. It was weird to be standing in the narrow hall across from Vikki's apartment. I could almost touch her doorknob. As many times as I'd watched Vikki with my binoculars through her windows from my cupola, I'd never been to her front door. I had no reason to visit.

Yellow police tape still marked the apartment off limits. It was quiet now. I walked behind Barbara across the hall to her door and asked if the police were still around. "I think they're inside. They're bound to be about finished. The apartment isn't that big, and they had a lot of people in there all night."

Barbara's big fluffy cat, aptly named Fluffy, met us at the door, winding in and out our legs. Since she was an indoor cat, I didn't know Fluffy from the neighborhood so I stooped to get acquainted. A cat lover all my life, I liked her right away. She was a sweet, loving cat who gave my hands kitty kisses as I rubbed her soft head.

Breaking away from Fluffy, I stood and glanced at Barbara's apartment. Neat and comfortably furnished. Her husband had been dead for years, and her only daughter was married and living in Oregon. Barbara had only herself to please. The furniture matched and was arranged attractively, so different from Miss Georgia and Mr. Clyde's overstuffed ramble-scramble existence.

Barbara opened an old fashioned roll top desk, revealing a stack of notebooks, each with a label printed with a Sharpie. I couldn't keep from noticing she had notebooks dealing with her neighbors, friends, her daughter, finances and anything else she deemed worth remembering. Barbara pulled a notebook from the neighbors' stack. "This is the one I kept on Vikki. It wasn't so much that I was nosy about her, although I admit to a little of that too," she said, lightening up and laughing a little. "Mostly, I wrote stuff in my notebooks so I had a record of what was going on around me. If I started thinking about something, it drove me crazy not being able to remember what I'd seen or heard or when it happened.

"Vikki took awful chances. A couple times when Justin came home from his job unexpectedly, when he got rained out or something, he barely missed running into Colton. Justin was good about calling Vikki before he came home to see if she wanted something to eat or needed anything from the store. It was thoughtful of him and gave Vikki a few minutes time to get Colton out the door. I'm not a mind reader, but it didn't take one to see that Vikki was heading for trouble.

"To tell you the truth, I was afraid Justin would catch Colton with Vikki some night and kill him. I never expected Vikki to be the one to get killed." Barbara handed the notebook to me. "Take it and I hope it helps. But, please, bring it back when you're finished. Truth be told, I couldn't have burned it. I've got some sweet stuff in there about Vikki. I don't want to forget the good times I had with her." Barbara's eyes got misty again.

I agreed she should cherish her memories of Vikki. "One other thing," she said, "my sister's picking me up in a few minutes and I'm going to stay at her house in Waynesville 'til this settles down. It makes me too sad to be around all this talk about Vikki. I've got to get away."

"Don't worry about your notebook, Barbara. I'll take it to my house right now and it'll stay there until I return it to you. Do you mind if I show it to Brit and Kristen since they're helping me?"

"That's fine. But don't let Mike see it. No. No." That was an easy promise to make and one I didn't worry about breaking.

Apparently an avid traveler, Fluffy trotted

unassisted into her carrier and I latched it and carried it downstairs. Fluffy and her carrier weighed more than I expected. There was some serious cat underneath all that fur. My arm ached by the time I carried her down to the first floor.

As soon as we walked outside, Barbara's sister, Rose, pulled into the driveway. I chatted with her while I settled Fluffy's carrier on the backseat. Barbara stored her suitcase in the trunk. When they got situated and buckled, Rose drove away and I waved good-bye to her and to my hurting neighbor.

Running through my mother's garden, zig-zagging around the rose bushes, I couldn't wait to get to the cupola and read Barbara's entries. Mom and Dad weren't home from work yet so I flew up the stairs to the cupola to show Brit and Kristen what I got from Barbara. My enthusiasm was shot down by their skepticism.

"Have you considered this notebook may be a record of when and what she fed Fluffy?" Kristen said.

"Or the life story of that cat of hers that lived to be twenty-three years old," Brit added. "Remember when it died, it got a front-page write-up in the paper?"

"It got a better and longer obituary than the retired sheriff who died the same week," Kristen replied, laughing. She and Brit batted stories about the cat and sheriff back and forth.

"Will y'all shut up about Barbara's cats?" I flipped through the pages randomly, half-way afraid a quarter-century record of feline hairball treatments and stool sample results would jump out at me. Brit and Kristen rattled my confidence in Barbara's note-taking.

But Barbara had delivered. "Not to worry," I told my bonehead friends. "Looks like Barbara's got everything in here."

I sat down cross-legged on my cot, eager to read. To begin, I checked last night's entry as a validation of Barbara's record-keeping ability. Brit and Kristen lay down on their cots to listen as I scanned and summarized the contents of Barbara's journal. "Vikki came home last night at nine-thirty, which jives with what Gene told the police about her getting off at nine and chatting with some high school friends. Colton came up the back stairs at nine-forty-five, carrying a six-pack of Heineken."

"What? You mean Barbara wrote down what kind of beer Colton brought?" Brit asked.

"She's very specific," I said, with an attitude.

"Uncle Mike called this one wrong. Barbara was willing to turn this notebook over to Drew, and Mike nixed it," Brit said.

I loved being one up on Mike and this was a big one. He better read some material on geriatric psychology. He might discover old people have some gems stored in their brains.

"Since Barbara's apartment door is directly across the hall from Vikki's door, I'm guessing she watched Colton out her peephole. I wonder though how she knew Colton was coming up the back steps so she could zip to the peephole in time to get all these details."

Kristen sat up, shrieking. "I know, I know. Remember that time Mr. Clyde showed us the back steps? They creaked something awful. We kept hopping back and forth on them, playing, because we'd never seen steps that made so much noise. And, they come up beside Barbara's living room wall so she could've heard Colton or anybody else for that matter."

"You're brilliant," Brit said. "Those steps are something else."

I nodded and read on. "Barbara reports fairly loud music coming from Vikki's apartment until about eleven. Then soft music until Colton left by the back stairs around midnight. Barbara made an entry this morning that she didn't hear Justin come home and didn't know he was in the building until he started screaming about two o'clock."

"So, does this mean Colton or Justin killed Vikki?" Kristen asked.

"Both were certainly with her and had the opportunity," I replied. "But somebody else could've gone to the apartment too. Barbara didn't hear Justin come home so maybe she didn't hear somebody else."

"I guess that's true. I wonder how long it'll take Mike to find out about Colton," Brit said.

"It depends on how many people knew about her having a boyfriend and how much they knew or didn't know," I said. "Start with Miss Georgia. She knows Vikki had a boyfriend but not who he was because it was always dark when he arrived. Rhonda knows Vikki was chasing Colton but she didn't see them together. For sure, Rhonda's not going to tell Mike anything, because all she knows is what she's guessed. Barbara's pissed at Mike because of what he said about her. She won't volunteer anything. You know, I wonder if anybody else who works at the diner suspected Vikki and Colton were having a fling."

Kristen laughed. "Dusty Rose is so naïve, I doubt she knows what an affair is. Can you imagine

Mike trying to interrogate her about anything having to do with sex?"

"Poor girl would have a stroke," Brit replied. "What about Gene though? Do you think he knew?"

"I doubt it. He doesn't miss much that goes on in that diner even if he does stay in the kitchen all the time, but it would've been limited to making sure Vikki got the bills right not who she was flirting with," I added. "I can't imagine Gene showing any interest in anything that didn't have to do with him making money. Anybody else who knows about Colton?"

"Ethan and Eric might know, but they won't mention it since it could implicate Colton in Vikki's murder. Man, I can't picture Colton as her murderer though. When we were watching them last night, the guy seemed crazy about Vikki. It's hard to imagine that he weirded out and killed her a little while later," Brit said.

I turned to the beginning of Barbara's notebook. "Let's see when Barbara started keeping tabs on Vikki." The first entry was about four months ago. Barbara described a fair young man--tall, wearing jeans, a suede jacket, cowboy hat and boots--coming to Vikki's apartment at ten o'clock and staying until midnight. She mentions Justin was working out of town. Vikki didn't wait long after her wedding to start running around."

"That had to be the naked cowboy," Kristen said. "It was still cool weather the first time we saw him in Vikki's apartment. He could be the fellow we saw with Ethan at the diner tonight. Rhonda said Vikki flirted with Ethan's friend, Eric. Of course, it was a hundred degrees outside today, so that explains why he was wearing flip-flops instead of cowboy boots."

"From Barbara's notes," I said, "it looks like Vikki dumped the cowboy and took up with Colton." The rest of the entries were details about Colton. "... a sweet boyfriend and partial to Heineken, Chinese food and daisies ... I bet Vikki got rid of those daisies before Justin got home for the weekend. Sometimes Colton and Vikki got dressed up and went out for the evening. Bet they went to Asheville where they weren't likely to run into anybody who knew she was married."

Colton's departure time from Vikki's apartment was noted but only if he left by midnight. I assumed that was Barbara's bedtime and her cut-off for snooping and note-taking.

"I wonder if Vikki was in love with Colton. I hadn't thought she might be serious about a boyfriend. I was thinking they were flings," Brit said. "It's kind of sad if she'd really fallen for Colton."

"It's even sadder if she fell for him and he's the one who strangled her," I replied.

Kristen agreed and added, "I'd say we have three or maybe four suspects with Justin in the most likely spot since he's the husband and Vikki was cheating on him. Then we've got the naked cowboy who Vikki dumped. Colton, the current flame that she seemed to really like. Maybe Ethan."

"Ethan? As far as we know, he wasn't involved with Vikki," I said.

"Mr. Clyde thinks Ethan's fishy," Kristen replied.

"We'll have to add half the population of Sugar Liquor if being fishy makes you a suspect for murder," I said, laughing.

Brit asked what motive the naked cowboy or Colton could have for killing Vikki.

"The cowboy's easy. He was mad at Vikki for dumping him," Kristen said.

"That doesn't compute," I said. "People get dumped every day. Most don't resort to murder."

"True," Brit argued, "but you never know a person's emotional state or their perspective on the relationship. Getting dumped affects people in different ways." She sounded more *legal* every day. It would be interesting to watch someday when Mike brought a case to court and Brit defended the accused. I'd put my bet on Brit.

"Okay," I said, "I concede the cowboy might be, and I say, might be, pissed enough at Vikki to strangle her but what about Colton? He looked like he was enjoying himself pretty good last night. I'd say his mood was amorous, not homicidal."

Brit wasn't ready to concede. "Maybe Vikki broke up with him later in the evening and he couldn't take it so he killed her." Anything was possible but it didn't seem likely. "How about Ethan? Maybe he had a thing for Vikki and she didn't respond."

"In that case, he should've killed the cowboy and Colton and eliminated the competition," Kristen was quick to reply. Brit and I laughed at her goofy solution.

"As much as we don't want it to be Justin, he still has the strongest motive," Brit said.

"Speaking of which," I said as movement next door caught my eye. "Justin's going in the front door of the building," I said. "Shall we go over?"

"To his apartment? What are we going to say? Did you kill Vikki because she was screwing around?" Kristen asked, laughing.

"Of course not, you moron. We'll express our

condolences and then we'll ask if he killed her," the lawyer in Brit suggested.

"Not far off, Brit. We'll go over and tell Justin how sorry we are about Vikki. After all, I'm the next door neighbor, and I'm supposed to do neighborly things. My grandma always taught me that little southern girls are supposed to show compassion, so it's time to put some into practice. Then, we weasel our way into Justin's apartment and talk to him about Vikki."

"He's going to see right through that," Kristen argued, looking at me like I was the world's dunce.

"Well, if we don't do something, he's liable to leave and we'll miss our chance." I started toward the door. "Vamos, y'all."

Chapter Nine

As my motley little detective squad snaked through Mom's garden toward Justin's apartment, I had second thoughts about our mission. My hasty decision didn't seem like such a good idea now that I was half-way to his house. After all, he had the strongest motive, perhaps the only realistic motive, to kill Vikki. And here I was, leading my friends to barge in on him. Not seeming like a good idea now.

But by the time I reached this conclusion, I was standing in front of Justin's door, yellow police tape still in place. Were the police inside? I didn't see any vehicles outside. "One of y'all knock," I told Brit and Kristen. Naturally they started squabbling over who had to do it. Kristen lost. She leaned across the yellow tape and tapped so lightly, it was barely audible. She hoped Justin wouldn't hear her. He opened the door right away.

"Hello, Justin," I said, trying to sound normal. "Hey, is it okay for us to be here?" Justin didn't seem to understand what I meant so I pointed to the tape.

"Are the police still here?" He shook his head no. "How'd you get in the apartment?"

"Simple. I ducked under the tape and used my key. I need some clothes."

"Did the police give you permission?" I asked.

"I didn't ask. All the clothes I own are in this apartment so I'm getting them."

Justin's blotchy face and bloodshot eyes had aged him way beyond his twenty-one years. He stood there looking at me blankly, waiting for me to state my business. He reminded me of the dejected high school boy Vikki used to kick around. Brit jabbed me sharply in the back, prompting me to get on with my sympathy spiel. I repeated the words my mother said in similar situations, thinking I sounded mature and sincere. Enough so that Justin's gaze dropped to the floor when I mentioned Vikki's name.

"Hey, if there's anything any of us can do to help you," I said, pointing to Brit and Kristen to include them, "please let us know. We really mean it."

"Yeah. Thanks," he said, his voice hollow. He didn't try to close the door on us so I waited for him to break the silence. I'd already said my bit and couldn't think of anything to add to it. "Y'all want to come in? I just put on a pot of coffee," he said in a monotone.

I nodded, pleased that I'd accomplished getting us invited into his apartment.

Standing behind me, Brit said in a tiny voice, "Thanks, Justin, but I have to--uh--do some stuff."

Standing behind Brit, Kristen added, "Me too. Some other time."

With that, my two best friends abruptly turned

and bailed on me, leaving me standing in the hallway facing Justin. I'm a quick thinker but I couldn't come up with even a pathetic excuse to get out of this. I'd already accepted Justin's invitation, so I ducked under the police tape and obediently followed him inside.

Nervously, I took a deep breath and a big whiff of stale cigarette smoke went up my nose, almost causing me to gag. From the looks of unemptied ashtrays, Justin smoked inside the apartment as well as during his al fresco chats with Ethan. With every step, I silently swore at Brit and Kristen. The minute I got out of this apartment, if I got out of this apartment, I was going to kill both of them for deserting me. Those were two murders I'd be able to solve without any trouble. I was already writing the first paragraph of the newspaper account in my head.

Justin took two mismatched mugs from a cabinet, filled them with coffee, pulled an almost empty carton of milk from the fridge and poked a spoon into a plastic sugar bowl. I retrieved two chairs from the living room and scooted them toward the table.

With knees threatening to buckle, I dropped into my chair. I was alone with a man the police suspected of killing his wife, and I was in the very apartment where it happened. I was so shaky, I could barely aim a spoonful of sugar into my coffee cup and definitely too rattled to pour milk. Justin didn't say anything. He busied himself adding sugar and milk to his coffee. He started to pass the milk to me but I shook my head no. He dumped the remains of the carton into his own coffee.

I couldn't think how to start a conversation. I

hadn't talked to Justin much ever so I didn't have an easy opener. When I was a freshman, I had a class with him and chatted occasionally but those topics seemed too much on target for this situation. *What's new? What'd you do last night*?

Justin broke the silence. "Actually, Amy, I'm glad you stopped by. Being in this place gives me the creeps," he said glancing around the tiny kitchen. "I'm outta here as soon as I grab my stuff."

"Where are you going?"

"My brother's place. The police are all over me and my mama's really upset. She's cried all day. I'm afraid Mike's going to arrest me and I'd rather not be at her house when it happens." He stared into his coffee cup. "Mike and Drew kept me at the station all night. Asked me a thousand questions. I kept telling them they were wasting their time. I wouldn't hurt Vikki much less kill her."

"You found Vikki's body. Is that what makes Mike so sure you did it?"

"I guess he figures I had the chance but he's wrong." Justin took a slow drink of his coffee. "It was like this. Materials didn't get delivered to our job site on time so the boss let us go home. The problem was that me and some of my buddies didn't get the message, because we'd gone out to eat and play pool. We didn't know work had been canceled until later when we got back to the motel where we stayed." Justin explained, by that time, most of the other guys had already left for home. "I was tired and thought about waiting until morning to drive home, but I decided to surprise Vikki." Who got surprised? Vikki or Justin?

"What happened when you got home?"

"I let myself in and found Vikki laying on the

floor. I tried to wake her up but I couldn't."

"When you found her, what did you think was wrong with her?"

"To tell you the truth, I thought she'd had too much to drink. It happens once in a while. I kept telling this same story to the police but they didn't buy it."

"Justin, you probably haven't heard, but I'm looking into Vikki's death. Brit and Kristen are helping. Maybe we'll find some evidence that favors you. Justin looked at me like I'd offered the detective services of Huey, Dewey and Louie Duck, complete with magnifying glasses and little plaid Sherlock Holmes caps.

"Well, can't do any harm." His face softened. "Thanks, Amy. Nobody else is on my side. By the way, good job of catching those good-for-nothing kids breaking in those stores. Thieving little punks."

We finished our coffee and Justin got up from the table. I rinsed our coffee mugs and set them in the drain rack to dry.

"I got to pack some clothes. Do you mind staying for a few more minutes and keeping me company? Going in that room tears me up inside," Justin said. He paused and took a deep breath before entering the bedroom. I followed suit by taking a deeper breath.

A bedside table lay on the floor, contents strewn across the floor. In the corner lay the lamp that likely had been on the table, the shade crushed, the bulb broken. The comforter was pulled half-way off the bed. Justin and Vikki's wedding photo hung off-kilter on the wall. I shuddered, picturing Vikki fighting her attacker, her struggle to save her life causing furnishings to fall and crash. Could these have been the crashing sounds that woke Miss Georgia?

Justin detoured around the spot where I guessed he found Vikki on the floor. I did the same, like avoiding stepping on a grave in a cemetery. The difference was that a girl I'd known died violently in this room last night and this was where her body lay until Ron took it away. She fell here when she could no longer fend off her attacker, when she lost the struggle.

I shook my head to get rid of disturbing thoughts about the horrific crime that had taken place within these walls. I needed to focus on something else, so I scanned the setting of countless nights of erotic teasing and pole dancing, the part of Vikki's life I knew and understood. Strobe lights, revolving lights, twinkling lights and even the dance pole were exactly as I'd seen them through my binoculars from the cupola. It was unreal to be in the room with them. Being in Vikki's lair was one of the weirdest experiences of my life.

Justin pulled clothes out of a drawer and a closet and stuffed them into a duffel bag. "You know, Justin, since you and Vikki were married, it's logical you'd be the person to find her. Aside from that, did Mike give you other reasons for thinking you did it?"

"Uh-uh. I didn't have any reason to kill Vikki. I told that to Mike over and over."

Justin shook his head, worn out, defeated. "But about that offer to help me. I'm desperate. I'd really appreciate anything you can do."

Before he finished packing and left the apartment, I asked him to start at the beginning and tell me everything he remembered about last night.

He obliged and, except for a few meaningless details, his story remained the same. "I was scared out of my mind. I ran out in the hall and started screaming for somebody to call an ambulance. My hands were shaking so bad I couldn't even turn my cellphone on. Thank goodness, people rushed out of their apartments to help me."

I didn't want to ask about Vikki's running around but it had to be brought out in the open. "Justin, don't get upset with me for asking this, but do you think Vikki was interested in another man? Maybe she got lonesome? Found a boyfriend?"

Justin's head snapped like I'd slapped him and slumped. "It's possible. Vikki changed after we got married. She didn't want to be around me when I came home. She took extra shifts at the diner on weekends and I'm sure she did it to avoid me. I asked her if there was another guy and she said no."

Justin got his razor from the bathroom and threw it in his bag and headed for the front door with me right behind him. "I got to get going. Take my cell number. Text me if you have any more questions or find out anything." I punched his number into my contacts and gave him my cell number. "I'm counting on you. Don't let me down," he said, his voice shaky and pleading, his eyes watery. With that, we stepped into the hallway. He twisted the lock on the inside of the doorknob, pulled the door shut, ducked under the police tape and ripped down the stairs without waiting for me. The main entrance door slammed behind him.

I took a slow, cleansing breath. Justin hadn't said or done anything intimidating, but being in that apartment put me on edge. Bad vibes from the room where Vikki died?

While I stood in the hall, my eyes drifted to the apartment door. Oh, my gosh. It was slightly open. The lock didn't catch when Justin closed it. I reached forward and touched it. It swung open. I knew I should lock it and leave the building but the temptation to go back in the apartment and snoop overcame my common sense.

I reached inside, flipped the lock, twisted the knob to make sure the door would open from the outside and gently closed it. Even though I was still mad at Brit and Kristen, I texted them to meet me at the back stairway.

I waited with the building's back door slightly open until I saw them emerge from Mom's garden. On the way up the steps I filled them in on what had happened.

The three of us violated the police tape, my second time if anybody was counting, and scrambled inside the apartment. I set the lock and inserted the security chain. We were locked in and the world was locked out. Brit said, "Don't forget that Kristen and I both have family plans so we better get on with whatever you have in mind." I agreed, not because I had anything to do, but because I worried we'd get caught. Since the police had the apartment taped off, they might return. But if they were still collecting evidence, wouldn't they have posted a guard? For sure, Justin wouldn't be back until he ran out of clean clothes and, Barbara, the only neighbor on the third floor, had left so we were safe from detection.

Since we were in the living room, I told Brit and Kristen, "We might as well start here." It was simply furnished with a discount store sofa and matching chair, coffee table, one end table and a few garage sale pictures hung erratically on the wall. Vikki wasn't much of a decorator. An HGTV devotee she was not.

I ran my hands behind and under the sofa cushions and found nothing more than a few pieces of stale popcorn and a couple lint-coated coins. Kristen flipped through a stack of fashion magazines and current and past issues of *Cosmo* scattered across the coffee table looking for anything stuck between the pages. Vikki wouldn't need her *Cosmos* anymore. Brit thumbed through CDs and DVDs stored in little multi-color plastic storage bins. We quickly exhausted possible nook and cranny hiding places in the living room.

The kitchen was next. When I was in there earlier drinking coffee with Justin, I didn't gawk out of politeness. Now with Brit and Kristen's help, we could do a job on it. I made a suggestion. "With all these cabinets and appliances, let's divide the room into sections so we can do it faster and make sure we don't miss anything." For once, we didn't have a long drawn-out argument over who was going to take which section. Each gravitated toward the closest area and got to work.

I looked in the trash can under the sink and found five Heineken cans in it. Since Barbara told us about Colton's six-pack, I automatically looked for the missing can. It was in the fridge, unopened and unconsumed. "Look, y'all, one beer. It looks lonesome."

The police seemingly had not attached any importance to the empty beer cans since they left them behind. They'd missed their chance to connect a second suspect, Colton, to the crime scene. I felt more than a little cocky catching their oversight.

Brit and Kristen looked behind dishes, inside pots and pans and through the sparse contents of the fridge. Apparently Vikki wasn't a fan of the Food Network either. Two Lean Cuisine frozen dinners, a box of pancake mix, two sticks of margarine and a partial carton of eggs seemed to be about it. Justin had polished off the last of the milk in his coffee. The kitchen took longer than the living room, but I was satisfied we'd given it a good search and left it in the same condition we found it.

Having searched the living room and kitchen, it was time for the crucial room, Vikki's bedroom and scene of the crime. I was dying to take a good, long look, and now I had my chance. I suggested we work together so all of us could see everything rather than one-third like the kitchen.

I opened a dresser drawer. Vikki's. Brit picked up one of Vikki's nightgowns. It was familiar from one of our binocular-watching sessions. As I rummaged through the drawer, it was clear Vikki had an extensive collection of sexy little nightgowns. Some with Victoria's Secret labels and others that came from K-Mart. "This is kinky," I said. "Let's cut out the Peeping Tom bit and look for anything that explains why somebody strangled Vikki. That's what we're supposed to be doing, not examining Vikki's choice of lingerie."

Kristen asked, "Do you think there's any point in doing this? Wouldn't the police already have found and taken away anything that's relevant to the case?"

"They didn't take the beer cans," I said. "If Mike hadn't made Barbara mad, she would've told him about Colton and the Heineken. The police could've matched Colton's fingerprints to the ones on the beer cans and proved Colton was in the apartment and included him as a possible suspect. As it is, they don't know that an important person in Vikki's life was with her here in her apartment the night she died."

"Sloppy police work," Brit added with a smug smile. Mike gave her a hard time about wanting to be a defense lawyer, so she couldn't wait for us to solve another one of his cases, but we weren't there yet. I gave Mike credit for being a great cop most of the time but if he'd missed anything, I intended to find it.

Suddenly I stopped rummaging in Vikki's drawers and listened. "Somebody's at the door," I whispered. "Be quiet. I'll go look out the peephole." What if it was the police? How on earth could I explain being in the apartment? As I tip-toed across the carpet, I expected to look through the peephole and find myself eyeball to eyeball with Mike.

Between worrying about what I was going to tell Mike and what he would do to me, I was trembling by the time I reached the door. I wouldn't put it past Mike to arrest me. Without touching the door or making a sound, I slowly swiveled my head to get my eye in position to look through the peephole.

It wasn't Mike or Drew or any other policeman. It was Ethan from downstairs. I was inches away from his pop-eyed convex face.

But Ethan wasn't knocking on the door. He was turning the doorknob trying to get inside. As I watched the knob rotate back and forth, I wanted to scream at him to stop. Did he think Justin was home and came up to talk to him? In that case, why didn't he knock? He wouldn't just walk in. Or had he seen Justin leave? Did he know I lingered in the hallway after Justin left and let Brit and Kristen in the back door? Was he being a concerned neighbor or a sinister snoop?

He tried the knob again and the rattling made my heart race. I could feel Brit and Kristen's hot breath on my neck. They must've followed me from the bedroom and were standing right behind me. I wanted to scream at them to back off. Their presence was freaking me out as much as Ethan's. I mouthed the word *Ethan* at them. Kristen's big blue eyes looked ready to pop. Brit held her hands over her mouth.

I stared at the tiny circle containing Ethan Matos' head. As abruptly as it began, the door knob stopped moving. Ethan turned and walked toward the stairs. I could hear his footsteps going down the uncarpeted steps one by one. When I thought he'd hit enough to be on the second floor, I silently slid off the deadbolt and opened the door a sliver. With my forehead pressed against the security chain, I heard his door close.

I turned around to tell Brit and Kristen that Ethan was gone and covered my mouth to stifle a scream. Brit held a gun in her hand. Kristen waved a stack of money.

"What the hell?" I asked.

"Appropriate question," replied Brit. "We found these in Vikki's closet. Come in here and look. It's too complicated to explain." My legs were so limp from my near-confrontation with Ethan and my idiot friends scaring me to death, I could barely walk. I grasped furniture to keep from falling as I followed Brit and Kristen to the bedroom. I reminded them to keep quiet so Ethan couldn't hear us. The idea he was directly below us creeped me out. I couldn't shake the image of his distorted face on the other side of that peephole.

The three of us squeezed into Vikki's closet. On the left side, the drywall extended only about three-quarters of the way to the ceiling. The upper wall was unfinished with the two-by-four studs showing. Brit said, "The gun and cash were wrapped in a plastic Wal-Mart bag, stuffed down between the studs, behind the drywall. A wooden cross-piece kept the bag from falling to the floor and making it irretrievable except by ripping off the drywall."

"How'd you find this?" I asked, incredulously.

"Brit rooted around in there with her little hands and pulled out the bag. It was an ingenious hiding place. Only somebody with little hands like Vikki or Brit could do it."

"Well done, y'all."

Kristen glanced at Brit who was still holding the gun. "What if that thing's loaded?" she asked.

"It is loaded, you moron. Not only that, the safety was off. You better be glad I was the one who found it. If you'd found it, you would've shot all of us waving it around asking if it was loaded." Brit, a sharpshooter since she was a little kid, carefully and competently removed the shells. Brit's whole family excelled at marksmanship. Their family reunions weren't complete without shooting contests that went on all weekend. In spite of my confidence in Brit's experience with weapons, I told her to lay it down, preferably with the business end pointing the other direction.

"What was Vikki doing with this stuff hidden in her closet?" Kristen asked. "Maybe she wanted the gun for protection but all this cash?"

"No way," Brit said. "The gun wasn't handy if

117

she was worried about somebody breaking in. Before she could've dug it out of its hiding place, somebody would've had her."

"New subject. Where did Vikki get this stuff?" Kristen asked.

"It's a safe bet she didn't pilfer it from Gene's. He'd miss a dime. Plus, she didn't need a gun to pilfer." I paused and added, "You don't think she and Colton robbed a store or something on one of their dates?" It sounded stupid even as I said it but it was so unreal to find that stuff in Vikki's closet to begin with.

"I don't think most people get dressed up for a date and then go out and knock over a convenience store. They don't keep that kind of cash on hand any way, and there's not much else open at night," Kristen said.

"True. Maybe they belong to Justin. Maybe he got mixed up with the wrong crowd on his construction job and helped pull a bank robbery," I said but took it back right away. That didn't sound like Justin. Although I didn't know him well, his reputation around Sugar Liquor was that of a decent guy. I couldn't picture him going into a bank brandishing a gun and wearing his mama's panty hose over his head.

Brit said, "Besides, if this stuff belongs to Justin, he would've gotten them out of the apartment before he went out in the hallway and started yelling for someone to call *911*. There's no way he would've taken a chance on the police finding something like this. Can you imagine what Mike and Drew would've made of these? So that brings us back to Vikki who had to be the one who hid the gun and cash, but where on earth did she get them?"

"Beats me," I replied.

"Me too," Kristen said, ending that discussion. "Okay, Brit, get on the chair and use your little hands to stuff them back in the wall."

"Hold on a minute, Brit," I said. "We can't leave all that cash here."

"Why not? That's where we found it," Kristen said.

"Because it's bound to be related to Vikki's murder," I said. "If we leave it hidden in this wall, it may never be found. The police didn't find it when they searched the apartment. And you can bet Justin wouldn't have left it behind if he'd known about it."

"Amy, you've lost what little mind you had. Are you seriously suggesting we take this with us?" Kristen asked.

"And the gun too," I added without hesitating. "They're a link between Vikki and her murder."

"Bad idea," Kristen said. "It's one thing to ignore police tape and search Vikki's apartment, but it's way different to remove things, especially something this potentially crucial. I say we leave them right where we found them."

"Kristen's right," Brit chimed in. "As much as you want to solve this case, removing evidence from an active crime scene is over the top."

"Y'all don't get it. This may be the clue, the only clue, to Vikki's murderer. Shush," I told them. "I hear something." I listened but I couldn't identify the sounds, kind of metallic and random. "It must be the police bringing more equipment. Let's get the hell out of here."

Brit and Kristen made a beeline for the front door. "Put that stuff back, Amy," Kristen hissed at me. "Now!" With that, they loped down the back stairs.

I ran to Vikki's closet, Kristen's words ringing in my ears, my fist clutching the bag of money and gun. The noises moved closer and louder. I dashed for the front door. Using fumble-fingers, I set the lock, closed the door securely, ducked under the police tape and bounded down the back steps.

The screen door of my house slammed as Brit and Kristen clamored inside. With metallic noises all around me, I stopped when I got to Mom's garden and hid behind a trellis, waiting for police vehicles pulling giant, rattling crime-detecting equipment to appear. I didn't know whether to cry or laugh when the weekly recycling truck rolled up in front of the apartment building, bottles and cans clanging as workers threw them into the truck.

All that anxiety and running for nothing.

On top of that, I had a gun and a bunch of cash in my backpack.

Chapter Ten

Out of breath, I huffed and puffed my way up to the cupola. Kristen and Brit were lying on their cots, red-faced and breathing hard.

"What was that thing?" Brit asked. "It scared the crap out of me."

Avoiding her question, I collapsed onto my cot. "No idea." I didn't want a lecture about inciting a riot and risking three heart attacks because the recycling truck was doing its weekly thing collecting beer bottles and tin cans.

When my heart slowed to a normal rate, I dumped the contents of my backpack on my comforter. Kristen scrambled off her cot, wild-eyed, ready to throttle me. "What the hell, Amy? I told you to leave this stuff in Vikki's apartment."

"What stuff?" Brit asked. "Oh, no," she said, jumping up when she recognized the bag. "Please tell me you didn't do this. If Mike finds out ... "

"Chill, Brit, he's not going to find out. I panicked because of those weird noises and stuffed the bag in my backpack. Anyway, this may be a major clue in finding Vikki's killer."

"It damn well better be," Kristen said. "You could get us in so much trouble."

"Hey, if anything happens, I'll take all the blame. Okay?" Kristen and Brit responded with skeptical stares. I didn't blame them. I wasn't sure I could make good on my magnanimous offer. We stared at each other like mute aliens.

Brit broke the silence. "Well, since the bag's here, we might as well take a look at it." She laid out five identical packets with matching paper bands around hundred dollar bills and counted the bills in a packet. "Whoa. There's five thousand dollars."

"Where did Vikki get her hands on that much cash?" Kristen asked.

"She sure didn't save it out of her tips from Gene's. You don't suppose she charged for her entertainment services, do you?" I asked, intending the question to be a joke.

"No, and even if she had," Brit said, ignoring my attempt at humor, "she couldn't have made any money in Sugar Liquor. Nobody here pays for *it*."

"Look, y'all," I said, "these are packaged for handling transactions. Nice, crisp bills. High finance. Or, fresh off the counterfeit press. I can't imagine where Vikki got her hands on all this."

"Nothing legit," Kristen said.

"Let's get this stuff put away." Pulling a spare *Hello Kitty* pillowcase out of a drawer, I said, "Hold this, Brit." With more caution than if I'd invited her to be the bag-girl on a rattlesnake hunt, her timid hands opened the case and held it while I slid the bundles to the bottom, taking care not to disturb the paper band wrappers. Not wanting to touch the gun, I took the pillowcase from Brit and motioned for her to put the gun on top of the cash.

"Okay, Sherlock. What are you going to do with it now that you've got it?" Kristen asked, her words smart-assed and accusatory. I didn't look at her face. I could feel her squinted eyes drilling holes in my non-functioning head.

I wrapped the excess pillowcase around the gun and money. *Kitty's* smiling, gentle face didn't realize her innocence had been violated. "For the time being I'll stick it in the back of a drawer until I come up with a better place.

"God, for a simple girl raised on a simple farm, Vikki sure had a lot of complicated stuff going on," I said. In fact, I seemed to be uncovering something new about her every time I turned around. How much more would I discover? I'd expected to wrap up this investigation quickly but the further I went, the more complex the case became. Every new discovery raised new questions about Vikki's life. Not only that but I was racing against Mike who had experience, manpower and resources on his side.

My manpower came from Brit and Kristen who helped me follow-up leads. My resources were gossips like Rhonda and Miss Georgia who kept the local grapevines humming with their news bits. Somewhere in the truths and half-truths, I'd find the key to Vikki's death. The mystery behind her violent death lurked in the murky corners of her life, not in Mike's crime detecting techniques and forensic science. I'd find Vikki's killer by following her sexy, capricious trail. Along the way, I'd figure out where the cash and gun came from and the link between them and Vikki's murder.

Brit and Kristen split on their way to family

events. Kristen's oldest sister was home for a few days from her petroleum engineering job in Houston and she and Kristen were planning a girls' night out. In order to spend time with her sister, Kristen not only ditched Brit and me but gave up going to watch her boyfriend, Scott, play softball. Kristen was very into Scott right now so foregoing an evening with him said volumes about her fondness for her sister.

Brit, who was related to at least half the county, was going to a big family dinner at Texas Roadhouse for her grandmother's birthday. Brit didn't have Kristen's problem of agonizing over missing out on a date with her boyfriend. At the end of school this year, she'd been abruptly dumped by Reese, her boyfriend for the past year. Brit was hurt and swore off boys forever. But lately she'd been paying attention to a certain blond lifeguard at the town pool. This was good. I didn't want Brit to end up a bitter old spinster.

I didn't have a boyfriend. I never seemed to have a thing for boys who liked me or vice-versa. If I didn't get in synch with a boy one of these days, I'd be the old maid of our threesome. My only invitation for the evening was to join my parents watching reruns of old comedy shows on *TV Land*. I declined to join them. Just as my parents had brainwashed me into appreciating classic movies, they also pulled me into classic TV. After a lifetime as an only child and eating cold cereal, I was enlightened by *The Brady Bunch* and longed to move in with them. A total package of brothers, sisters, and a cook. I felt restless and at loose ends with both my best friends missing. More than usual, I wished I had a Brady brother or sister to hang out with.

With nothing to do, I borrowed Mom's car. I

thanked the Universe that my parents both taught biology and went nearly everywhere together for work and academic events. Even better, they had similar interests and hung out together in their leisure time. Mom's ownership of a vehicle was more a statement of her status as an independent twenty-first century career woman with a PhD from Duke than her need for transportation.

My favorite hangout, the *Chatterbox*, was a long, low building jam-packed with booths, tables and counter stools. This place rocked on big nights like home football games but on this summer night, business was slow. Quiet suited my mood.

I got an end booth and sat with my back to the wall, legs stretched out on the seat. Not ladylike, as my mother would be the first to point out, but comfortable because I planned to stay a while.

I hated to think how gross I'd looked today sluggishly dragging my hot, sweaty self around the parking lot pushing finger-blistering grocery carts. For the first time in my life, I'd be overjoyed to see school start and put this stupid summer job behind me.

Bless my parents to the bottom of their education-loving hearts that they didn't allow me to work during the school year. They were afraid a job would take too much time away from my studies. Hallelujah and *adios* to grocery store carts at the end of summer.

Brit, Kristen and I were all good students and spent a lot of time on school work, if for no other reason than to get us out of Sugar Liquor. We dearly loved our hometown, but no way did we want to spend the rest of our lives here. A big world full of amazing opportunities awaited a zealous news reporter, an exceptional computer scientist and a clever defense attorney.

Considering I'd had a shower, shampooed and styled my hair, changed clothes and cooled off after my hellish afternoon at work, I was revived and looked pretty decent. My hair, although naturally curly, was manageably tamed with de-frizzing mousse and glossed with spray shine. Tonight, my hair hung free and loose. I was sick to death of that damp, moldy ponytail flopping along behind my head. It made me cringe to touch it.

My large, round hazel eyes topped by naturally high arched brows made me look inquisitive and intelligent, the ideal facial expression for a reporter. I was tall and slim like Kristen, although I didn't have her exquisite beauty, and I definitely wasn't cute and petite like Brit. Even so, I was satisfied with my looks. I smiled and the face in the window reflection smiled back at me. It told me this summer would pass and I would be right with the world again.

Opening my journal, I started reading the entries I'd made since last night. I had so much to write that I'd jotted down brief notes rather than trying to put them into a readable narrative. I'd done the same with each new development until I had an amazing collection of bits and pieces to organize. Until I saw it written down, I didn't realize how much had happened in such a short time and how much progress I'd made in determining who knew what and when, as well as who didn't know what and when about Vikki's life and death.

My information was in the haphazard order it'd been gathered from Miss Georgia, Rhonda, Barbara and Justin. I wished I'd brought my laptop, my indispensable partner in ordering my thoughts and in phrasing them in perfect news-ese lingo. Oh, well, I'd start by organizing my notes on a legal pad while I was here and enter everything into my computer when I got home.

Making a list of all the people who might be suspects in Vikki's murder was the easy part. I started with Vikki's two possible boyfriends, the naked cowboy and Colton. At this early point, I included rumors and gossip as well as who passed them on to me. If I'd heard the same info from two sources, I considered that verified-ish and marked the item with an asterisk.

Using Mike's supposition of opportunity, I put Justin in first place on my list. I separated what I knew about him into two columns, the facts that supported he was Vikki's killer and the ones that tended to exonerate him. The good news for Justin was that, as far as I knew, Mike's evidence against him was based on opportunity.

"Hey, Amy, how's it going?" I was so engrossed in my suspect list that I didn't hear Cody Evans approach. Cody, a hottie who lived next door to my grandma on the other side of town, towered over my table. I'd known him since we were kids but had never quite adjusted to his grown-up size. "Okay if I sit for a minute?" he asked. Trying not to look too eager, I nodded casually to the other side of the booth. Cody deposited his well-built linebacker body into it.

Cody was several years older than I was and had been popular in high school, partly due to his athletic ability and partly due to his good looks and adorable personality. It was safe to say I would never have gotten anywhere near this close to Cody Evans if he hadn't been my granny's next door neighbor. I had a major crush on Cody when I was a freshman and he was a senior but he never knew about it. If he'd found out, I would've been too embarrassed to go to my granny's house ever again.

"Man, can you believe what happened to Vikki? It must have been a wild night in your neighborhood." My cappuccino arrived and Cody told the waitress he'd have one of the same. "Habit I picked up at college," he admitted with a self-conscious smile. "Everybody drinks lattes and cappuccinos." I smiled. A man-of-the-world image suited grown-up Cody

"So, Amy, with your reputation for being a crime buster, are you working on Vikki's murder?" I was flattered that Cody, who'd been away at UNC at the time, had heard about my exploit. "How'd you catch those low lifes?"

With a little bragging on my part along with due credit to Brit and Kristen for their help, I gave him the abbreviated version of how my calculated stake-out led me to catching the juvenile punks in action. "Beating Mike's officers by a mile was how I zoomed to the top of Mike's Shit List."

Cody laughed. "I can believe that. He must've been pretty salty."

Since we were on the subject of crime, Cody asked what I knew about Vikki's murder. I gave him a general rundown including that the police suspected Justin because he was the one who discovered Vikki's body.

"Plus having a motive sure doesn't help him either," Cody said.

I stopped in mid-drink of my cappuccino, upper lip coated with foam, sputtering, "What motive?"

A guy and girl came in and sat down in the next booth so Cody lowered his voice and leaned across the table toward me. "Because of the way Vikki's been running around on him. Everybody in our crowd's been talking about it." Tell me I hadn't heard Cody correctly. If their friends knew about Vikki, how could Justin not know? I was speechless. "You didn't know about Vikki?" Cody asked.

"Not until recently," I replied. I wasn't about to admit I didn't know something that sensational until last night. "On top of that, I thought only the snoops in her apartment building and people from the diner knew what was going on."

I waited for Cody to respond. He was in the same high school class with Vikki and Justin, and he'd been friends with Justin since they were kids. "All I know is that Vikki was running around with some guy named Colton, and Justin was bent out of shape that she was going to run off with him."

Justin's voice in my head telling me Vikki wasn't running around was being drowned out loudly by Cody's voice across the table telling me he did know. I asked Cody how long Justin had known about Colton. "About two weeks. He called me weekend before last to hang out because Vikki was working an extra shift at the diner. Justin was drunk and really worked up that Vikki might leave him. I didn't want to be around him in that condition so I took off with some other guys."

"Do you think Justin was upset enough about the possibility of Vikki leaving him to kill her?"

"I don't know. He ought to be accustomed to her ways by now. Personally, I think he should've said *adios* to Vikki years ago but he couldn't give her up. You're a smart girl, Amy. What was wrong with

Vikki?"

"I'm afraid you'll have to refer that one to Dr. Freud," I said in complete honesty. Cody smiled, saying Vikki would've been a challenge even for Freud. "Seriously, Brit and Kristen and I have deliberated at length, and we've decided Vikki requires more attention than one man can give her. I think she's been tired of Justin for months."

"In my opinion, Justin should've helped her pack her bags and let this Colton character have her. Uh-oh," Cody said, glancing at the big wall clock. "I have to pick up my kid sister from her dance class." Cody drained his cappuccino and got up to leave. Would it be unseemly if I begged him to stay? Oh, Universe, do something.

It worked. After a couple steps, he turned and came back to my table. "Hey, Amy, you busy Saturday night? Want to catch a movie?" Was Cody asking me for a date? Just so it wasn't because he was bored from being home for the summer and desperate for company. Never mind, it didn't matter. I accepted. Amy Jackson was going to the movie with Cody Evans. Yay, yay, yay!

I decided to wait until Brit and Kristen and I were all together to tell them about my date with Cody. I'd get a bigger bang out of my announcement. Me and Cody. How sweet was this?

In the meantime, I had to tell Brit and Kristen that Justin likely knew Vikki was running around on him. Even if they were with their families, I had to get in touch with them. Kristen's voice mail answered. I left a terse message to call me immediately and then texted her to be sure.

I tried Brit next. "What the hell do you want, Amy?" she whispered. "You know I'm at Granny's party."

I told her to slip away for a few minutes, that I had breaking news on our investigation. She called me back a few minutes later.

"What's that weird noise, Brit?" I asked.

"I'm in the ladies' room. They're toilets flushing, dork. Talk fast. I can't stay in here all night like some weirdo." Barely taking a fresh breath, I blurted out what Cody told me. "You mean Justin lied to us? Oh, my gosh, he couldn't have a stronger motive for murder than jealousy. Man, I can't believe this," Brit said, her voice brittle. She was plenty pissed-off at Justin. I asked her if Mike was at the party. "Of course, he is. It's for his mama."

"Sweet talk Mike and see if he'll tell you what he thinks Justin's motive was. I don't think Vikki's affair with Colton is common knowledge. We hear everything in town and we hadn't heard it." Brit said she'd see what she could pry out of Mike and agreed to come to the cupola as soon as her grandmother's party fizzled out which shouldn't be long. Her family tended to lose interest in socializing when there were no shooting contests on the agenda.

Chapter Eleven

It was after ten o'clock when I left the *Chatterbox* and started home. On impulse, I detoured by way of Riley Street looking for Colton Matos' condo. Barbara had his address in her notebook so I'd scribbled it into my journal. I parked on the street in front of Colton's unit, curious about this man who partied with Vikki the night she was killed.

Lights were on in the condo so I assumed Colton was home. I sat in my car watching and hoping someone would appear or something would happen. Cody made it clear Justin didn't want Vikki to leave him. If that was true, it wasn't good news for Justin. Colton's presence in Vikki's life didn't look good for him either. Hanging out with Vikki was like working in a fireworks factory. The odds were against you.

Sitting huddled in a parked car in the dark waiting for answers that weren't going to appear was not what reporters did, especially when that reporter was Amy Jackson. I desperately wanted to crack this murder case and get a big story out of it, big enough to catapult me to the ranks of bona fide investigative reporter. That meant taking charge and asking somebody some questions. Like--say--Colton Matos.

I opened the car door, picked up my backpack from the passenger seat, flung it over my shoulder and walked to Colton's condo. On the way, I ran several opening scenarios through my head. Friendly or professional, which was best? I didn't know and decided to use the one that came out of my mouth first. As soon as I pushed Colton's door bell, second thoughts bombarded me.

Did reporters appear uninvited and unexpected on people's doorsteps? Of course. I saw them on TV news all the time, barging in during the worst tragedies in people's lives, asking intimate, heart wrenching questions. I, on the other hand, resolved to be more sensitive.

Wearing plaid pajama bottoms and a dark t-shirt, Colton opened the door. This was the first time I'd seen him except when I was spying through Vikki's window and that was only his back. Wow. Rhonda's gushing didn't do him justice. No surprise Vikki was attracted to him. He looked like Ethan but more appealing, more open, more approachable with a face that was ready to have fun and a mouth ready to laugh.

"Colton? I'm Amy Jackson. Vikki's next door neighbor. Can we talk?" I tried to sound friendly.

"Why?" The word came out slowly. Puzzled, he looked and acted like I'd just winged my way out of an unknown cave.

"Because you were in Vikki's apartment the night she was killed."

He opened his mouth to protest but I interrupted. "My friends and I saw you. I know about the Heineken and Chinese take-out and daisies." Guilt chewed at my conscience for adding that last personal part. That was not part of my compassionate approach.

Running his hand through his hair, Colton took a deep breath and, when he exhaled, his previous expression of good cheer slipped away with it. "Who are you and what are you doing here?" I repeated my name and purpose. "Amy Jackson. I didn't kill Vikki. I liked her and we had some good times together. I had no reason to be angry with her."

Colton pulled the door open for me to come inside. "I'll talk to you for a minute because I don't want you running all over town spreading rumors I killed Vikki." Was that a threat? "You're too young to be a cop so what's your interest in Vikki's death?"

"Well, I solved a string of juvenile break-ins and got a good write-up in the *Asheville Citizen-Times*, and I desperately want to be a news reporter. So if I solve Vikki's murder, I can write a dynamic first-hand account of my investigation for the Charlotte or maybe even the Atlanta papers." Colton reacted to my journalistic ambitions as if he or I or both of us had just awakened from a coma.

I walked past him into the foyer. His condo was impressive. A coveted open floor plan that TV decorators gush about. Contemporary furnishings. Masculine in neutral, earth colors. The ultimate bachelor pad.

Taken by his upscale living situation, I asked, "What do you do for a living?" As I heard the words come out of my mouth, I sounded exactly like my mother nosing to find out how he could buy into this pricey complex and afford such expensive furniture.

"I'm a pharmacist at Kelly's. What do you do, beside snoop on your neighbors and investigate murders?"

I said, "I'm a rising senior in high school and I'm going to the University of North Carolina to major in journalism." I left out the cart-return girl bit. It made me look stupid. Correction, it was stupid.

"So you're trying to pin Vikki's murder on me so you can write a sensational story. I hate to be the one to thwart your journalism career, but I had nothing to do with Vikki's death. What kind of stupidity possessed you to come here anyway? If I were the murderer, I'd kill you for planning to expose me in your career-building newspaper article." I didn't know if he was serious or making a joke but his tone scared me. It was get-the-hell-out-time for me.

"You're right," I said, agreeing with him. "I shouldn't have come here." I turned to leave.

"No." He grabbed the doorknob, blocking me from it. He trapped me. I braced, expecting an aggressive move from him. Instead he motioned for me to sit down in his living room. My legs quivered and threatened to drop me on the floor. I collapsed into the first chair in my path.

"You came here thinking I had something to do with Vikki's death so let's get the facts straight," he said. "Yes, I had something going with Vikki but I wasn't in love with her and I made that clear to her all along. She, on the other hand, said she'd fallen in love with me and wanted to leave Justin. It was time to break it off with her. I was going to tell her last night but I wimped out. She was in such a happy mood and had such a big evening planned, I couldn't bring myself to ruin her plans. Like I said, I cared for her and I wanted, for her sake, to end this as gently as possible. Believe me, breaking up with her was the only thing I planned to do last night. I didn't need to kill her to do it."

"Why are you telling me this?"

"If you know about Vikki and me, the police will find out soon if they don't know already. So I might as well start getting my story out there. I have nothing to hide. I had no reason to kill her. Do you get that?" I nodded and gave him passable marks for being convincing.

"If you want my opinion, Justin killed her. Vikki said he was out of his mind she was going to leave him. But she would've left him whether I broke up with her or not. That marriage was over."

"That seems to be the consensus."

"Which proves my point. Justin killed her to keep her from leaving him. Jealousy is powerful."

"Someone told me that Vikki had seemed jumpy and nervous for the past few weeks. Do you know if she was worried about anything or anybody? Did she say if Justin had threatened her, especially if he was reacting so strongly to the idea she was leaving?"

"Vikki rarely mentioned Justin to me. In fact, Vikki didn't talk about anyone much. I don't think she liked or got along well with many people. She and my brother, Ethan, who lives in the same building, weren't on good terms."

"What was that about?"

"Beats me. Even when I stayed with Ethan before I bought this condo, he wasn't friendly with Vikki, although he seemed to like Justin okay."

"Wonder what happened?"

"I don't know except Ethan didn't like Vikki and tried to get me to stop seeing her. I chalked it up to objecting because she was married."

Colton thought for a minute. "Something did happen recently. I was at Vikki's apartment and we decided to go to a club in Asheville, but I needed a tie and jacket. I didn't want to take the time to go home, so she and I stopped at Ethan's apartment for me to borrow a tie and jacket from him. He wasn't home so I used my key back from when I lived with him to let us in. I turned on the TV in the living room for Vikki, because I decided to take a quick shower.

"When I finished dressing, Ethan was home. He and Vikki stood glaring at each other. Later, I asked Vikki what happened. She said nothing happened, to drop it. Vikki didn't mention it again and I forgot about it." I asked how Ethan and Vikki reacted to each other after the incident. "Ethan didn't act any different. Vikki kind of ignored Ethan unless she had to talk to him. Like when he came in the diner."

"One more question, what time did you leave Vikki's apartment the night she died?"

"Around midnight. I came straight home because I had to work the next morning. I have to be wide awake and alert." he said. "And before you ask, Vikki was very much alive when I left. I didn't know about her death until people started talking about it in the store this morning. Even then, I couldn't believe it was true."

While I was mulling over this new twist in Vikki's tangled life, someone knocked on the door. Colton said to me in a whisper, "It's Ethan. We're going to watch the end of a baseball game."

"I don't want him to see me here. What'll I do?" I asked. Colton yelled toward the door that he was coming and grabbed me by the arm with one hand and my backpack with the other. Pushing me out the sliding glass doors, he shoved my backpack into my hands. He closed the doors, drew the drapes and left me standing in the dark. My heart was beating like crazy. Trying to get off Colton's patio, I stumbled into big, heavy flower pots. Bruised, battered and scraped, my shins throbbed as I hobbled toward Mom's car.

Although Colton sounded sincere about his last night with Vikki, the fact remained that he was in her apartment until late. And Ethan? What happened between him and Vikki to make them dislike each other? All in all, Ethan scared me lots more than Colton or Justin.

Chapter Twelve

Still freaked out from my unorthodox and unladylike exit from Colton's condo, I ran up the stairs to the safety of my beloved cupola. Fortunately my parents had gone to bed, so I didn't have to explain my frantic bolt up the steps. If it hadn't been for Colton's quick-thinking to toss me out the sliding doors, I would've been face to face with Ethan in an inexplicable situation. For sure, he would've recognized me after Brit drew attention to us at the diner. With my increasing uneasiness about him, I didn't want Ethan to connect me to Vikki or Justin or Colton or my house or neighborhood or the grocery store parking lot or dumpsters or anything else.

I flopped down on my cot to get my head together. Right away, I got a text from Brit. She was parking in my driveway and would be up in a minute. When I heard her high heels clicking up the stairs, I ran to the door. "Looking hot, Brit," I told her. She was wearing a very short, coral strappy dress and high white wedgies. Her big bunch of black curls was pulled into a high ponytail nearly the size of a basketball. For a change, she looked like a sexy seventeen-year-old instead of an over-ripe twelve-year-old.

Brit opened a dresser drawer and got out pajamas she kept at my house. She pulled the bottoms up under her dress and then slipped it over her head. She slithered into her tank top and was almost set except for hanging up her dress on our little kitty cat coat rack and setting her shoes under her cot.

"So what's the big news?" Brit asked, lying down on her cot. Hildy, who'd followed Brit up the stairs, jumped up on the cot with her and snuggled. Hildy loved sleepovers. More people to cuddle with.

Without trying to explain my motivation which even I didn't understand, I told her about going to Colton's condo. Brit sat up straight and her mouth flew open. "Amy Jackson. Are you out of your frigging mind?"

"Yes, or I wouldn't have gone, but listen." I began by telling her that Colton thought Justin killed Vikki. "It's another vote against Justin although Colton's vote doesn't really count, since he was in Vikki's apartment that night and had as much opportunity as Justin."

Brit must've been thinking the same thing, especially in her capacity as Justin's quasi-legal defense counsel. "Okay, what are the chances that Colton did it?" she asked.

"I don't think he was passionate enough about Vikki to kill her. He'd only known her for a short time, and he said he wasn't in love with her. According to Colton and Rhonda, Vikki was crazy about him, so our previous hypothesis that she broke up with him and he was devastated enough to kill her doesn't hold up." Brit thought that over. "Hey, you remember how everybody said how cute Colton is? Well, it's true. He's cute. Adorably cute. Not only that but he gives off vibes that he'd be a lot of fun. I can see why Vikki fell for him," I said.

"We saw his playfulness first-hand through her bedroom window. I wish he'd been at the diner with Ethan and Eric," Brit said.

"Yeah, me too. I believe Colton when he says he wasn't in love with Vikki. There was something about seeing him in his own condo, in his own space among his own personal things that made me see how far apart he and Vikki really were. He lives in a world Vikki knows nothing about. When I arrived at his condo, a Mozart CD was playing. Books on Impressionist art were piled on the coffee table. For all Vikki knew, Rembrandt was a toothpaste and Beethoven was a movie about a dog. Vikki and Colton lived on totally different planets. I doubt Vikki realized it but I bet Colton did."

Brit asked, "Did you find out why he and his brother and the blond one moved here? Sugar Liquor's never been a lure for hunks, especially three at one time."

"I don't know about Ethan and Eric, but Colton's a pharmacist at Kelly's."

Brit said, "Colton's sounding better and better."

"I agree. He looks like Ethan but his personality is kind of like Ethan on uppers.

"One more thing, Brit. Colton said Ethan and Vikki had an argument, but I don't know if it has anything to do with her murder. It was some time ago. In fact, Colton says Vikki and Ethan didn't like each other and kept their distance. I wonder why he disliked her so much."

Brit answered promptly. "Maybe he didn't like a married woman chasing his younger brother."

"Yeah. That's what Colton thinks." I asked Brit if she talked to Mike about Justin's motive.

"Yeah, but you won't like what he said," she replied.

"Big surprise. So what did he say?"

"His exact words, 'Stay the hell out of police business.' But that's not the end of it. He wants to talk to us in the morning." I asked her if he knew anything specific we'd done or if he was fishing. "Fishing, I think. I was afraid he was going to say something in front of my mother but he didn't, or she would've been in my face. I don't want to get in a fight with both of them. One at a time is enough."

Kristen called. She'd just got out of the movie and read my text to contact me immediately. She spoke carefully since she was in the car with her sister who'd graduated from college, found a real job and got inducted into adulthood. Kristen was afraid her sister would rat on us to their parents.

Grabbing my cell, Brit talked to Kristen long enough to tell her that Mike wanted to see us in the morning. Kristen said she had to get it over with so she could go to work on time. Brit called her uncle and told him we'd meet him at the police station at eight o'clock.

Brit and I were sleepy so we called it a night but I couldn't go to sleep. My investigation had to remain secret if I was going to beat Mike at finding Vikki's murderer. If he heard what I was doing, he'd shut me down in a flash.

Too wired to sleep, I sat up and looked out the

window at the apartment building next door. Only last night, we'd watched Vikki entertaining a man I figured out wasn't Justin. Twenty-four hours later, Vikki was dead and her windows dark.

I glanced down one floor at Ethan's apartment. Even though his drapes were closed, I could see a sliver of light where the panels didn't quite come together and a shadow as Ethan walked around the room. I'd never noticed but that streak of light could tell me if Ethan was home. I didn't really care though because I intended to stay clear of him. That scene behind the grocery store had *dodgy* written all over it.

Brit said something and when I turned to ask what, I realized she was mumbling in her sleep, probably dreaming she was in a war of words with some prosecutor. My gaze settled on my kitty decal-coated dresser where a gun and five thousand dollars reposed in the back of a drawer. My parents would flip out if they knew I had a gun in their house. They were so anti-guns. NRA members they were not. I had to dispose of this one soon so my parents would never know it had dwelled under their gun-free roof.

Attempting to rationalize my rash actions, I told myself it was right to remove the cash and gun from their hiding place. Granted I'd made the decision in a moment of panic, but my intuition said it was right. Given Justin's bad experiences in the apartment, he'd move out as quickly as he could pack up. I was totally convinced he would've removed the money and gun if he'd known about them. Meaning, they would've remained in the bedroom closet wall forever unless a future tenant happened to find them. By then, the connection to

Vikki and her murder would be lost. Yeah, it was better I took them out of the apartment.

I checked the neighborhood one last time. A flash of light at Vikki's bedroom window caught my eye and then disappeared. I waited for the light to reappear but it didn't. It must've been the reflection from the headlights of a passing car. Suddenly I felt terribly drowsy, gave Vikki's dark window a final glance and lay down ready to drift asleep.

Chapter Thirteen

Kristen and I arrived at the police station ten minutes early. Seven-fifty AM on the dot.

The door to Mike's office was partially open and, I could see him talking on the phone. In turn, he had a direct view of Kristen and me sitting in the waiting area if he'd chosen to look in our direction. When Brit arrived, I said, "Mike's deliberately ignoring us."

She giggled. "Good. Maybe he'll forget about us."

Whether it was to irritate us or whether Mike was genuinely occupied with the business of the taxpayers of Sugar Liquor, he kept us waiting until eight-ten before he summoned us into his office. Kristen was fidgeting, worried about being late for work.

Foregoing niceties, Mike closed the door and sat at his desk staring at us through exhausted, puffy eyes. "Somebody broke into Vikki's apartment overnight and trashed the place," he said without any preliminaries. "Any ideas who it was or what they were looking for?"

Whoa. We didn't expect that and shook our heads.

Brit spoke. "If the break-in happened during the night, how'd you find out about it so early this morning? Did the neighbors hear something and call you?"

"Nope. Nothing so dramatic. Clyde discovered the broken lock on Vikki's door when he went up this morning to check Barbara's apartment. He called on his cell and waited in the hall until we got there."

"So nobody heard anything? Isn't that kind of unusual since you said someone trashed the place?" I asked.

"Yeah, but Barbara's gone to her sister's in Waynesville, and Ethan Matos said he went to bed early last night and didn't hear anything. The two of them would've been our best chances for information since Barbara lives across the hall from Vikki, and Ethan lives in the apartment directly beneath her."

So Ethan said he went to bed early. How did he define early? He was at Colton's condo around ten-thirty and I saw him moving around inside his own apartment around midnight. That hardly passed for an early bedtime in Sugar Liquor which steadfastly followed small town tradition of rolling up the sidewalks at seven o'clock.

"Any chance it was random vandalism?" I asked.

Mike shook his head. "No. Someone was searching for something and wanted it badly enough to take the risk of going to a third story apartment. Increased likelihood of being discovered and less chance of being able to split in a hurry. Vandals look for easy targets."

I mentioned to Mike that Mr. Clyde usually locks the front door around eleven at night, and I wondered if the burglar got in the building before then.

"Not necessarily. The locks on that building aren't complicated, plus, thieves are getting better and better at opening supposedly secure locks. That little gang of thieving riff-raff you caught cracked some fairly sophisticated locks, and they didn't have experience or brains." I got Mike's point.

"Let's get to the reason I told y'all to come down here," he said. His calm, even tone relaxed me. This wasn't going to be so bad after all. I sat, looking at my toes, evaluating my pedicure color and debating whether to go with dark purple or lime next time.

Mike's sizeable fist came down so hard on his desk that his coffee cup dove for the floor, leaving its contents trailing down the wall. Jolted out of my toe fetish, I jumped, my butt clearing my chair seat. The reaction went down the line, first Brit, then Kristen. It would've been funny if it hadn't been for Mike's clenched teeth and his face glowing red underneath his tan.

"I hear you've been asking questions about Vikki after I told you to butt out. But no, you went right ahead as if I hadn't warned you. Amy, I know all about this reporter career you want, but this isn't the time or place or way to go about it. Damn it," he yelled, "you're going to stop snooping right now. Not only is this a vicious murder but Vikki's apartment has been broken into. I don't want to hear of you three asking a single person one single thing about Vikki. Any part of that you don't understand?"

Knocked speechless by Mike's ferocity, we shook our heads.

Mike lowered his voice to a civil tone and asked, "Before you leave, is there anything you want to tell me? Either about Vikki's death or the apartment break-in?" Yeah, right. In your dreams, Mike. We all shook our heads again. Mike grunted and told us to get out.

As soon as we escaped from the police station, I told Brit and Kristen about the flash of light in Vikki's apartment. "I bet it was the burglar's flashlight, not a reflection of car headlights like I thought. Another thing, Ethan lied to the police about going to bed early. He was still up when I was looking out the window at midnight. His lights were on and I could see glimpses of him moving around."

"You think the burglar was Ethan?" Kristen asked.

"He had the best shot at pulling it off," I said. "Lives in the building."

Kristen and Brit were due at work soon so they left. My shift didn't start for a while yet, and I didn't care if I was late. The grocery store wouldn't fire me. Nobody else in Sugar Liquor was dumb enough to want my job. Anybody below my grunge level was looking for work that was illegal.

I headed toward home but that wasn't my destination. I wanted to get into Vikki's apartment to see if the burglar had searched the closet wall where the money and gun were hidden. If the burglar knew they were in that wall and he or she reached behind the drywall and couldn't find them, then the burglar would've ripped the wall apart looking for them. I wanted to see what condition that wall was in this morning. Somebody out there was bound to be pretty salty about their missing cash. Just so they didn't connect its disappearance to me or my cupola.

Mr. Clyde was filling bird feeders outside his living room windows. He and Miss Georgia loved to watch birds visiting their feeders throughout the year. I didn't pay attention to their bird-watching talk but I was glad it was a pleasurable past-time for them. I walked up to him. "Got a favor to ask you, Mr. Clyde."

"You name it, Amy," he said, smiling.

"You may not be so eager when I tell you what it is. I want to get inside Vikki's apartment for a couple of minutes and figured you'd know the best way to go about doing it. Just between us," I whispered, "I want to do it when Ethan's not home. He makes me nervous."

"He makes me nervous too. I never know what he's a-thinkin'. He don't say nothin'." Mr. Clyde motioned for me to sit on a garden bench and he joined me. "I know you're a-tryin' to help Justin 'cause Mike's lookin' hard at him. But I don't want you to get in trouble or get hurt."

"I'm not going to do anything but take a quick look at something Mike overlooked."

"The police put a padlock on the door to protect Justin's stuff until he decides what he's a-goin' to do. I know for a fact he'll never stay there again. He told me so hisself. How long you think you need?" Mr. Clyde asked me.

"Half an hour at the most."

"I've probably got an old key that'll work on that lock. Ethan leaves about eleven o'clock every morning. That too soon?" It was fine with me but it didn't give Mr. Clyde much time to pick the lock or whatever he was going to do. "Go home and wait for me to call you. Okay?"

It didn't take long for Mr. Clyde to call and I hurried back over. He was standing inside Vikki's apartment waiting for me. "How'd you get in?" I asked him.

"Easy," he replied with a satisfied smile. "I called the police department and told them I heard water a-drippin' and needed to get in to check it. They sent somebody right over with a key for the padlock." He dangled the key in front of me, laughing.

"I'll hang around outside to watch if anybody unexpected shows up," he told me and trotted down the stairs.

I zipped through the living room. It was intact except for sofa and chair cushions on the floor. The CDs, DVDs and magazines looked undisturbed. Did the burglar know what he was looking for was too large to be hidden among them? The kitchen was a different story. Pots and pans and dishes covered the countertops, table and floor. Every item had been taken out of the cabinets and left on the closest surface in stacks or sitting around. At least, the burglar was smart enough to do a quiet search and not wake up the whole building.

The bedroom was worse than after Vikki's murder. Someone had taken it apart. The mattress was shoved off the bed, covers wadded up and thrown in a corner. Even Vikki's night gowns were strewn on the floor. Without thinking, I stooped and picked them up and stuffed them in an empty drawer. Although it was kind of creepy to touch a dead girl's undies, it seemed obscene to leave her personal possessions helter-skelter. They were a big part of who Vikki was, at least the part I'd seen through my binoculars for the past six months. The dresser stool lay on its side. I set it upright and carried it to the closet so I could stand on it to check the upper wall. I ran my hand up and down inside the wall. It was exactly as Kristen, Brit and I left it. The burglar hadn't ripped the drywall apart.

While returning the chair to its place in front of the dresser, I stepped on a bracelet. Vikki's jewelry box lay open under the dresser with its contents scattered all over the floor. I bent down and scooped up a few pieces and dropped them in the box. Suddenly I felt someone watching me. I raised my head slowly expecting to be confronted by Ethan. Instead, Justin stood in the bedroom doorway with tears in his eyes.

"Amy?" Justin asked.

"Oh, Justin. You startled me." Damn Mr. Clyde. He was supposed to be my look-out. My heart pounded as I grasped for words. Above the drum rolls of my heart, I barely heard myself talking. "I'm so sorry about the break-in, Justin. God, you've had enough without this. I came up here with Mr. Clyde while he was checking a plumbing leak and when I saw things in such a mess, I couldn't help but try to straighten up a little. It didn't seem right that Vikki's things should've been treated like this." I hadn't planned to say that but I meant it. "I folded her clothes and put them in the dresser drawers. I just started picking up her jewelry."

"Thanks," he said. "That's sweet of you." He looked around the disheveled room without reacting. "I came over to start packing. I don't want Vikki's folks to have to pack up her things. They're out of their minds over her death."

Justin's droopy face reminded me of a hurt child. I moved him from the possibly guilty column to the possibly innocent column. "I have an hour before I have to go to work, do you want some help?"

Before Justin could answer, Mr. Clyde burst through the open door, huffing heavily from charging up the stairs. He didn't look surprised to see Justin so he must've discovered he was in the building. To bring Mr. Clyde up to speed, I quickly repeated my cover story.

"I'm done with that leakin' pipe. I can he'p pack too," he said. "That is, if you want me to." Mr. Clyde solidified our cover story and even added the part about the police bringing a key for the padlock.

"I'll take all the help I can get. I can't stand to be in this place."

Mr. Clyde grabbed an empty box. "I'll pack up your music albums and movies."

Justin started pulling clothes out of the closet. He folded and stacked them in piles on the bed. I sat on the floor and sorted Vikki's jewelry. Justin gave me a weak smile and thanked me again for helping. Except to answer our occasional questions about packing, Justin had little to say. We worked in near silence.

While I packed, I figured out that while Mr. Clyde was watching the front door, Justin must've come up the back stairs, probably to avoid entanglements with his neighbors.

I crawled under the dresser and ran my hands under the bed until I collected all the jewelry I could find. I didn't end up with any odd earrings so I stuck the pairs in the little slots in Vikki's jewelry box. The bracelets and necklaces went in little drawers. When

I finished, I closed the jewelry box and put it in the bottom of a box. I emptied Vikki's drawers and closet, folding and packing their contents until four large boxes were full. Vikki might not know how to cook or decorate, but the girl knew how to shop.

Circling the bedroom, I gathered up framed photos of Vikki, some from when she was young, and wrapped them in newspaper to protect the glass. A cute baby, she was unmistakably Vikki right from the beginning. Her blonde hair had changed shades as she'd experimented with colors ranging from her natural childhood corn silk to brassy blonde. Her photos were a collage of the hottest blonde looks from the past two decades. Vikki's hair color changed, but her pale blue eyes and a smile that always looked a little naughty stayed the same. Throw in a sexy body, a generous helping of natural boobs and Vikki was a knock-out. It was sad she hadn't used her looks to better advantage.

Handling and packing Vikki's personal possessions made her death more poignant. Her clothes, jewelry and even her twinkling lights were packed and would soon be hauled away. I was surprised by my sadness for Vikki, especially since I'd never really liked her.

When I finished packing the last box, I asked Justin for tape, sealed the boxes and wrote *Vikki* with a Sharpie on each. I checked my watch and told Justin I had to go to work.

"Thanks for your help, Amy. I appreciate it. Hey, I was just thinking. I don't have any need for Vikki's lights. I won't be doing any dancing for a long time. You take 'em. You and Brit and Kristen can use 'em when you're having a party."

My first impulse was to say no because it

seemed creepy to take things from a dead girl but I decided why not? They were party lights so I accepted. Mr. Clyde said, "I'll take them down to my apartment when I finish and you can pick them up later." I couldn't wait to tell Brit and Kristen I'd inherited Vikki's lights. They'd crack up.

One sure thing about Vikki, she knew how to have a good time. I couldn't see how she veered from the good times highway to getting mixed up in something that ended in her death. Where did she get the gun and five thousand dollars? Who would come looking for that money? And where would they look? As hot as the weather was, I got the shivers.

Chapter Fourteen

When Brit and Kristen finished their days' work and arrived at my cupola, I had plenty to tell, but Brit only half-listened. Unusual since I was speaking legal defense, her first language. Her faraway stare, locked in a frown, puzzled me. I looked at her with fixed, raised eyebrows waiting until she spilled it.

"I did something today that would so get me fired from my job. Y'all have to promise never to tell anybody and I mean never. If Uncle Mike finds out, he'll kill me because he was my character reference for the job." Kristen and I stared at Brit in disbelief. She loved working at the courthouse. No way would she deliberately do anything that would cost her job or put Mike on the spot for recommending her. She was fond of her uncle.

"While I was entering my usual dull data today, I accidentally hit a key sequence that brought up what looked like gibberish. I was half a second away from going to another screen when it hit me I'd found a list of codes or passwords for some town and county departments. Nobody was around so I saved all of them to my flash drive.

"I don't know how I found them or if they're even authentic but I thought Kristen could give them a try. Maybe one is police records. If it is, we can take a look at what evidence they have against Justin and other suspects."

Stunned, I stared at Brit. On the other hand, Kristen sprang to life. She yanked her laptop out of its case and got ready to search before Brit could produce the flash drive from her backpack. We sat on each side of Kristen so we could see the screen although I doubted anything Brit discovered by accident would produce usable results. Kristen, on the other hand, was upbeat as she typed her way into and out of various county and town office records. If we needed to know when somebody bought their house or check how much their property taxes were or how many DUI arrests they had, we were in luck. I doubted Brit's info would lead to the secret stuff. So far, everything we'd seen was public record and obtainable without going through all this.

Then suddenly, Kristen shouted. "Oh, my gosh, I'm in the police department," she said, typing so quickly, I couldn't read the screens as they zipped by. "Hold on, girls. We're in. I'm tingly. Let's hope I don't set off World War III."

"If Mike finds out, it'll be worse than World War III," I said.

"Here it is," Kristen said. "The file on the murder of Vikki Ann Wilson."

On the screen, we read a report on Vikki's murder including the evidence collected so far and a list of assignments that needed to be done. The last entry, notes from the investigating officers, had been posted a half-hour ago. I complimented Mike. This organized system had to be his doing, he was a put-together kind of guy.

Kristen clicked on the first item. A photo of dead Vikki sprawled on the floor of her bedroom filled the screen. We gasped at the grisly image. I wanted to turn away but my eyes were fixed on the screen. It had been one thing for me to envision Vikki murdered and another to see proof of it. A slow motion film played in my imagination. Vikki clawing at her attacker, struggling to get free, the rope pulling tighter around her neck, digging into her flesh, cutting off her breath. My stomach flip-flopped at the terror and pain Vikki endured. She fought back with all her might but in her final, conscious moments, she knew she was losing. Rhonda had talked about how scared Vikki must've been and I realized for the first time what a horrible, frightening death she'd suffered.

Kristen kept clicking on more photos of Vikki and the disarray in her bedroom came up. I couldn't take any more. I'd seen enough photos of Vikki lying lifeless in her hot pink lace night gown. Earlier that evening, she'd had so much fun showing off in it. Who knew it would be her death garment?

"Look for something about the investigation," I told Kristen.

"The medical examiner's preliminary report lists the probable cause of death as strangulation by ligature. Is a ligature the rolled up negligee?" Kristen asked.

Brit nodded. According to the medical examiner, the marks on Vikki's neck were abrasions caused by the ligature scraping against her skin, consistent with injuries expected from a victim struggling to get free from her attacker. No other injuries were found on her body. Toxicology tests were ordered. However, no drugs or medications, other than Vikki's birth control pills and a half-full bottle of Tylenol, were found in the apartment.

The photos and description of how Vikki died left me shaky. This was a brutal, raw side of life I'd never encountered. "You know," I said to Brit and Kristen, "I started this investigation so I could solve Vikki's murder and write a sensational story about it. And, of course, we were all in it because of our competition with Mike. But things have changed. It's not about my ambition or our quest to be one up on Mike. It's about finding a monster who inflicted a senseless, horrible, painful death on a twenty-one year old girl. Nobody should have to endure what Vikki did."

"You're right," Brit said. "And we're trying to help Justin prove his innocence." Our little defense attorney didn't stray far from the tree of justice.

"Then we better see what the police have to say about Justin," Kristen said, clicking on a screen which brought up the police case against him. His vital statistics, including his lack of previous arrests or charges, were unimportant to us. I already knew how old he was, that he was born in this county, and I'd never heard he'd been in trouble. In a small county like ours, everybody's criminal record was truly public knowledge. Everybody remembered every time anybody, including parents and grandparents, had a run-in with the law.

Kristen scrolled past the biographical stuff and found what she was looking for. Drew had talked to everyone except Barbara and no one had heard

Justin come home the night Vikki died. Efforts to contact Justin's construction co-workers who were out with him earlier that night were not going well. They lived all over western North Carolina as well as eastern Tennessee and northern Georgia. Drew was working on getting their home addresses from the construction company, although I didn't see what talking to them would prove. Whatever time Justin got home, it would only have taken him a few minutes to kill Vikki.

"Uh-oh," Brit said. She pointed to an entry at the bottom of the page and summarized it. "Justin and Vikki got into an argument at Millie's Café a couple weeks ago. Sounds like it might have been around the time Rhonda said Vikki started getting jumpy. A half-dozen people were in the café but not close enough to hear what Vikki and Justin were arguing about. A couple came forward and told the police about it in light of Vikki's murder."

"Bummer for Justin," I said. "On the other hand, couples argue all the time, especially those two. Being married to Vikki must've been like waiting for an explosion. Anytime, anyplace. Boom."

"Yeah. I don't see any hard evidence here against Justin. Mike's probably threatening him to try to get him to talk," Brit said.

Kristen scanned through more pages of police evidence. "What is this about?" she asked scrunching her shoulders to move closer to the screen. I tried to read along with her but she scrolled too quickly. Stopping on a page, Kristen said, "Oh, my gosh. Mike has a file here on Mr. Clyde."

"A file on Mr. Clyde? As a suspect?" I asked.

"Yeah. Drew's reports say Mr. Clyde was missing from his bedroom at approximately the time Vikki was killed and that he had a key to her apartment."

"Miss Georgia already told us that. She thought she heard a crashing sound and woke up. Mr. Clyde was in the bathroom," I said.

"According to Drew's report, Miss Georgia *thought* he was in the bathroom. She didn't get up to check." Kristen was right. "And remember, she told us she went back to sleep before he came back to bed."

I wanted to cry. "Mr. Clyde a suspect? It's not possible. He didn't have any reason to kill Vikki."

"They lived in the same building," Brit said. "Who knows what might've happened between them?"

I didn't like the insinuation in Brit's voice. Mr. Clyde hitting on a young girl like Vikki? It was a sick thought and I couldn't imagine it happening. I'd never heard any talk about Mr. Clyde being a womanizer, even when he was young. Knowing the police considered Mr. Clyde a suspect freaked me out. He couldn't kill anybody. But inside, I knew that seemingly harmless people do bizarre things sometimes.

Kristen closed Mr. Clyde's file and moved on while I was still working on convincing myself he couldn't be responsible for Vikki's death. "Mike's got officers checking out Dean and getting statements from Rhonda and Dusty Rose," she said.

"It figures since they worked with Vikki. Dean and Dusty Rose are spooky enough to do it but not Rhonda. Who else is Mike checking?" I asked.

"Second floor neighbor, Tommy Miller, and some folks we don't know," Kristen added.

"Sounds like pretty much the whole town except Colton who was in her apartment that night."

Turning my attention back to the police files, I saw a surprising entry. "Look at this," I said pointing to the screen. "Mike ran a check on Ethan too. He only came up with a fender bender and an unpaid parking ticket. Not exactly the life of hard crime Mr. Clyde suspected. Wonder why Mike checked Ethan. Another neighbor? You know though, Ethan's name keeps surfacing in our investigation. He's always in the shadows. What do we know about him?"

Kristen frowned. "Not much. He's Colton's brother, they're from Illinois, he's close-mouthed, he runs some kind of computer business from his apartment, he has good taste in cars, and he likes the Chicago Bears. From what Colton told you, he didn't like Vikki and had an argument with her. Oh, yeah, he has secret, creepy business meetings behind the shopping center. That cover it?"

"Pretty much," I replied. "But let's look at some coincidences. Ethan was the first neighbor to go to Justin's aid. He gave CPR to Vikki so that means he was very likely home at the time she was killed. He tried to open the door to Vikki and Justin's apartment while we were searching it. That was really creepy. Plus, he told the police he went to bed early when Vikki's apartment was burglarized, but I saw him moving around at midnight, long after he was supposed to be asleep. Mr. Clyde's right that Ethan's fishy."

"Appears that way," Brit concluded, "but we haven't linked him to Vikki or her death."

"One possibility is that Ethan hit on Vikki early on and she turned him down," Kristen said. "Maybe he's been sulking all this time. To make it more of a put-down from Ethan's point of view, she went out with his brother and maybe Eric. Ethan was probably pretty salty about that. And the day Colton said Ethan and Vikki had words, what if he came on to her that day and she told him off?"

"From what Colton said, Ethan was the one doing the telling off," I replied. Brit said she doubted Ethan would hold a grudge this long just because Vikki wouldn't go out with him, and if he was pining for her or looking adoringly at her at the diner, Rhonda would've picked up on it. True. Rhonda didn't miss much. Kristen reluctantly agreed. So that left us with the question of what the trouble was between Ethan and Vikki. Other than Ethan's realistic objection to his brother being involved with a married woman, I didn't know anything else.

I saw no possibility of a previous history between Vikki and Ethan. He was from Chicago and, for sure, Vikki had never been to Chicago. It was doubtful she'd ever been out of North Carolina except to go to Myrtle Beach, South Carolina, every summer since she started working enough to pay for gas and a cheap motel room.

Other than Colton, the only connection between Ethan and Vikki was living in the same building. "Maybe there's something to that," I said.

"Yeah, something that had nothing to do with romance. Neighbors get put out with each other all the time," Brit suggested.

"What could be bad enough for him to kill her?" I asked.

"We've had people killed right here in Sugar Liquor over things that were so trivial, they were worse than silly except somebody ended up dead," Kristen reminded us. "Like when that father killed his son over the TV remote control. How stupid was that?" Pretty stupid in everyone's opinion, including the jury that found him guilty.

"If we're going to find out anything about Ethan, we're going to have to get into his apartment and take a look," I said. "Maybe there's something that will shed light on this feud between him and Vikki. Maybe she knew something about him that she shouldn't or caught him doing something weird, like that business meeting behind the grocery store."

My ever present chorus of naysayers chimed in. "No way. I'm not going in Ethan's apartment. Do you remember how scared we were when he nearly caught us in Vikki's apartment?" Kristen asked. "And you want to risk him catching us in his own place?"

"Kristen's right," Brit said. "If Ethan catches us, well, it can't have a good ending."

"Back off. Ethan's not going to catch us. Bring your binoculars over here and I'll show you how we pull this off." Reluctantly, Kristen and Brit moved over to my cot. I explained how to look for slivers of light between Ethan's curtains, how to see shadows of him moving around. His apartment was dark tonight. Ethan was gone. "There's no time like the present. Let's go kick some ass."

"Hold off a second with the ass-kicking," Kristen said. "I want it on the record that I am absolutely opposed to breaking into Ethan's apartment but if you're determined to go, I'll go. But we've got to get organized. We can't do this without a plan."

Oh, yes. We so excelled at planning and our plans worked so well. They were flawless and went off without a hitch.

"Okay," I said. To save an argument, I agreed with Kristen that we needed a plan. "Brit, you be our look-out. I'll take Kristen with me inside Ethan's apartment. She can try to get into Ethan's computer while I poke around looking for whatever there is to find."

Kristen loved anything to do with computers so she got into the spirit. She was *mucho* better at it than Brit or me so that part of the plan made sense.

Brit's lack of enthusiasm made me grind my teeth, but she accepted her assignment without a showdown. The legal part of her brain was telling her it was illegal to break into a man's home even if he was over-the-top fishy and suspicious.

Since I was fairly new at breaking and entering, I didn't know what tools or supplies to take. The three of us batted around a few ideas of what to take and ended up grabbing random stuff. Brit emptied junk out of our draw-string bags into the trashcan. The bags were smaller than backpacks and less cumbersome. "They'll work great," I told Brit. Into the bags went our three emergency flashlights Mom bought for us in case the power went out during a storm.

Wearing our bags on our shoulders, we slipped down the stairs, careful not to let my parents hear us. One advantage of living in a big house was that sounds didn't carry far. We made it out the back door and into Mom's flower garden.

"It's awfully dark for eight o'clock," I remarked, glancing at the darkening sky.

"It's supposed to storm," Brit replied.

The back parking lot of the apartment building was dark so there wasn't much chance of anyone seeing us. We continued around the corner of the building to the side parking lot. No sign of a black BMW with a Chicago Bears front license plate. Doubly satisfied Ethan wasn't home, we scouted the best place for Brit to keep watch. After a round of bickering between Brit and Kristen, I chose a spot behind a stone wall in the garden. "Okay, Brit," I told her, "you have a clear view of the parking lot driveway and front door from here. And you're perfectly hidden."

"If you see Ethan, text us immediately," Kristen told her. Brit opened her mouth. I was certain she was about to tell Kristen she had enough sense to do that without being told but closed her mouth. Thank goodness. I wasn't in the mood to listen to the two of them.

"Oh, no. Miss Georgia and Mr. Clyde's windows are dark," I said to Brit and Kristen. An unexpected snag in my plan. "They're away. I was counting on him to help us get into Ethan's apartment."

"Can't you remember anything, Amy?" Brit asked. "This is the night he and Miss Georgia always go to their son's house to eat." She gave me a look that reminded me of Mike's sneer. Maybe the idea of Brit getting into the legal business wasn't so hot after all. She was going to end up being as self-righteous and smug as Mike.

Kristen and I set our phones on vibrate. I'd check the message from Brit since Kristen would need time to shut down Ethan's computer, assuming she could get into it. I planned to put things back in order as I went so I could be ready to clear out with a few seconds notice.

After I settled Brit in her hiding spot, I led Kristen to the back of the building. "Exactly how are we going to get into Ethan's apartment?" Kristen asked.

"Good question." I didn't have a Plan B. Yet. Kristen rolled her eyes.

The logical entry to the apartment building was

the back door, but I didn't hold much hope even as I approached it. I pushed and shoved but it was solid and didn't budge. Kristen fished a bobby pin out of her bag and poked it in the lock but nothing clicked.

I moved on around the building until we were on the side facing my house. Ethan's apartment was just above us on the second floor. "Here's our doorway," I said, feeling pretty resourceful. Kristen looked around and asked where. "This old pine tree. It's close to the building. We can climb up it and scoot out on a limb to get into Ethan's window. The branches give us something to hang onto. I doubt Ethan locks his windows since he's on the second floor. A lot of people in Sugar Liquor don't even lock first-story windows."

"Amy Jackson, are you seriously suggesting we climb this tree and go in Ethan's window?" Kristen asked. Her sarcasm clearly conveying she didn't think much of the idea.

"It's either the tree or break down Ethan's front door. What'll it be?"

"Your idea. You go first," Kristen said.

Myra McJunkin's windows, with open drapes, were directly below Ethan's. Myra and Sandy were sitting on the living room sofa watching TV. I didn't have to worry about being quiet on their account. They both had hearing problems. The TV was so loud, I could hear it through the closed window.

I didn't want Kristen to know how nervous I was, so I grabbed a branch and started climbing like I knew what I was doing. Right away, I plunked my hand on top of a big blob of sap. I yanked it back and reached for a different branch. Pine needles stuck to the sap. My palm was coated with yuck. I'd forgotten this part of tree climbing.

"O-o-h, there's a bug crawling on my leg." I let go of the branch I was clutching so I could flick the bug off. The branch slapped Kristen in the face.

"Damn, Amy," she whispered. "Can't you do anything right?" I didn't tell her my leg-devouring bug was actually a twig.

In spite of sap-covered hands, imaginary bugs and rattled nerves, I made steady progress up the tree until I reached Ethan's window. I put the bug incident behind me and my enthusiasm returned.

"Isn't this exciting?" I asked Kristen who was standing just below me.

"It'll be more exciting if we don't get shot."

Chapter Fifteen

Assuming Ethan's apartment was laid out like Vikki's, my perch on a tree branch was outside his bedroom window. I almost laughed thinking that if Ethan had gone to bed early tonight, as he had falsely claimed last night, I was getting ready to pop through his window while he snoozed. That wouldn't actually be funny but it would make for a bizarre encounter. I didn't know what he'd do, but I'd be racing Kristen down this tree.

As I edged along the branch, I remembered Mr. Clyde saying the building's old window screens were discarded after a new heating and cooling system was installed. When I got close enough to the window, I saw he was right. No screens. One less obstacle.

I gently nudged the bottom window. As I'd correctly guessed, it was unlocked and slid up easily for an old house. With little effort, I raised the window high enough to shimmy through. Before I entered though, I stuck my head through the curtains half-expecting to see Ethan's large slumbering body in his bed, but the covers were smoothed out nice and flat. No Ethan. No snoozing body.

The bedroom door was open so I could see into the living room where a streak of hallway light entered the apartment under the front door. As far as I could tell, there were no other lights or sounds in the apartment. This was further confirmation that Ethan wasn't home so I wiggled inside, Kristen behind me. I didn't know if Tommy and Rachel Miller who lived across the hall were home. Being truckers, they were usually gone on long cross-country hauls. Even so, I put my finger to my lips reminding Kristen to be quiet. Mr. Clyde said the tenants were pretty jittery since Vikki's murder. They had every right to be on edge, and I didn't want to do anything to rattle their pumped-up nervous systems.

During our snatch and grab packing, Kristen threw in hair clips, of all things. Digging them out of her bag, she used them to hold the curtain panels together, so no one outside could see our flashlights flickering around. Pretty clever. How many burglars include hair clips in their breaking and entering tool kits? As soon as Kristen got the bedroom curtains securely fastened, I held my flashlight pointed at the floor, so we could see to get into the living room without tripping over anything. A window on the front of the building could be seen from the driveway and street, so Kristen double clamped the living room curtains before we made our way to the kitchen and bathroom. She clipped those curtains too. Now we could get down to business.

Kristen headed straight for Ethan's computer.

She hit Enter and the screen lit up asking for a password.

"What now?" I whispered.

"You're so lame. Remember, I'm in the computer business. Most people choose obvious passwords, but we're out of luck if Ethan used his first puppy's name. How about *Bears* because of his license plate?" she said. "Nope. Didn't work. Give me some ideas, Amy."

"O-kay," I said, trying to summon up what info I knew about Ethan. "Chicago? Illinois? BMW? Beemer? German Engineering?" Kristen typed quickly, ignoring my last suggestion. I was running out of ideas. "Cubs? White Sox? Wrigley? Bulls?" In desperation, I went with a long shot. "At Colton's condo, I saw a photo of Ethan in his purple college football uniform. I forgot to tell y'all, he played for Northwestern. Wildcats? Is that their nickname?"

"No idea but here goes. Yay. It is and we're in," Kristen said gleefully. "See. I told you passwords are usually meaningful. That's why people get hacked."

Kristen started clicking her way into Ethan's files. "Let's see what we got here. Ethan was working on business when he left," Kristen told me. She scrolled through pages of what appeared to be accounting records. "I don't understand what these numbers mean," she said. I stood over her shoulder, trying to decipher columns of numbers which meant nothing to me. I was a word person, not a number person. "I'll put this stuff on my flash drive," Kristen said. "I'll print it at home and see what my cousin, Andy, thinks. He'll know what kind of records they are."

"Good idea," I told her. Andy was an accountant and we could depend on him to keep his mouth shut.

So while Kristen prowled through Ethan's files, I began a systematic search of the apartment. Ethan's kitchen had less of everything than Vikki's, which was the barest kitchen I'd ever seen. This one was pathetic. No wonder Ethan ate at Gene's all the time. He had no pots and pans nor food to cook. His fridge contained a half-gallon of milk, mustard, salsa and two six-packs of bottled beer with a couple missing. Since my parents were beer connoisseurs, I recognized the label from a pricey micro-brewery in Asheville. The Matos boys liked good beer. I opened and closed cabinet drawers. Nothing to cook in them either. Not anything to eat at all except a couple bags of tortilla chips, mini-pretzels and an unopened jar of dill pickles.

Finished with the kitchen, I started on the living room. Half was furnished as a sitting area with a plump, chocolate-colored suede sofa and chair and large flat-screen TV. The rest of the room was taken up by Ethan's office set-up. A plain metal desk, filing cabinet, computer, printer and fax. His claim that he was running a business from the apartment seemed legit.

Kristen whispered to me, "Take a look. These are odds on sporting events. On the previous screens, there were odds on winning casino games and poker. Ethan must be into betting. Didn't Brit say she overheard him and Eric talking about playing poker when they were at Gene's Diner?"

"Yeah, poker's really hot now, especially on-line. A lot of people from school play," I replied.

"This looks like more than playing poker," Kristen said. "I'll save everything suspicious."

We'd been in Ethan's apartment fifteen minutes

and I didn't want to push our luck, plus I heard thunder in the distance and speeded up. For once the weather forecast was on target. As soon as I'd checked the coat closet and Ethan's bedroom, we'd call it a night. I told Kristen to be ready to shut down and get out in five minutes. She nodded.

I opened the closet which apparently served as overflow hanging space for Ethan's clothes. They were in dry cleaning bags. No point in checking the pockets but I flipped through the hangers looking for little plastic bags containing coins or anything the drycleaners found in the pockets. Nothing. As I started to close the door, I noticed a large cardboard box on the floor behind Ethan's clothes.

An unexpected storage area about three feet wide by eight feet deep had been built behind the clothes bar to take advantage of otherwise unusable space. The ceiling began sloping behind the clothes and continued until it almost touched the floor at the back of the closet. The building must have been converted into apartments by a contractor who worked by the seat of his pants. So far, I'd discovered the drywall in Vikki's closet had been left unfinished, Ethan's kitchen cabinet doors and drawers stuck and a very weird closet.

I immediately bumped my head on the sloping ceiling, proving my point. Holding my hand over my forehead to prevent a repeat, I stooped to a crouching position to reach the box. Lifting the flaps disappointed me. Just ordinary office supplies. I moved on. The box behind it was heavy so I tugged and scooted it toward the front of the closet where the ceiling was high enough that I could sit upright.

"Uh-oh, Kristen, check this out." She ducked and sat beside me while we stared at a box of bubble wrapped hand guns. I counted nine. I unwrapped one of the guns, careful not to touch anything that might set it off. Remembering Brit's procedure when taking the bullets out of the gun in Vikki's apartment, I kept it pointed away from us and checked it. This one wasn't loaded, thank goodness. I knew nothing about guns except my parents' admonitions never to touch them. I laid the gun near the closet door with the intention of putting it in my draw-string bag when I finished the closet.

Kristen helped me close the box and put it back in the same position I found it. With my eye for detail, I defied anyone to tell it had been tampered with. I started to scoot backwards to get out of the closet when I saw another small box pushed all the way to the back of the closet. Belly-crawling, I reached it, pulled it toward me and scooted backwards. Maneuvering into a cross-legged, hunched-over sitting position, I opened one flap enough to shine my flashlight inside. I whispered for Kristen again and she came scrambling back into the closet. Bundles of money filled the box. "Don't these look like the stacks from Vikki's closet?"

"Sure do. Same wrappers." Kristen replied. She quickly counted a stack of hundred dollar bills. Just like Vikki's. Except there's a lot more bundles here."

This was way more than coincidence. How many people keep a box of guns and large sums of cash stored in their closets?

To establish an irrefutable link between Vikki and Ethan, I had to be certain the two sets of guns and cash were perfect matches, and the only way to do that was to put them side by side.

Time was ticking away and the frequent booms of thunder warned me to get out of Ethan's apartment. "Kristen, stick five bundles of cash in my bag so we can compare it to the stuff from Vikki's. I think we've hit the mother lode."

"Whoa, Amy. I agree with your logic and I agree this is where Vikki got her goods but what if Ethan misses his money?"

"We'll have to hope he doesn't, and he has no reason to suspect us anyway. If Ethan's involved in some illegal business, he'll blame his crooked associates for the loss. You know the old saying about no honor among thieves. This has to be where Vikki's money and gun came from, but I have to know for sure. The question is whether Ethan gave them to her willingly or she took them without his consent. My vote is that Vikki helped herself."

Kristen didn't look convinced. "I don't think we should take them."

"Not this argument again, Kristen. I'm taking them." End discussion. I crawled out of the closet and put the gun and cash in my bag. She squinched her eyes at me. "Not now, Kristen," I snapped at her. She could vent her disapproval another day.

Kristen sat down again at Ethan's computer. She was obviously miffed but continued working. "Okay. I've been through all Ethan's files that I can get into. A couple minutes and I'll be finished. I need to leave Ethan's computer the way he left it. How about you?" she asked.

"I want to take a quick look at Ethan's bedroom and bathroom, although I don't expect to find anything incriminating. It'd be hard to top stashing money and guns in a coat closet. From my limited perspective, they verify Mr. Clyde's claims that Ethan was fishy and established a powerful link between Ethan and Vikki." How much more was I going to dig up on Vikki? Was there no end to her secrets?

As I suspected, the bedroom and bath only contained Ethan's clothes and personal items. He had a lot of trendy clothes with expensive brand names. He didn't skimp on the cost. If all he had to do was take a stack of bills out of his closet and head for the nearest Tommy Hilfiger store, he could afford to splurge.

I came back into the living room and told Kristen, "Let's go. The storm's getting closer and I sure don't want to be in the pine tree with lightning bolts targeting us." Besides that, the increasing wind added to the creaks and groans of the old apartment building, making me more nervous than I already was.

Kristen shut down and waited while the screen went dark. I glanced around the room making sure everything was exactly as we'd found it, including leaving the closet door open a couple inches. Nothing about the room's appearance should alert Ethan it had been searched.

A strong gust of wind rattled Ethan's front door which really freaked me out. I froze in place. The door opened. Kristen and I didn't have time to hide or even turn off our flashlights. Ethan was standing in the doorway. Why didn't Brit warn us? She let Ethan catch us.

"Amy? What the hell are you doing here?"

"Colton?" I asked, recognizing his voice. "Is that you? How did you get in?"

He closed the door and flipped on a lamp, causing us to blink after being accustomed to near darkness. "I used a key," he told me angrily, dangling the keys in the air. "The question is--how did you get in here? I'm guessing you didn't use a key. Even Clyde, the caretaker, doesn't have keys for Ethan's locks."

I was too scared to speak. Kristen stood motionless beside me, offering no help. I didn't see any way out of this so I blurted out the truth. "We climbed a tree and came in through Ethan's bedroom window."

"You what?"

I stammered, "I--I'm trying to find Vikki's murderer."

"Oh, spare me. Let me guess. You have a new theory. Ethan killed Vikki. Does this mean I'm off the hook? Or do you think we're in cahoots and teamed up to do it?"

"I think Vikki was involved with Ethan," I said in a squeak.

"That's crazy. I already told you there was nothing between them. They didn't even like each other." I wanted to tell him that I didn't mean romantically involved, that I meant involved in something illegal, but before I got the words out, a deafening boom of thunder directly overhead made us all duck. Our heads, with goofy grimaces, were half-buried in our shoulders. I jerked and hurt my neck.

"Kristen and I have to get out of here," I told Colton. I didn't want to get fried climbing down a stupid-ass pine tree. That's not how I wanted the *Sugar Liquor Times* to write up my departure from this world.

"You didn't answer my question. Who's the murderer? Me? Ethan? Both of us?"

"I think I've decided it's not you." Colton was just starting his career as a pharmacist. He had everything to lose if he got on the wrong side of the law. I really doubted he was mixed up in this business.

"Lucky me. I'm cleared but my brother's your main suspect. Still not a good day for the Matos brothers."

I was certain Ethan was connected by guns and money to Vikki, and the chance of an innocent explanation was zip. If self-centered Vikki happened upon some scheme, illegal or otherwise that was good for Vikki, she'd go for it, even if it was with Ethan, someone she disliked.

"Yesterday, Kristen," I said, nodding at her so Colton knew who she was, "and Brit, our other friend, and I found a gun and five thousand dollars in Vikki's closet."

"That's bull. Vikki was lucky to have five dollars. You sure it wasn't Monopoly dollars?"

"I know the difference."

"Then it must belong to Justin. Maybe he robbed a bank," Colton suggested, the bitter tone of his voice revealing his dislike for his dead girlfriend's husband.

"I don't think Justin robbed a bank and I don't think the stuff belongs to him," Kristen spoke up. "Amy and I figure he would've gotten them out of the apartment before the police arrived. If he didn't kill Vikki, he sure wouldn't have taken a chance on the police finding evidence of another crime he'd committed. And if he's her killer, he would never have left anything that made him look even worse at the scene of Vikki's murder. Justin's got more sense than that."

Colton mulled over what Kristen said. "Okay. For the time being, I'll concede Justin's not a bank robber. But where on earth do you think Vikki got her hands on that kind of money? She told me everything and she never mentioned it. She would've bragged like crazy about having five thousand dollars."

"Maybe because she got them from your brother."

"Are you hung up on that again? Give it a rest. Ethan and Eric run an import business called EE Imports, and Vikki wasn't their partner or anything else to them. Think about it. What could Vikki contribute to running a business? Nothing. That's what.

"Ethan and Eric buy big lots of household items like lamps and picture frames and vases from Asia and wholesale them to stores. They lease a warehouse over on I-40 at Wrigley Road Exit. And they don't deal in cash. Do you think a business would send a sack full of cash with their driver to pay for merchandise?" Colton had a point. It didn't make sense and Vikki certainly didn't know anything about business. Anything beyond lip gloss and mascara shades were over her head.

I asked why he thought Vikki had a gun. "No idea. Maybe she got it for protection since Justin was gone so much."

I was deliberating telling Colton about the guns and cash hidden in Ethan's hall closet when loud music by Jay-Z shattered our silence. Kristen and Colton jumped but I beat them clearing the floor first. Finding cash and guns and getting caught snooping in Ethan's apartment, followed by thunder that had caused me severe neck injury was enough to shake even a seasoned reporter, much less a newbie like me. This combination of nerve jarring events topped off by Colton's staccato cell ring tone sent me off the Fright Meter scale.

"Yo. Right-o," he replied after listening briefly. "That was Ethan," he told me. "He's going to meet me here in a few minutes. I ought to keep you here to face Ethan with your accusations, but I'm so sure you're wrong, I'm giving you a break. Get out of here and leave investigating to the police."

I was already heading for the bedroom window and our tree. Kristen was right behind me. Colton yelled at us, "For God's sake, you can't go down that tree. You'll get killed by lightning." He had a point. The storm crashed and raged directly above us. "Go down the back stairs. Ethan can't come in that way. I still have his key."

Colton opened the apartment door and we dashed past him. As far as I knew, he hadn't paid any attention to our draw-string bags. Kristen and I were so scared our legs dragged behind us as we tried to run down the stairs. We looked like cartoon characters with our heads leading, way out front of our spinning feet.

Lightning lit up the sky and rain pelted us as Kristen and I ran to the side of the building to find Brit. She was still hidden behind the garden wall, soaked to the skin. "Why didn't you dumbasses answer? Amy, I've been texting you frantically to let you know Ethan just went in the front door. It would've served you right if he'd caught you. But since he didn't kill you, I'll take care of it myself."

"Sorry, Brit. I was running down the stairs and shaking so badly, I didn't feel my phone vibrate," I said. Kristen told Brit to shut up and we ran all the way to my house. Kristen came in for a second to drop off her bag and its contents. She ran right back out, late for her family get-together.

Brit called her mom to let her know she would be home shortly. Even though she was totally pissed at me, she still wanted to hear what Kristen and I found in Ethan's apartment, plus she needed to dry off and change clothes.

Mom and Dad were watching TV. Brit and I stuck our heads in the door and said hello to them. I told Mom that Kristen had already gone home and Brit would be leaving soon. Mom required an update on houseguest count.

Brit was a mess. The full brunt of the storm had dumped on her. Ringlets of hair were plastered to her face and neck. Her ponytail was a soggy mass of curls. Even worse, she was still red-faced furious I didn't respond to her texts. "I was scared to death. I thought for sure Ethan caught you. You don't know how close I came to calling *911* to come and save you," she yelled at me. I hugged her and thanked her over and over but she wasn't ready to accept my apologies. Once she got dried off and into clean clothes, she'd mellow. She didn't hold a grudge nearly as long as Kristen.

To divert her attention from her waterlogged condition and her fury at me, I emptied the contents of the drawstring bags onto Kristen's bed. Brit immediately picked up the gun. She checked to see if it was loaded. "This is identical to the gun we found in Vikki's apartment," she said, reinforcing my conclusion.

"I'll get the gun and bundle of money out of the drawer and we'll compare them," I said. When I laid the packets side by side, the bands around the bills were identical and the amounts were the same. "We have our proof that Vikki and Ethan were connected, and I don't think it had anything to do with importing vases."

Brit dried off and put on a clean pair of shorts and a top. She used my hair dryer which made her hair frizzier. Not an improvement but it stopped dripping on her dry clothes. She kept on her wet flip-flops. They didn't matter.

"Why didn't you text us about Colton?" I asked before she left. Brit looked at me with a blank expression.

"Colton? What are you talking about? I didn't see him."

"Colton caught Kristen and me in Ethan's apartment. He must've come up the back stairs, the same way he got to Vikki's apartment. The scene with him was scary as hell but he let us go. Frankly, I think he thinks I'm a nut case."

"He'd be right about that. Does he know you took *those* from Ethan's apartment?" she asked with a glance toward Kristen's cot. I assured her he did not.

I walked down to the back door with Brit. "You don't know how scared I was, Amy. If you'd been one minute later coming out of that building, I would've called the police for help. Right now you'd be explaining to Mike what you were doing with a gun and five thousand dollars in your draw-string bag." My heart pounded at the thought.

When she drove away, I went to the TV room and snuggled with my parents to watch TV Land. Right now I needed some old-fashioned comfort.

Chapter Sixteen

A little before eight AM, I finished dressing for my meeting with Kristen and Brit at Gene's Diner. At the last minute, I panicked and ran up to the cupola and stuffed my Hello Kitty pillowcase and its diabolical contents in my backpack. I was scared to carry it around with me, but I was more afraid of leaving it in my house.

Kristen's cousin, Andy, agreed to look over our documents if we'd buy him breakfast. Out of college for only a year, Andy was living at home with his parents while trying to dig himself out from under a pile of college loans.

Looking quite the young professional in dress slacks, short-sleeve shirt and tie, Andy arrived at the diner seconds ahead of me. He waved and waited at the door for me to catch up. Like Kristen, he was tall, slim, blond and over-endowed with self-confidence. He was six years older than I was but I'd known him pretty much all my life. Of course, I knew everybody in Sugar Liquor except for the few new people, like Ethan and Eric and Colton, who moved into town occasionally.

Kristen and Brit already had a booth, so Andy and I slid into the empty side. We ordered right away since none of us needed menus. Breakfast selections were good old' southern greasy traditional fare. Thank goodness. Some things were too good to tamper with.

"I don't have much time before work, so let me see your papers while I'm waiting," Andy said.

Kristen passed me a folder of print-outs from her flash drive. I held them firmly in my hand before turning them over to Andy. "I'm not supposed to have these documents so don't flash them around while you're looking at them and don't tell anybody what you read. Okay?"

"FYI, Amy, I learned not to blab client information in Accounting 101. Since y'all are paying for my services with the *Super Deluxe Breakfast with Three Eggs, Ham and Extra Home Fries*, technically you're clients, so don't lecture me on the ethics of my profession, okay?" Oh, my gosh. He sounded way too much like Kristen.

Andy laid the folder flat on the table, placed his arms on each side of it and sat in a casual, slumped position. As soon as he opened the folder, he started rifling through the papers, putting them in a different order.

Our breakfasts arrived in record time and Brit, Kristen and I dug in. "Andy," Kristen said, sounding like his mother, "stop reading and eat while your breakfast's hot." Andy was so engrossed in the documents, he wasn't aware his food was on the table. Surprised to see his waiting food, he set our papers aside and ate.

When Andy polished off the last bite of his second biscuit dripping with strawberry jam, he pushed his plate aside and picked up the stack of papers again. Double-checking they were in proper order, he studied them. I waited eagerly for him to decipher the columns of numbers. His interest, which began as studied professional attention, turned to astonishment. "Where in the hell did y'all get these?" Andy asked, a little too much on the loud side.

"Put a lid on the volume, Andy. You're supposed to keep a low profile which does not include shouting so the whole damn diner can hear." Kristen's tone sounded amazingly similar to the one he'd just used on me about ethics.

"We got the papers from a friend," I said, answering his question before he and Kristen got going at each other. Calling Ethan a friend was stretching it, but it was as much as Andy needed to know. "We figured out some of the pages list odds on various events and casino games. We assume our friend's into betting."

Andy leaned toward the center of the table, motioning us to lean forward until we almost bumped heads. He whispered, "Your friend's into more than betting. This is not something your friend pulled off the internet to increase his or her chances of winning over at Harrah's on the Cherokee Reservation. This is illegal stuff and your friend is on the operations side, not the playing side. From the sums of money going into and out of these accounts, this is big time.

"The info about odds is available on the internet and no big deal. What is a big deal are the records showing large sums of money coming into your friend's account from losing betters and going out in payoffs to winners. It's all spelled out here in black and white. There's lots of money moving around in these accounts and it's dirty money. I don't know how y'all met this friend but you need to find some other friends as in immediately. Y'all are swimming in the wrong pond. This one has some nasty characters in it," Andy said in a paternal voice. "Y'all aren't betting, are you?" That question was directed at Kristen.

"No way, dummy. I'm not risking my hard-earned dollars on some scheme statistically rigged to take them away from me." Andy looked questioningly at Brit and me and we shook our heads vigorously. Gambling wasn't my thing. I sucked at Uno.

Andy's attention returned to Kristen's print-outs. As soon as he finished reading one page, he quickly flipped to the next. Judging from Andy's eager reaction, it looked like Kristen hit the jackpot on Ethan's computer. "Y'all didn't get this from some high school kid who's gotten in way over his head, did you?" he asked.

Kristen looked at me to answer. I realized by letting Andy see the printouts, I'd set myself up so that I had no alternative but to trust him to some extent. I couldn't risk having him telling his friends that I got my hands on somebody's bookie records. In a little town like this, how long would it take before Ethan started hearing bits and pieces about three teenage girls passing around print-outs of illegal gambling records? How long before he figured out the documents belonged to him? And that one of the teens doing the passing was his next door neighbor?

With our heads still huddled in the middle of the table, I said, "I'm investigating Vikki's murder and trying to help Justin prove he didn't do it. The gambling evidence turned up accidentally." Since Andy was Kristen's cousin, I figured it was better to keep quiet about her part in acquiring the documents. "I don't know how but I think this gambling business is related to Vikki's death."

"You think Vikki was part of this? Are we talking about the same Vikki Wilson?" Andy asked incredulously. "No way," he said, answering his own question. "This is so over Vikki's head. She wouldn't have grasped the first thing about how it worked."

"Duh. I didn't say Vikki was the ring leader but I do believe she figured out some way to horn in on the action. I think Brit, Kristen and I are going to come up with some answers to what was going on very soon. In the meantime, keep this to yourself. We're paying clients. Remember?" Looking worried, he nodded.

"Look, Andy, it's like this. You want to help Justin, right?" Brit asked. Andy had been best friends with Justin's brother for years. That's the way it was in Sugar Liquor, everybody had connections with everybody else, usually good ones, which was true in this case. Brit tapped into that friendship and counted on Andy's loyalty to Justin's brother to keep him quiet.

"You know I want to help Justin and I'll keep quiet for the time being, but you have to promise me you'll stay away from this so-called friend." We nodded. Our promise seemed to satisfy Andy.

"Okay. I got to get to work." With that, Andy handed me the folder and thanked us for breakfast.

"You've been a big help. We appreciate it,"

Kristen told him. Her voice was warm with genuine admiration for her cousin's abilities.

Brit seconded Kristen's thanks. I reassured Andy I'd keep my distance from my friend's gambling business.

Andy left the diner and crossed the street to walk to his office.

None of us were due at our jobs yet, so we sat down for another cup of coffee. I raised my refilled cup in a toast to Kristen. "You're a genius."

"I agree," she said jokingly. "What did I do this time?"

"Asking Andy to take a look at our papers was brilliant," I replied.

"Absolutely," Brit said, raising her cup too. "And I think we can count on Andy to keep quiet. He's got his professional ethics and he doesn't want to harm Justin's chances."

"You know something I wonder about," I said to Brit and Kristen. "Colton said Ethan and Eric were in the import business. I wonder if that's for real or if it's a cover for the gambling operation. I hadn't thought much about Eric other than as a possibility for Vikki's naked cowboy, but after seeing him with Ethan at that spooky meeting behind the grocery store, don't y'all think Eric must be in as deep as Ethan?"

"I think being at the meeting behind the grocery store incriminates the whole bunch of them. That was over the top weird," Brit agreed.

As usual, Kristen thought of a computer solution to my question. "I can research Ethan and Eric's import business on my laptop. Certain documents listing owners of businesses and some kinds of info have to be filed with local or state government and are public record. I don't know the exact law but I bet I can find something. The only problem is I don't dare use my office computer since my company designs software that enables businesses to catch employees doing personal activities like bidding on stuff on eBay and online shopping during work hours. I'll have to do it during lunch." I laughed at the irony of Kristen catching herself with software she helped design.

Kristen and Brit rushed off to work, but my shift didn't start for a while yet, so I had another cup of coffee while I decided how to proceed with my case. In some ways, I wondered if I was making a mistake by focusing my investigation on Ethan, but then I remembered the guns and the money. Vikki's murder and Ethan and this gambling operation were all tied together.

Checking my watch, I realized I had a couple hours to kill. My shift had been scheduled by the devil himself to fall during the hottest part of the day, the better to torment me.

I couldn't sit around doing nothing so I walked home. Mom and Dad had left for work so I took Mom's car and drove to Colton's condo. I didn't know if he'd be home but I had to face him sooner or later to talk about Kristen and me being in Ethan's apartment. I was hoping he wouldn't be home so I could postpone the inevitable. From my parking place on the street, I had a clear view of him through the sliding glass windows. The same sliding glass windows through which I had been ungracefully tossed night before last. Colton was sitting at his dining table working on his laptop. I dreaded facing him because he was angry with me and justifiably so. I gathered my courage and walked to his door and rang the bell.

"Oh, hell, what now?" he said in greeting.

"Hi. I'm really sorry about last night," I said meekly. "I'm returning copies of documents Kristen and I took from your brother's computer." I handed him a copy I'd made of Kristen's printouts. "Colton, you don't know me much at all and this is hard for me to say to you but I think your brother's involved in some bad business. Kristen saved this information from Ethan's computer before you caught us and printed them at her house. Ethan and Eric may have a legitimate import business like you said, but Ethan's involved in an illegal gambling operation and, from his records, it's a big one. I think Vikki's death is connected to Ethan."

"You are so off target, Amy. How many times do I have to tell you that Ethan and Vikki had nothing to do with each other? Not personally, not business-wise, not any wise. Can't you accept that?"

"I have proof they were connected."

"Impossible."

"Then I'll show you." I tried to take off my backpack and open it but it was an awkward maneuver since I was standing.

"Sit down." Visibly annoyed by my intrusion and accusations, Colton remained standing. I unzipped my backpack and gently removed my *Hello Kitty* pillowcase holding its dark secrets. Colton stared at kitty's large, innocent face topped by her pink hair bow like she was a zombie.

I started pulling plastic bags out of my pillowcase, looking like a magician who was never going to get to the rabbit. I laid them on the coffee table and gathered my courage. "Remember I told you about finding a hand gun and five thousand dollars in Vikki's apartment?" Colton nodded. I gently removed the gun from the bag and laid it on the table. Colton flinched. "It's not loaded," I told him. He didn't act like he had much confidence in my gun-handling skills. He gently edged the barrel away from us. I picked up another bag and withdrew the stack of money, still with the original paper band around it. Colton reached for it and flipped through it.

"I didn't believe it was real," he told me. He laid the money on the table. "Okay, you've convinced me. I believe Vikki had a real gun and real money. What does this have to do with Ethan though? It doesn't connect Vikki to him."

"But these do." I opened another plastic bag and pulled out a gun and stack of money. I laid the gun beside the one from Vikki's apartment, and even a novice like me could tell they were identical. The cash was an obvious match too. "I found these in boxes in Ethan's living room closet last night. Colton, I know it was wrong to go into Ethan's apartment and remove this stuff, but I had to do it to follow my leads in Vikki's murder and help Justin. He thinks he's going to be arrested for her murder."

Colton ignored the part about Justin. "You're saying you found one set of these in Vikki's apartment and the other set in Ethan's apartment?" I told him I didn't claim to know what the connection was between Ethan and Vikki, but this was proof there was one.

"And another thing to think about—if Eric's in business with Ethan, maybe he's in the illegal gambling part too. What do you know about him?"

Colton hesitated before answering. "He and Ethan go back a while. They knew each other in

Illinois."

"Was Vikki ever involved with Eric?"

"No. I heard she hit on him when he first came to town. Ethan said Eric wasn't interested." So Eric wasn't the naked cowboy after all.

"I'm sorry to be the one to tell you about Ethan, but it's better you know." I glanced at my watch. "I have to go to work," I said to Colton.

Suddenly I regretted my hasty decision to bring my evidence against Ethan to Colton's condo and lay it out before him. I hadn't thought far enough ahead to realize that he probably wouldn't let me leave with it. Without the link between Vikki and Ethan, my case against Ethan was dead in the water.

Colton was deep in thought so while he was zoned out, I slowly began putting my stolen goods into their plastic bags. So far, he hadn't paid any attention to what I was doing. Working in slow motion, I loaded my loot into the pillowcase. Colton turned toward me, only half-way paying attention. His forehead was creased, processing what I'd told him. He didn't speak or try to stop me. He wasn't reacting right and freaking me out. He should be irate I was leaving his apartment with evidence connecting his brother to a murdered girl.

"Colton, aren't you worried this evidence is going to link your brother to Vikki's murder?"

"I don't know what's going on but Ethan didn't kill Vikki."

"You don't get it, Colton. This links him and Vikki. Doesn't it bother you that I'm leaving here with it?" Was I crazy? Why did I say that? I was practically inviting him to snatch the pillowcase out of my hand.

"Not in the least. You stole it. It's yours. I don't

want that stuff in my condo."

I looked carefully at his eyes to see if he was bluffing. Surely he didn't mean what he said. "So you're not worried about Ethan being implicated in Vikki's murder?"

"I'd be worried if I thought he was involved with her death, but I know he's not. Whatever else Ethan's doing, he can figure out for himself. I'm not getting involved. However, I'll give you a word of advice. Don't carry this stuff around with you." He paused. "Turn it over to the police now. Let them deal with it."

My breathing almost stopped as I pictured myself walking into Mike's office with my *Hello Kitty* pillowcase and laying guns and large amounts of money on his desk, admitting I took them from Vikki's and Ethan's closets, without their knowledge. I pictured my frightened, bewildered face trapped behind metal bars. As many warnings as Mike had given me to stay out of police business, he'd slap me in jail before I could insist on my one phone call.

"Going to the police is not an option," I admitted.

"I figured you'd say that. So get rid of it. I'm warning you."

"I'll hide it where nobody can find it," I said, thinking out loud. I knew the perfect place. Pisgah National Forest. I went up there on my work breaks, so I wouldn't look suspicious if anyone saw me. Plus, there were millions of nooks and crannies under logs and rocks.

"Do it before somebody misses their cash and comes with a bigger gun looking for it." He scared me.

"Colton, are you going to tell Ethan about me

breaking into his apartment and having the guns and money?"

"You're saying they're evidence against him. He deserves to know." I took that as a yes.

I decided to try to recruit Colton as an ally. "Why don't you help me get to the bottom of this Vikki-Ethan business? I could really use your input. Meet me and Kristen and Brit at Gene's when we get off work. Say around five and we'll talk this through."

"Look, Amy. I'm not getting involved in your investigation. As you pointed out so eloquently, I was in Vikki's apartment the night she died, and a convincing case could be made against me for being her killer. And you've developed a case and collected evidence against my brother. I can't do anything about that, but I will give you my best advice about how to handle the money and guns. You've got a dangerous problem, the proverbial hot potato, as they say. I can't meet you at five though. I have to cover part of an extra shift at the pharmacy this afternoon but give me your cell number. I'll text you when I get off and we'll get together then. I don't know what's going on but I can promise you that Ethan didn't kill Vikki."

Colton had a lot of confidence in his brother. I didn't.

Chapter Seventeen

I carried my backpack holding my *Hello Kitty* pillowcase filled with guns and money up to my bedroom. The more steps I climbed, the more this stuff weighed me down. An albatross around my bent neck. Colton was right. I had to get rid of this stuff. As soon as I got dressed for work, the guns and cash were out of my house once and for all.

For the past few hot, miserable days, dressing for work meant putting on as few clothes as the grocery store would allow me to wear in public. That didn't take long so I ran up to the cupola to check my email which included the usual daily offers to cleanse my colon. Gross. Or how about cheap life insurance? I hoped my parents wouldn't need to collect that anytime soon.

While I was shutting down my lap top, I caught a glimpse of Colton going in the front door of the apartment building next door. My heart thudded. He said he was going to tell Ethan about my revelations and, apparently, he was on his way to do just that. I hoped Colton wouldn't tell Ethan who gave him that info. If Ethan killed Vikki, he had nothing to lose by quashing me like an ant with a tiny backpack full of tiny notebooks and pens scurrying down the sidewalk. With Mike and Ethan both after me, my future looked bleak. Upping my life insurance might not be such a bad idea.

When I got ready to leave for work, my backpack felt heavier than the last time I carried it. With my own albatross hanging around my neck, lines from Coleridge's *The Rime of the Ancient Mariner* ran through my head:

> *And from my neck so free*
> *The Albatross fell off, and sank*
> *Like lead into the sea.*

I could only hope to be rid of my albatross.

Fairly confident Colton was still in the apartment building, I pulled Mom's car out of my driveway and drove by way of the old back alley once used for delivering supplies to the rear of houses on my street. I slowed to a crawl past the back of the apartment building, eyes keen for Ethan's car. No cars were in the back lot, but not satisfied with my partial view of the side lot, I turned around and went back for a better look. I eased far enough into the lot to see the few vehicles parked there. No black BMW. Ethan wasn't home. Justin's pick-up was there though. He must've come back to finish packing. Mr. Clyde was right. Justin was out of that place as fast as he could move.

Although it was inevitable that Colton would tell Ethan some or all of what I'd discovered, chances were good it hadn't happened yet and I welcomed any delay. As I backed out of the parking lot, I wondered if Colton was in Ethan's apartment alone, if he'd reluctantly opened the coat closet, pushed Ethan's clothes aside and found the telltale boxes. When Colton saw all those guns and cash for himself, would he still be so confident in Ethan's innocence?

Colton wasn't my concern right now. Getting rid of my pillowcase topped my agenda. The more I thought about stashing that stuff in the forest, the better the idea sounded. I had to hustle if I was going to hide it before work. I definitely couldn't leave it in Mom's car in the shopping center parking lot. Too risky. What if the car caught on fire and the firemen found ten thousand dollars of charred bills and two scorched guns inside it?

As I drove through town, I checked the rear-view mirror every few seconds to see if any cars were following me. I knew I'd crossed over the line into paranoia but I couldn't help it. Colton scared me. He'd done a major job on my self-confidence. Making random turns, zig-zagging around downtown, I took the highway that led to my job. I couldn't keep my eyes off the rear-view mirror. I felt like the whole world was stalking me.

While I was busy concentrating on the road behind me, a car making a left turn stopped in front of me. I slammed on my brakes, tires screeching, so close to rear-ending it. I was way too close to a Clemson Tigers decal on the back window.

What if I had an accident, and while lying unconscious, the police found the cash and guns? Hunched over the steering wheel like a little old lady on a Sunday afternoon, I focused on the road ahead and made it safely to the shopping center parking lot. I pulled into a parking space in a quiet corner, stopped and put the car in Park for a few minutes to recover my cool after my near-accident and my ongoing what-if scenarios.

Feeling as calm as I was likely to get with my explosive pillowcase on the seat beside me, I put the car in Drive, turned around, made a right turn at the intersection and sped down the highway into the forest. In a couple minutes, I pulled into my work break haven and drove all the way around the one-way loop road, eyes peeled for suspicious people or cars. Like me, for example. I was the most suspicious acting person in the whole forest. I even made me nervous.

A group of senior citizens occupying a picnic pavilion lugged boxes and baskets from their cars. No threat there. Three women I recognized as daily exercise walkers were doing their warm-up stretches beside their cars. No problem with them either. There was no one else in the area. I made a second lap that took me back to my usual picnic tables beside the river.

Staying in my car, I fitted plastic bags inside each other. I grabbed handfuls of them from the garage at home, since I wasn't about to stick my pillowcase under a nasty rock where slimy worms could crawl on kitty's sweet face. When I'd layered what seemed like enough bags to make a super watertight sack, I transferred the guns and money from my backpack into my newly constructed storage bag. In a stroke of luck, I found an old piece of brown burlap in the garage. The color of soil and dry leaves, I wrapped the burlap around my package. My camouflaged loot was ready for its new hiding place.

Without glancing in my direction, the trio of walkers, engrossed in chit-chat, chugged past. It'd be ten-fifteen minutes before they lapped past me again.

With the burlap package tucked in my backpack, I got out of the car trying to look laid-back and casual, instead of clumsy and herky-jerky. I locked the car and put the keys in a zipper compartment of my backpack, carefully zipping it and checking twice to make sure the keys couldn't slip out. Ready to head down the path to the river bank, I halted when a flash of movement coming from the wooded area in the center of the loop road caught my eye. It flashed again. I turned and crossed the road. Lurking behind a tree, I poked my head out for a look.

Geez, it was just an old guy turning newspaper pages. Another of the daily regulars. Sitting on opposite sides of the table, he and his buddy came to the forest every day, drank coffee and read the paper. Like me, they had their signature table.

Satisfied the area was secure and my preparations complete, I hurried down the river bank with my backpack. There was no shortage of possible hiding places--rocks, logs, prickly bushes, secret nooks. The perfect hiding place was here and I'd know it when I saw it. It had to be concealed well so some kid looking for creepy-crawlies under rocks didn't discover it or some nosy old fisherman walking along the shallow river bed didn't stumble across it.

As I walked, I bent down to swat a fly off my leg and saw my hidey hole, a tiny hollow spot with straggly weeds growing in front. Easing the weeds aside, I discovered a little niche that angled off to the left. The little side cavity was the perfect spot. With that decision made so easily, I looked up and down the river and toward the road in the recreation area. No one in sight. With exaggerated care, I slipped my burlap bundle into the dark hole and pushed it as far as it would go. Careful in my movements, I fluffed the weeds concealing the opening and left the ground undisturbed. No signs that someone had stuffed two handguns and ten thousand dollars into a hole along the river bank.

Dipping my dirt-covered hands in the river, I rinsed them and wiped them dry on my backpack. Counting the number of footsteps back to my car, I drew a map. Brit and Kristen had never been here with me since this was my respite from work. They probably couldn't find the loot even with my map but they could give it a shot. My mind refused to dwell on the reason I wouldn't be returning for the package myself.

Circling the loop twice, nothing was amiss. The newspaper guys were still sitting at their picnic table. The exercise trio was into their second lap. The senior citizens were buzzing around their pavilion. No other cars had parked along the loop road.

Stressed out before my day even began, I drove, hands trembling, toward the grocery store for my despised shift.

I was in the parking lot gathering carts when Kristen called me. Holding my cellphone between my ear and shoulder, I kept pushing carts. With any luck, as long as I was moving, no one from the grocery store would notice my forbidden phone usage during work hours.

Kristen excitedly reported she'd finished

researching Ethan's company on the internet. "I found out tons of stuff. He and Eric opened EE Imports about six months ago. They registered the company name and listed their base of operations as the warehouse on Wrigley Road like Colton said. The mailing address is Ethan's home address next door to you. I wish I could print all this stuff but my boss might catch me," she said.

"New topic. I took another look at Mike's police records. There's nothing more on Ethan than what we already knew. There's a report on Eric but it's clean. If they were in the illegal gambling business there, they stayed out of reach of the law. Ethan and Eric both majored in Economics at Northwestern University and graduated the same year, so chances are they've been friends since college." That jived with what Colton said about their friendship going back some years. "Seems like they could've put a high-class education like that to better use than running an illegal gambling operation," Kristen added.

Yeah. I wished I could go to a classy school like Northwestern, but it was double or triple my modest budget. "Good job, Kristen. What would I do without my in-house computer expert?"

Kristen laughed it off but I meant what I said. She was terrific in her computer world.

"Just so you know," I said, "I went to see Colton and showed him Vikki's and Ethan's cash and guns to prove there was a connection between them."

"You did what? You're going to get yourself killed or arrested. I'm guessing the first."

"Nice prospects." Neither one had anything going for it. I assured Kristen nothing bad had happened. At least, so far.

"Colton still insists there was no connection between Vikki and Ethan and that Ethan had nothing to do with Vikki's death," I said.

"After all we went through to get that stuff, he didn't keep our evidence, did he?" I could hear her squinting her eyes.

"No. That was the scariest part of all."

"How so?" Kristen asked.

"After I showed the stuff to him, I suddenly got scared he'd take it away from me but Colton said he didn't want the guns or money in his possession."

"For real? He let you walk away with proof his brother was involved with Vikki in a criminal way?"

"Not only let me walk away with it. He insisted."

"Weird," Kristen said, sounding kind of weird herself. "Hey, Amy, I got to get back to work. Any more surprises?"

"Yeah. Colton told me to get rid of the stuff. He really scared me so I took it up in the forest and hid it. I drew a map for you and Brit in case anything happens to me."

"Don't talk like that. You're scaring me." Good. I was tired of being scared by myself. I donated a share to Kristen. After all, she was with Brit and me in Vikki's apartment. And Colton saw her with me in Ethan's apartment.

Before Kristen clicked off, I quickly told her about Colton going to Ethan's apartment and still being inside when I left for work. "That doesn't sound good," she said and hung up.

I gathered stray carts in the parking lot and headed back to the store with them. At least, the weather was cool and the cash and guns were buried.

At five o'clock, Kristen, Brit and I met at Gene's.

I'd hated my afternoon at work as usual but, for a change, Brit hadn't saved the state of North Carolina from catastrophe and Kristen hadn't thwarted a sabotage of worldwide communications, so they had no significant accomplishments to report.

Instead of leading us to our seats, Dusty Rose's eyes followed the linoleum squares to the right side of the diner which was our cue to follow her eye instructions. She made a faint gesture with her hand which meant we could choose our own booth. My mood always improved after being in Dusty Rose's company for a few minutes. Watching her made me realize that in spite of my crappy summer job, I had college and a career to look forward to. Poor Dusty Rose was already imprisoned in her life's career. She'd never have a chance to be the lead dog. Dusty Rose's scenery, the inside of Gene's Crummy Diner, wasn't going to change.

Brit and Kristen studied the map to the location of the money and guns but no light bulbs popped above their heads indicating they got it. The way they kept turning the map around and around, they'd never find the spot by the river. They couldn't even get north and south in the right position. So much for them ever finding the stash.

We decided none of us were hungry for a meal, so we ordered coffee and apple pie with vanilla ice cream. Gene's pies should be on the cover of *Southern Living* magazine.

We finished eating and still no text from Colton. "Why don't we stop by his apartment?" I said to Brit and Kristen. "He worked the afternoon shift so he might've gone home. If nothing else, Colton has to understand that I didn't start out to *get* Ethan. My goal was finding Vikki's killer and helping Justin prove his innocence. Ethan's connection to Vikki materialized along the way."

Now that I'd disposed of the guns and cash, the burden of the albatross had fallen from my neck taking my neck ache with it. Only Brit, Kristen and Colton knew I had them. Brit and Kristen wouldn't tell. Colton's connections were too complicated for himself and his brother to rat on me. I felt calmer. This was going to work out just fine.

We all hopped out of my car at Colton's condo, and I led the way to the front door. Instead of Colton answering the doorbell like last night, there was silence. I rang again. No response. Disappointed, we trotted back to the car. "Let's go to the drugstore and find out when he gets off," I said, eager to talk to him.

I drove us to the pharmacy, and we took a place in line behind an old woman who'd tried to telephone a refill for a prescription but gave the number incorrectly. Her prescription hadn't been processed. The woman was hateful and the young female clerk was losing her cool. "I'm sure I gave the correct numbers." The woman kept insisting she was right even though it was time for her to shut up and let the pharmacist get on with fixing her meds. Brit, who was all for putting on evidence, said to Kristen, "I wish the clerk would play the telephone recording and put that bat in her senile place."

The woman finally stepped aside to wait until her prescription was refilled. "I know I gave the right number. That girl can't hear," she mumbled. I squeezed past her to reach the window.

I craned my neck looking for Colton, but he was nowhere in sight. I assumed he was at the back counter filling prescriptions for other idiots who couldn't read their prescription numbers.

"Hi," I said to the clerk who was decked out in a white jacket and a grumpy expression from dealing with the last customer. "I'd like to see Colton Matos, please."

"Mr. Matos isn't here."

"I thought he was working today."

"Yes. But he's not here. Say, are y'all friends of his?" she asked, suddenly interested, her tone softening. She leaned across the counter and confided to me, "Colton should've been here hours ago. We've being calling him all afternoon. No answer. The manager's big time worried about him. He didn't call or anything. So not like Colton."

"Definitely so not like him," I agreed. "The three of us are Colton's friends," I said, pointing to Brit and Kristen, grossly exaggerating our relationship to the tardy pharmacist.

"Maria, these girls," she said to another woman behind the counter, "are friends of Colton. They're looking for him too."

An efficient-looking woman wearing a white jacket and troubled expression trotted right over. "I'm the pharmacy manager. Do you know where Colton is?" I explained I didn't. Just so she'd know, I told her I'd already checked at his condo. She nodded. Since she couldn't help me, I left her standing at the window with an anxious look.

"So what do you think happened to Colton?" I asked Brit and Kristen as we walked to the car. "I saw him go in Ethan's apartment building about eleven. I'm sure he was there to tell Ethan what I told him. If we think Ethan killed Vikki, wouldn't he kill Colton because he knows too much?"

"His own brother?" Kristen asked in disbelief.

She adored her sisters so much that harming a sibling didn't exist in her world. "Hold on a minute," Kristen said, stopping us in our tracks. "We can't look for Colton unless we know what kind of car he drives. I'm going back and ask those pharmacy people. I bet that girl knows. Y'all get the car. I'll be right back."

By the time I got my car and dodged my way through the parking lot traffic, Kristen was standing in front of the store twisting her head back and forth looking for us. "Got it," she said. "Colton drives a 2014 silver BMW. The Matos boys like their BMWs. Y'all should've seen me. That old woman was back at the window paying for her meds and I weaseled in beside her at the counter instead of waiting behind her. She opened her mouth to object but I gave her my back-off stare." That stare was enough to scare a pack of wolves.

Brit asked me, "Where do we start looking for a 2014 BMW?"

"At his condo. If he's not there and his car is, then we'll know he's riding with someone else, probably Ethan." I drove through Colton's condo parking lot, up and down the street in front and along the nearby side streets. His car was nowhere in the area.

I parked and the three of us trotted to his door. No answer. I walked around the building to his sliding doors and peered inside. I could see the living, dining and kitchen areas. To make my snooping round complete, I found his bedroom window and looked through it. His bed was empty. The entire condo was empty, as neat and tidy as it had been this morning.

Next stop, Ethan's building. The back lot was

empty so I drove into the side lot. No BMWs of any color. Justin's pick-up was gone too. "I wish I knew where Eric lives. I could swing by there too," I said.

"No problem," Kristen said, surprising Brit and me. "Don't y'all know anything? That kind of information is on the business documents they had to file with the state. I ran by home after work and printed them. I figured we'd need them. Aren't I clever?" I could do without the self-congratulations, but it was clever of her and I told her so. The print-out of the document was in her backpack on the back seat floor, and after some digging, Kristen produced the street and number.

Eric's address was a relatively new townhouse. They were popular rentals with young professionals, the few we had in Sugar Liquor. Most kids who went off to college never came back except for family visits. Mike was the rare exception. Each home in Eric's complex had two designated parking spaces in front of the unit. Eric's slots were empty.

Whether it was coincidence or by plan, neither Ethan, nor Eric, nor Colton was home. "I only know one other place connected with them," I said to Brit and Kristen.

"EE Imports. Shall we give it a try?" Kristen asked.

"Suits me," Brit answered, "but I have to report in." Kristen and I needed to do the same. We called our moms, saying we were hanging out for a while. No way, did we mention we were looking for a missing pharmacist whose brother was a major player in an illegal gambling operation and likely connected to Vikki's murder. No point in activating their parental freak-out radar.

Chapter Eighteen

Thirty minutes later, I buzzed along I-40, closing in on EE Imports. Kristen scanned the exit signs watching for Wrigley Road. "This is probably a big waste of time," she said, undermining my expectations.

I defended my plan. "Colton knows about everything, and he knows Ethan's part of an illegal gambling ring. By now, he's probably warned Ethan."

"Man, if I were Ethan, I'd be destroying evidence and *getting out of Dodge City* before the sheriff shows up," Brit said.

Half-listening to Brit, a broader theory was taking form in my brain. For the first time since Vikki's murder, the pieces of information I'd collected were jelling into a rational scenario. "Colton was close to Vikki and Ethan and knew both well," I said to Brit and Kristen. "He, of all people, would've been aware if anything was going on between them. He says there's no link. That they don't like each other."

"Rewind there, Amy. The guns and money link them," Brit said.

"Not so fast," I said. "They link Vikki and Justin's apartment to Ethan's apartment. What if Justin, not Vikki, was mixed up with Ethan? Remember Mr. Clyde said Ethan was friendlier to Justin than anybody else in the building? That they talked when Justin went outside to smoke? I sort of passed it off that Justin and Ethan met in the yard by chance, but what if they planned it that way? What if they met outside so they could talk without being overheard?"

"Hold it," Brit said. "Justin's big hands couldn't have hidden the money and gun in Vikki's closet. It took someone small like Vikki to do it."

She had a point. "Yeah," I said, "Whether it was by intent or bad luck, Vikki plopped herself in the middle of something that got her killed. For now, we've got to find Colton. I saw Justin's truck in the parking lot when Colton arrived at Ethan's apartment. I assumed Justin was at his apartment packing but what if?"

"What if what?" Brit asked, frowning.

"What if Colton told Ethan about us finding money and guns in both apartments and then Ethan told Justin? If Ethan and Justin were in something together, they knew their secret was out," I said. "Colton could be in serious trouble because he knows too much."

"You're getting way off track," Kristen said.

I didn't think so. Ethan and Justin teaming up made more sense than Ethan and Vikki being in cahoots. From what I knew about Vikki, she wasn't made of long-term, trustworthy relationship fiber.

Justin, on the other hand, was hang-dog steadfast and loyal. If he partnered up with somebody, even Ethan, he'd stay committed.

"I'm worried about Colton. It's been six or seven hours since he failed to show up for work. According to the pharmacy girl, that's totally out of character for him," I said. "His disappearance must be related to this mess."

"As far as we know," Kristen said to me, "nobody's seen Colton since you saw him going into Ethan's building."

"Right. It's Justin's building too and he was home when Colton arrived."

"If Colton isn't at EE Imports, I don't know anyplace else to look for him. Did you turn up anything in your computer search, Kristen?"

"Afraid not. The documents only list basic info about the import business owners. I already told you all that stuff."

"Have we heard mention of any locales associated with the gambling business or how it operated?" Brit asked.

"No." It was a secretive, reckless business as far as I knew.

"If Colton's not at the warehouse, we'll have to contact Uncle Mike," Brit said.

"Oh, yeah, that'd be a smart move. We'll end up in jail." Kristen had a good point.

Even worse than the possibility of going to jail, I felt responsible for Colton's disappearance. I'd set everything in motion against him by barging into his condo blabbing about a Vikki-Ethan-Justin conspiracy.

The reality of facing Mike and going to jail quieted Brit and Kristen, giving me a chance to run my new theory through my head again.

Mentally shifting names, I repositioned the main characters in my guilty-innocent columns. Early on, Ethan rated a penciled-in slot as a bad guy and now made a permanent leap to the guilty column. Eric was tight with Ethan so he joined him in the guilty column. Justin, who'd been in the innocent column, downgraded to the maybe column.

"Slow down. Wrigley Road's the next exit," Brit said. My sweaty palms clenched the steering wheel and prompted me to crank the air conditioning to its coolest setting and the fan to its highest. As soon as I pulled onto the exit ramp, Brit said, "I see the EE Imports sign on a building. How do we get over there?"

Wrigley Road turned out to be a one-way access road taking us the opposite direction from where we needed to go. By making a sharp U-turn, I fixed the problem by heading the wrong way on the one-way. "You're going to get us killed." Kristen's shrill voice caused me to slam on the brakes, locking our seat belts.

"What if you get a ticket? Uncle Mike will find out." Brit said.

"Would y'all hush? How can we crash, Kristen? The road is flat. The land on either side of the road is flat. I can't even run into a ditch. And there are no cars in sight to crash into us or for me to crash into, and there's no police car and no cop to write a ticket." I shut them up until their next outburst.

The sun was beginning to set, but I could see well enough to drive with the headlights off. It gave Kristen something new to worry about. Ahead of me, Ethan's warehouse, topped by its prominent sign, stood among a row of stark buildings in an old farm field. Plain and ugly with no landscaping or customer appeal, the buildings were intended solely for storage and shipping. Easy-on, easy-off the interstate for truckers, if they knew what they were doing.

A solitary vehicle, a silver BMW matching the pharmacy girl's description of Colton's car, occupied the parking lot. Was it a good or bad sign that his car was here? I could make a worst-case argument for either its presence or absence.

Brit and Kristen eyeballed the scene before they slipped out of the car. Grabbing Mom's emergency flashlight from the passenger seat's storage drawer, I joined my waiting friends. Their worried glances toward Colton's car did nothing to allay my apprehension.

As soon as I closed the car door, heat and mugginess enveloped me. The high temperature of the day was hanging on with no cooling evening breezes to whisk it away.

I glanced down the row of garage-type loading dock doors at Ethan's building. In the middle was a single door leading into the warehouse. With wary faces and hesitant footsteps, my trio tiptoed toward it. Other than a hum of traffic on the distant interstate, I detected no sounds of life.

Offering no clues what lay beyond, I half-expected the door to fling open revealing the individuals on my suspect list lined up with guns aimed at our heads. I nodded to Kristen to try the doorknob. Unlocked and without a squeak, the door opened.

As I stepped inside the dark cavernous space, a blast of stagnant, hot air more sweltering than outside, smacked me in the face. A fresh round of sweat dripped off my forehead. Brit and Kristen gasped.

This place needed some serious air conditioning or, at least, some mega-fans to get the air moving. I didn't think it was possible but the inside of the building was hotter than my hated grocery store parking lot.

A rosy glow, cast by a brilliant coral sunset entering the warehouse through the open doorway, provided enough light for us to get the gist of the place. Like the outside, the interior was utilitarian with no windows. Row after row of stacks of large, plain cardboard boxes awaited loading onto trucks.

I could hear my own raspy breathing as well as my friends' breaths. I couldn't remember ever being in a space devoid of sound, as if all life had been sucked out of it. As I waited, watched and listened, I became more inclined to believe the absence of vehicles other than Colton's, and the absolute lack of noise or movement meant no one was on the premises. Unless, they lay in wait to ambush us.

The worst of my worst-case scenarios was that Ethan or Justin had taken Colton away with them. The warehouse's location provided handy access to the interstate and was less than a half-mile from one of many entrances to Pisgah National Forest. In those thousands of acres, someone could hide out until doomsday. If I wanted to disappear or dispose of someone--like say--Colton, that's where I'd go. Common sense told me to make a run for Mom's car and flee but I couldn't. I intended to follow this case to its conclusion. However, my decision shouldn't cause harm to Brit and Kristen. I said to them in a whisper, "Y'all can wait outside."

"No way," Kristen mouthed to me.

"Forget it." Brit gave me an offended look.

"Thanks, y'all," I said. "I have to try to find Colton. I feel guilty."

We inched our way through the building, eyes and ears alert. The sun, slipping lower behind the Great Smoky Mountains, dimmed the interior. I opened my mouth to warn my friends to be quiet and careful. Before I got a word out, Brit, clumsy as ever, tripped and fell into a stack of boxes. Like dominos, they set off a chain reaction, causing a couple nearby stacks to plummet.

If anyone was in this hot, miserable place, that commotion would bring them running, guns in hand, ready to blow us away. Kristen stopped in mid-step. Brit lay sprawled among boxes with more boxes on top of her. She didn't move a muscle except for blinking back tears. Was she hurt or scared?

Standing in place with clenched eyes, I willed all my senses to thrust their energy into hearing, giving me an edge if anyone was sneaking toward us. An extra minute's warning might give me time to come up with a plan, although my frightened mind was drained.

After waiting for what dragged like hours, no one came to investigate the ruckus. I gave it a couple more minutes and decided we were safe. For the time being.

Kristen and I trudged through a pile of boxes to free Brit from her cardboard dungeon. Before we reached her, a couple of bumps came from the front of the warehouse. Kristen jumped. Pie-eyed, Brit still lay where she'd landed. I jerked my head toward the direction of the commotion and waited, with pounding heart, for a gunman or a horde of gunmen to surround us.

No gunmen or anyone else showed up. I tiptoed toward the front door. A stack of boxes, rendered unstable from Brit's fall, fell in a delayed collapse.

With weak knees and shaky hands, Kristen lifted a box off Brit and stumbled backwards. "What the hell?" Kristen said. "This threw me off balance. I was prepared to pick up a hefty box. This feels like feathers. What kind of household stuff is this?"

"Yeah, the boxes are so light, they didn't hurt when they hit me," Brit said, crawling out, wiping her tears, injury-free.

I picked up a box and shook it. Nothing moved around inside. Kristen shook a couple boxes and agreed.

"Did you notice the boxes didn't thud when they hit the cement floor? They bounced like a box full of cotton balls," Brit said.

Fishing in her backpack to retrieve her nail clippers, Kristen used the file to slit the packing tape. In the dark, the box looked empty. I stuck the flashlight inside and, as I'd guessed, nothing. Kristen and I grabbed other boxes and opened them. "What's going on? What kind of fool ships boxes with nothing in them?" she asked.

"If you ask me, this whole household import deal is phony. Just a front so EE Imports looks legitimate. I bet none of these boxes contain anything," Brit declared, waving her arms at the remaining columns of boxes.

This bizarre case made me long for that bunch of juvenile brats I caught. That was easy compared to being in a dark, silent warehouse full of empty boxes looking for a missing pharmacist.

I cut a winding path through the building's spacious square footage, each wary step bringing me to a new stack of boxes, and the possibility whoever was mixed up in this phony import business lurked in secret to pounce on us. With Brit and Kristen following in tight formation, we threaded our way around cardboard towers, reluctant to check for enemies but forcing ourselves forward. We couldn't leave without making a clean sweep of the warehouse. I was so scared, I could hardly breathe.

In spite of my circuitous route and determination not to overlook anything or anybody, we approached the back wall, marking the end of the building and our search. Desperation to finish and get out of this place pushed me to hurry. Rounding the last stack of boxes and seconds from completing our task, I came to an abrupt halt.

Hidden by the fake trappings of fake business activity was a metal door in the back wall. Where did it lead? Outside, I hoped. I didn't want to see any more of this building. My shaky fingers turned the knob. The door didn't budge.

Focusing the flashlight on the door knob, a key in the lock convinced me this was an exterior door. Giving the key a twist, the lock clicked. The sharp sound ricocheted off metal walls, making more noise than the boxes toppling to the floor. My legs wanted to run to my car and not look back.

I pushed the door open expecting farm fields.

A blast hotter than hell engulfed us.

Instead of being outside, we faced a small, windowless room.

"Amy, get me out of here. I can't take this," Kristen said, clutching my arm.

"Don't freak out. I'll do something," I said,

trying to sound calm as her breathing got faster. This wasn't the first time she'd panicked in a tight place but never to this extreme. The combination of fear, heat, darkness and being closed in proved to be the tipping point for our claustrophobic. If Kristen went off the deep end, I feared we couldn't complete our mission. "Take deep breaths, Kristen. That's right. Good girl." My consoling voice sounded like me talking to Hildy when she was trying to hack up a hairball.

"Look, Kristen." I aimed the feeble flashlight beam in front of her, hoping a look at her surroundings would stave off a meltdown.

We stood in the doorway looking at what might have been intended as an office but contained only odds and ends of junk now. No desks or file cabinets. Sweeping the flashlight beam across the wall, I halted on an object in the far corner.

Brit screamed, her hands clasping her cheeks. Kristen covered her eyes to block the sight.

A man, tied to a chair, slumped forward, his chin resting on his chest. I couldn't see his face but I recognized his clothes. He'd been wearing the same clothes earlier in the day.

"Colton?" I whispered, approaching him. "Are you okay?" Of course, he wasn't okay. He looked dead.

"It's me, Amy. And Brit and Kristen. We've been looking everywhere for you. Can you hear me?" I asked. My voice sounded high-pitched and tinny.

He moaned faintly. At least, he wasn't dead. Yet. He looked closer to dead than alive.

Facing a bigger crisis pushed Kristen's claustrophobia into the background. She scuttled to where I stood and leaned close to Colton, screwing up her face. "His lips are parched. He needs water badly. See if you can find the freaking light switch, Brit, so I can see." We no longer whispered. If anybody else was in the building, our presence had ceased to be a secret.

Brit felt her way around the walls and clicked a switch. An overhead bare bulb provided needed light.

Kristen retrieved a full bottle of water from her backpack. Holding it close to Colton's lips, she tilted it slightly so that it dripped into his mouth. I watched his throat hoping to see him swallow. He didn't. With a steady hand, Kristen controlled the droplets so he didn't choke. Brit's anguished face looked like she expected him to die. I was inclined to agree with her, but I couldn't stand here waiting for him to pass.

"Colton," I said, forcing my voice to sound confident, "we're going to get you out of here." He was running out of time.

Although Colton showed no awareness, I spoke to him as if he could hear me. "Brit and I are going to untie your ropes." Hard tied knots were no match for two sets of experienced, freshly manicured fingernails clawing at them. A lifetime of untangling dainty sterling chains was getting ready to pay off. As Brit and I loosened the ropes binding his wrists, Colton began to wobble. "Don't worry. Brit and I won't let you fall," I said. Kristen held onto his chin and kept his head upright with one hand while she trickled beads of water into his mouth.

Brit and I wedged ourselves against Colton's sides, pressing our bodies against him to keep him from toppling while we worked on the ropes. "Just a few more seconds and you'll be free," Kristen murmured to Colton as she rubbed water on his face and through his hair to cool him. This tender side of her didn't surface often.

When Brit and I got the ropes loose, I said, "Let's stand him up and try to walk." Struggling under his weight, we'd barely gone a few inches when he drooped forward, almost falling. We staggered, trying to regain our grip on him. Kristen let go of his head and grabbed him around the waist. We clumsily maneuvered him back to his chair and dropped him in it. "That didn't work," I said. "The three of us barely missed landing in a heap on the floor and taking Colton with us. It's going to take all three of us to get him up." Brit and I kept Colton balanced on the chair while Kristen dripped more water into his mouth. He must be parched from the overbearing heat trapped in this small space.

Panting, we took a minute to catch our breath.

Colton was tall, well-built and dead weight. Or maybe just dead, since he hadn't shown much sign of life since we found him. Re-evaluating our seemingly impossible task of moving him, I said, "We're going to have to get smarter to get him out of here."

"Did you see any kind of a cart or wagon we could use?" Kristen asked.

"I didn't see anything," Brit said. "Not a single apparatus to move so-called heavy merchandise."

"This warehouse set-up is so lame," I said. "What a lousy, amateur job. I could've come up with something more real looking than this."

We had to make another attempt to get Colton out of this building before Ethan or Justin or Eric or their criminal buddies returned to finish him off. In his condition, it wouldn't take much. If we kept jostling and dropping him, we'd end up killing him ourselves.

And if we didn't get out of that agonizingly inferno of an office, we'd all be goners. An air conditioner poking through the wall caught my eye until I noted its derelict condition. Its number one problem was lack of a cord and plug. They lay on the floor, snipped to pieces.

"We've rested long enough. New plan. Kristen and I are tall so we'll hold Colton up and walk him out of here. Brit, you clear a path through the fallen boxes and hold the flashlight."

Kristen and I got on each side of Colton. "Use that *lift with your legs* thing we learned in health class." My helpful reminder triggered a new eye squinting session. "Let's lift," I said, ignoring her. "Easy does it." We had him standing and propped between us.

Brit hopped up onto Colton's chair and draped his arms around our shoulders. "If y'all can hold onto his hands, it should help keep him upright."

"Good idea, Brit. Okay, Kristen, put your arm around his waist. Or, would it feel more secure if you held onto his belt?"

She tried both. "Belt," she said, gripping it tightly.

"Grab onto his arm like Brit said." I did the same. His body hung lifelessly between us. It was all we could do to keep him and ourselves from collapsing onto the floor. Whether we could move forward was a separate issue.

"Small steps," I said. We looked like ventriloquists who'd lost control of our dummy's movements as well as our own. As Kristen and I wobbled our first step, we dragged Colton with us.

"Stop," I said. I needed a moment to steady myself. Brit crouched, stuck the flashlight under her armpit and pulled Colton's feet forward so they were straight under his body. Baby steps, rest, more baby steps, more rest, we made it to the office door. A small milestone and some blessed relief from that oven of an office.

Leaning against the door frame, Kristen and I took a breather. Sweat, mixing with sun block, ran down my forehead and burned my eyes. The more I wiped, the worse they stung. Everything associated with moving Colton was grueling. While Brit cleared boxes for us, she spotted a light switch. The three of us stared expectantly at long fluorescent lights on the ceiling when she clicked the switch. Nothing. What was wrong? Wrong switch for those lights? Bulbs burned out? Crap.

Resigned to working in the dark, Brit held the flashlight beam and we trudged on. Brit pulled Colton's feet forward again.

It was slow, torturous going but I saw a possibility that our rhythmic motions might work if time and our strength held out. My shoulders ached from the weight of Colton's arm and body hanging on them. Kristen's delicate features twisted in pain. Brit flashed the light toward the front door, sighing that it wasn't getting any closer. Our progress was measured in inches, not feet or yards.

Thank goodness for my mother's flashlight. As darkness descended, without the flashlight, we wouldn't be able to see. Now and then, I thought I felt Colton trying to put weight on his legs but it was too brief to tell. More likely Brit got his legs propped straight under his body and they held him for a few seconds. Colton moaned and I pressed my ear close to his mouth hoping for a recognizable word.

Moments later, his legs twitched and jerked, making it even harder for Kristen and me to hold him up. It was like trying to hold onto a giant, sweaty eel. If we dropped him, we'd never be able to get him off the floor.

"What's wrong with him?" Kristen yelled at me.

"What he's been through, it could be anything." I said. "Brit, come help us."

"It must be something caused by the heat or being tied up," I said. "Heat seizure? Cramps? Dehydration? Poor circulation?"

They all sounded possible considering his situation.

"What should we do?" Brit asked.

None of us had first-aid training other than what we got in Health class at school, and it didn't cover anything like this. We only knew what to do in clear-cut cases like getting a piece of steak caught in our throats in a trendy restaurant. On top of not knowing what to do, Kristen and I couldn't do anything because it took all our strength to hold him up.

"Let's put him down on his side," Kristen said. With care, we started to lower him but his sweat soaked body slithered out of our grasp, dragging us down with him. While Kristen and I disentangled ourselves from Colton and each other, Brit kneeled at Colton's feet, laid the flashlight on the floor, pushed his pants' legs up to his knees and massaged his legs. Colton moaned. Brit kept at it.

"I got to get something," I said, rummaging through my back pack and pulling out a bottle of Midol pills.

"For God's sake, Amy. This is not the time to

worry about a few cramps." Brit words came out downright mean. In our twelve-year friendship, she'd never spoken so hatefully to me.

"Seriously, Amy," Kristen said, agreeing with Brit, "suck it up."

"They're not for me. I'm going to give them to Colton."

"Whatever's wrong with him, it's not cramps, you fool." Brit was still fired up.

"I think I know that, Brit. They're basically pain relievers with some other stuff in them. Maybe, they'll relax his legs. Help me get some down his throat. Without choking him," I said.

"And how do we do that?" Brit asked.

"Oh, I know," Kristen said. "My great aunt has a problem swallowing. I've watched how she takes medicine. She takes a big drink, coats her pills with applesauce to make them slippery, puts them in her mouth, takes another big drink and down they go. We need something greasy to lubricate the pills. Ideas?"

Giving Kristen a smug smile, Brit produced a tube of lip gloss. Kristen smiled her approval. "Okay, Brit, help me sit him up." Dripping with sweat, they pushed him upright. "Brit, prop your body against his back so he doesn't fall over. I'll stay on this side and steady him. Amy, get on his other side."

"Okay, everybody set?" Kristen asked, handing me a bottle of water. "Amy, hold his head up and dribble water slowly into his mouth. Easy does it. He's parched so use your fingers to wet the inside of his mouth. Keep doing it." My fingers were dirty but, under the circumstances, it didn't matter.

I couldn't see or hear Colton swallowing but the water didn't back up. I took that as a good sign.

Encouraged, I continued giving him drinks, keeping his mouth wet.

"Brit, see if you can hold him by yourself." Little but strong, Brit forced her back tighter against Colton's back and dug her heels into the floor.

Kristen got an extra bottle of water from her backpack, poured water into her hands and rubbed it on his face, through his hair, gently moistening his neck, back and arms.

"Okay, his mouth is plenty wet. Let's do the Midol before he dries up," I said.

Brit smeared lip gloss all over the pill and passed it to me. It slipped through my hands, landing on Colton's pants' zipper. With no time to waste, I went after it. Kristen's eyes and mouth widened while I groped our patient's crotch. It wasn't a time for humor, but I wanted to laugh at what Colton would've thought if he'd awakened.

Scooping up the slippery little pill and, holding it between my pinched fingers, I put it on his tongue. "Push it as far back as you can," Kristen instructed. I gave the pill a flick with my index finger and it disappeared from view. "Okay, give him water," Kristen said briskly, sounding like a surgeon getting ready to suture. Again, I dripped water into Colton's mouth. "I saw his throat move a little bit," Kristen said. "Let's hope he swallowed the pill."

Brit greased another Midol and we repeated the process. He didn't gag or choke and the water and pills stayed down. As hot as the warehouse was, it was nothing like that horrible office. We took turns giving Colton water and cooling his face. In time, his leg twitching slowed. Was it the massage, water or Midol that did it? Or the combination? Or did it quit by itself?

When his body settled enough that Kristen and I could hold him, we hoisted him upright and, with Brit lighting the way, resumed our slow progress toward the door. One step at a time, we pulled and dragged Colton toward the front door. It loomed closer with each back-breaking step. If only Kristen and I could hold out long enough to reach it. Every muscle in my body throbbed or cramped.

Brit said, "When we get close to the door, give me the keys and I'll go get the car. Y'all drop him in the back seat and I'll sit with him." I nodded in agreement, telling her in one-word spurts that the keys were in my shorts' pocket.

"The Asheville hospital's our best bet," Brit said. "It's the closest to here and I know how to get there." In a few minutes, we'd be on our way to the emergency room with Colton. Hang in there, fellow, I told him silently. Only a few more steps ...

Chapter Nineteen

"Hold it right there," a man yelled. In spite of the heat, shivers rushed through my body. I swiveled my head, trying to follow his echo bouncing around the warehouse, until a blinding flashlight beam coming from the doorway told me where he was. His voice already told me who he was.

"Justin! Colton's dying. We've got to get him to the hospital fast."

"No way, Amy," Justin said. He flipped a switch just inside the door, and light flooded the front half of the building. The back lights remained off.

"I'm here to finish him off," Justin said, nodding at Colton, "before I high tail it. Good thing I came back. Looks like the goody-two-shoes butted in and tried to save him."

"If you won't help, get out of our way. We're taking him to the hospital. You're in enough trouble without adding his murder to your problems," I said.

"You got that wrong, Amy. In a few minutes, I'm outta here. Y'all are the ones in trouble." I monitored Colton's condition, pleading with Justin to help us. "Do you have a hearing problem, Amy? He's not going anywhere. Drop him on the floor. Now."

My muscles were exhausted. I couldn't hold him any longer anyway. Kristen and I tried to lower him gently to the floor but he slid through our hands again. "Good," Justin said, giving the unmoving heap on the floor a disgusting glance. "Looks like the bastard's gone. Guess y'all aren't very good at life-saving."

"Justin, why did you leave Colton in that horrible room to bake? If you planned to kill him, why didn't you do it and skip the torture?" I asked.

"For your information, I planned to do just that but some trucks pulled in to load. The drivers and guys doing the loading would've heard the shots. I cleared out until they left and stopped back to finish him before I get out of here for good. I thought the heat might save me the trouble."

"That's horrible. You knew he'd die an excruciating death." My faith in humanity plummeted multiple notches.

Brit yelled at him. "Justin, are you crazy? We've been trying to help you. We were on your side."

"Yeah, I know, Brit. I had me some regular little *Charlie's Angels*. Y'all almost had me convinced I was innocent."

"But you *aren't* innocent, Justin," I said, resigning myself to the truth. "You killed Vikki. And I know why."

"Well, if you're thinking I was jealous of her dumbass boyfriend laying there on the floor, you're way off base."

"You didn't kill her because of her fling with

Colton, and you didn't try to kill Colton because you were outraged he was fooling around with Vikki. You killed her because she stole money from Ethan that came from your gambling operation. Either Vikki or Ethan told you what she'd done. When she wouldn't tell you where she hid the goods, you killed her."

"Not bad, Amy. But as the politicians say, you didn't connect all your dots."

"Meaning what?" I asked.

"You're right about Vikki but Ethan didn't tell me. I don't think he even missed the cash. Careless dumbass."

"How did Vikki find out you and Ethan were involved in the gambling ring?"

"After she found the money in Ethan's apartment and helped herself to a generous share, she knew he was up to something shady. At the same time, I started bringing in more money from the gambling operation. I told Vikki it was overtime pay from my construction job but she didn't buy it.

"While I was away at work, she started nosing through my things and kept digging until she found a duffel bag full of money, packaged identically to what she stole from Ethan. The boss gives it to me every month to pay our guys.

"When I came home two weeks ago, Vikki told me what she'd done and hit me up for more money. It blew my mind. I told her she had to give it all back, that I'd be killed if any cash was missing. I'd given Ethan his share to make the north Georgia payments, and I was responsible for that too.

"Vikki wouldn't budge. Greedy little bitch tried to cut a deal with me. When I wouldn't play ball, she threatened to go to the police and take the bundles of cash she stole from Ethan and me as evidence. She was mean enough to do it too." I believed that. "When I got home Monday night, I begged her to give everything back, but she laughed at me saying she didn't care if the boss did kill me.

"I went crazy and strangled her. If I was going to get my hands on that money, I'd have to find it by myself."

"Did you find it?" I asked. Did he have any idea I had some of it?

"Hell, no. I tore that apartment to shreds. I don't know what she did with it. I'm taking what I've got left and getting out of here."

Thank God, he didn't suspect I had the missing cash. He'd squash me like a bug.

Foolish Vikki. By refusing to return his loot and threatening to go to the police, she'd trapped Justin. He either had to face his mob boss and admit he'd lost tens of thousands of dollars or face the police and years in prison.

Brit and Kristen stood beside me, still and speechless, taking in Justin's angry confession. The meek teenage boy Vikki kicked around had finally kicked back. After years of taking her crap, he stood up to her. She never thought he'd do it.

Considering Justin admitted to us he killed Vikki, left Colton in a stifling room to die and came back to make sure or finish the job, the three of us were in big trouble when Justin high-tailed it. The only reason he was talking so freely was because he didn't intend to leave us alive to tell any stories.

"Justin, you low-life," Kristen yelled. "You killed Vikki? She was your wife, for God's sakes."

"Spare me your sermon, Kristen. Vikki played at being my wife for a couple months before she started cheating. She wanted to leave me for Colton. I didn't care if she left. But not until I got my money back. Me, Ethan, Eric and a couple guys from my job had a good thing going. I wouldn't let Vikki ruin it. I won't let y'all ruin it either."

Justin pulled out a gun and pointed it at me. His face, twisted by anger and greed, said he had nothing to lose. "So long, girls," he said, glancing at his watch. "I got to hit the road. Ethan didn't show up to make his pay-off to the Georgia boys this morning. The stinking rat and Eric took their cash and bailed.

"Nobody knows about this place but Ethan and Eric so if I was you, I wouldn't put any hopes on anybody showing up to save you. *When* somebody finds you, it'll be too late."

"Hold on, Justin, you can't do this," I protested.

"I can and I am. I'm not leaving the three of you to blab everything you know to Mike. Give me some credit for brains. I can save myself or the three of you. I choose me.

"Now turn around and walk slowly toward the back office. No funny moves." He glanced at Colton. "I reckon he's done for. Leave him there." Colton hadn't moved or moaned since we dropped him.

Brit and Kristen looked at me with question marks in their eyes. What could I do to save ourselves? If we didn't make some kind of move, Justin would shoot us or lock us in that sweltering office.

We had nothing to use as weapons. Nothing but stupid empty boxes. A lousy piece of cardboard against a gun?

An idea, although a lame, long shot, came to me. I flashed eye signals to Brit and Kristen, getting wide, puzzled eyes in return. At least, I had their attention. If I made a move, they'd follow suit. Standing in a raggedy circle, I switched my gaze back and forth from one to the other to keep their attention on me. They tensed their bodies, ready to make a desperate move.

"Y'all walk slowly toward the office," Justin ordered.

I took three steps and hurled my body into a stack of boxes. From the barrage of thumping noises, I knew Kristin and Brit did the same. Boxes tumbled and rolled like a brown avalanche. Thrown off guard, Justin looked up. The boxes pummeled him and he reeled backwards, landing on the floor.

Scrambling to our feet, Kristen and I pounced, throwing ourselves on top of Justin and pinning him down. Brit went after the gun. Justin swore and kicked but he couldn't shake us. Our surprise attack gave us the edge we needed.

Still wrestling Justin for his gun, Brit yelled to us, "Help!" Kristen grabbed two large handfuls of his hair and yanked repeatedly. Her thinking face morphed into a warrior face. I chomped down on Justin's gun arm with all my jaw strength. He screamed from the double whammy.

When pain forced him to relax his grip on the gun, Brit snatched it away from him. Gun in hand, she sprung to her feet like an acrobat. With the gun aimed squarely at Justin's head, Brit ruled. Justin, as well as everybody in Sugar Liquor, knew about Brit's family's obsession with guns. He also knew she wouldn't hesitate to pull the trigger and her aim wouldn't miss its target.

Justin collapsed into the pile of boxes, his scheme to make easy money thwarted. He'd killed

Vikki and Colton and would face murder charges for them, plus whatever crimes he'd committed in the illegal gambling business.

The only winners in this mess were Ethan and Eric who'd split with a hefty sum of mob money. Of course, they'd be looking over their shoulders for the rest of their lives to see if their criminal colleagues were gaining on them.

Kristen and I crawled away from Justin, draping our exhausted bodies over a pile of boxes. My legs and back wouldn't allow me to stand. My heart was pounding and I couldn't take in enough air to satisfy my lungs. Worse than my physical agony was the sad loss of Colton. We were so close to getting him to the hospital. I wanted to rip Justin apart for what he'd done to Vikki and Colton. Two young lives wasted.

Brit guarded Justin, resolute and unflinching. She was in her natural element. She was on the right side of the law, and she had a gun in her hand. Her world was in perfect synch.

"Just for the record, Justin, how did you think you could get away with killing Vikki?" Brit's authoritative voice left no doubt her question required an answer.

Justin responded, breathless, bitter and hateful. "I was counting on y'all to pin Vikki's murder on Lover Boy. Let good old Colton take the rap. He was at the apartment with Vikki nearly every night, and I figured nosy Barbara would put Mike on Colton's trail. Mike would find Colton's fingerprints all over the apartment, including his Heineken cans and it was bye-bye Colton.

"All I had to do was play the grieving husband and wait for Colton to go down, except Mike didn't listen to Barbara, and his guys didn't pay attention to the beer cans. I still had y'all on my side. I sure didn't plan on y'all actually stumbling on the truth though."

"You wanted us to find the truth. And, just so you understand, I didn't *stumble* on the truth. I *found* it."

"Well, you found the wrong truth, Amy," he said.

Justin had fooled me. I'd believed he was still Vikki's kicked-around high school boyfriend. How well he'd hidden his transformation from pathetic victim to ruthless murderer. When and how did he conjure up the hatefulness to kill two people?

If nothing else, I'd come out of this experience suspicious of everyone. I was on the path to being as cynical and distrustful as Mike.

Chapter Twenty

Brit held the gun on Justin and standing beside her, Kristen stood guard, the contempt on her face daring Justin to move. I wasted no time pulling my cell from my shorts pocket and dialing *911* to order a posse of law enforcement officers in short order.

In spite of the dispatchers testy attitude, I kept my cool, gave the address and told my story in sequential order. "I need police and an ambulance on the double."

Madam Dispatcher had a problem grasping that I and my two seventeen-year-old-friends were in an abandoned warehouse holding a gun on Justin Wilson of Sugar Liquor, who'd admitted he killed his wife, had likely killed a pharmacist and was an operative in an illegal gambling ring. What part of that was so hard to believe?

"Put the gun down immediately," she said.

Put the gun down? Right. That'd be a smart move. "When Justin leaves, he'll grab the gun and while he's going out the door, turn around and shoot us. We're not giving up the gun," I said, beginning to lose patience.

"Considering Justin's already killed one person and probably two, we decline to be Numbers Three, Four and Five. When an officer comes through this warehouse door and slaps handcuffs on Justin, we'll relinquish the gun, not a minute before that."

Although Brit kept the gun aimed steadily at Justin, his eyes darted wildly like a trapped animal looking for an escape route, searching for anything he could use as a weapon to attack us and retrieve his gun.

The dispatcher said, "A county deputy is on his way to Wrigley Road." I wanted to scream at her to tell him to turn on the siren and put the pedal to the metal, but it wouldn't get him to us any faster.

Once I was off the phone, Kristen nodded for me to stand with Brit guarding Justin, and she went to check on Colton. She gave him drinks and doused his face and hair but shook her head.

Justin's face was flushed and beaded with sweat, his eyes glaring and desperate. Given half a chance, I believed he'd slit our throats. It nagged at me that we hadn't searched him for other weapons. "It's too risky to get close to him," Brit said, her decision final.

As long as Brit had the gun, she could shoot him before he pulled a knife or anything else out of his pockets. She kept her eyes glued to him, barely taking blink breaks. Justin heard me make the 911 call. His time was running out. I expected him to lunge at us or make a break for the door.

"Dude, don't let him get away," I said.

"I'm not planning on it," Brit replied, calm and in control.

Not sounding like a deputy or ambulance driver, a voice boomed through the warehouse. "This is the FBI. Drop your weapons." FBI? What the hell? It had been less than five minutes since the dispatcher said the deputy was on his way. No way could she have gotten the FBI here too.

For a moment Justin looked like he was going to have a stroke but a glimmer of recognition and relief swept across his face and he laughed. "Ha, Ha, FBI. That's a good one, Ethan. Where'd you get that FBI vest? EBay? You rat, I thought you and Eric double-crossed me and split with the money."

What was going on? Instead of a deputy showing up with open handcuffs to clamp on Justin, my enemy in the form of Ethan had shown up to rescue him. This wasn't supposed to be happening. Justin said Ethan and Eric vamoosed.

"Justin, Colton's car is parked outside. Where is he?"

"Oh, him. He took off with some friends to go to Asheville. Met them here so he could leave his car. We've got to get out of here and deliver that cash to the guys pronto. You got your share? Mine's in my truck. I bet Big Sam's got everybody looking for us. We don't want him to think we were trying to run out on him. You hear me, buddy?"

"Loud and clear. We'll talk about that in a minute," Ethan said, stepping closer, revealing he held a gun. Eric stood beside Ethan, his gun drawn too. Both wore FBI vests. I agreed with Justin they were knockoffs.

Ethan nodded to Brit. "I'll take over now, young lady. Put your gun down."

Brit didn't budge. For starters, she looked too stunned to do anything. And if she gave up the gun, we'd be at the mercy of Ethan, Eric and Justin. Kristen whispered to me, "My God, we're going to die in a shoot-out with mobsters."

Brit against Ethan and Eric? This was turning into *The Gunfight at the OK Corral,* but I couldn't remember if the good guys won. Brit was a terrific shot but could she take both Ethan and Eric before they got her? If shooting broke out, they'd hit some or all of us.

Justin started getting to his feet, jubilant that the arrival of Ethan and Eric turned the tide in his favor. Ethan shouted, "Don't move."

"You and who else is going to stop me?" Justin asked.

"Me, Eric and our back-up team. That's who." He yelled, "Come on in." I braced, expecting some hillbilly version of the mafia to come stomping in, spitting tobacco juice, shotguns blasting.

A gang of people entered the warehouse, swarming around Justin who stared at them. "These aren't our guys," he yelled at Ethan.

Brit and Kristen looked at me for answers but I didn't have any. I expected a county deputy and got the whole freaking FBI. Were they real FBI or gangsters in fake FBI clothes? I would've felt more secure with a county deputy in a standard county uniform.

In a calm voice, Ethan said to Brit, "Please hand me your gun. I know this is confusing but Eric and I and these other people are FBI agents. Months ago, we infiltrated a local gambling operation, and we're shutting it down today and arresting everyone connected with it, including Justin."

I focused on the faces of the FBI agents, recognizing some of them from the meeting behind the grocery store. FBI agents meet behind dumpsters?

Reluctantly, Brit handed the gun to Ethan. "Thanks. You're doing the right thing." Ethan asked me, "Do you know where Colton went?"

I nodded my head. "He's over there," I said, pointing to the spot where Kristen and I dropped him. "I'm afraid he's dead," I added in a soft voice. Ethan jumped over boxes, throwing others aside to get to Colton. He yelled at Eric to call for an ambulance. "One is supposed to be on its way as well as a county deputy," I said.

Ethan yelled at Eric again. "Find out where that ambulance is and tell the dispatcher the FBI needs it here. Now!"

Justin's head snapped every time anyone spoke or moved. His shirt, drenched with sweat, clung to his body. When his eyes settled on Ethan, Justin's face contorted in hatred. It was sinking in that Ethan was an FBI agent who had come to arrest him, not save him.

"Ethan, you double-crossing bastard. I got you and Eric into my business so you could make some big money and all the time, you were planning to bring me down. I hope you rot in hell." Justin's outburst got louder. Additional agents surrounded him and took him out of the warehouse.

"So Ethan really is an FBI agent?" Kristen whispered to me.

"I hope so. He's got all the guns on his side," I replied. The back-ups, directed by Eric, were spreading out all over the warehouse, moving boxes, searching, probing.

Ethan sat on the floor beside Colton. He leaned forward and talked quietly to his brother, but as far as I could tell, Colton didn't respond. Kristen, Colton's makeshift nurse, went to Ethan. She dripped water into Colton's mouth as she'd done earlier. She poured water in Ethan's hand and together they rubbed Colton's face and arms. I didn't know if their efforts helped Colton but it gave them the satisfaction of doing something while we waited for the ambulance.

Sirens wailed in the distance. Ethan wouldn't have to wait much longer. Before the sirens wound down, paramedics burst into the building, quickly surrounding Colton. Kristen backed off to give them room to work. "Is Colton responsive?" I asked. She shook her head.

The paramedics quickly hooked Colton to all kinds of tubes and wires and monitors. I took that as a good sign. Maybe he was alive. "Ready to transport," an EMS attendant said. Ethan summoned Eric to tell him he was going to the hospital with Colton.

"May we go to the hospital and see how Colton is?" As soon as I asked, I realized I had no business butting into a family situation, but I felt responsible for pulling Colton into this horrible situation.

"Uh--sure," Ethan answered. "Let's go," he said, motioning Brit and Kristen to get with it. "In fact, you three can fill me in on the missing parts of the story while we wait at the hospital." Ethan hopped in the ambulance with Colton and I followed with Brit and Kristen in Mom's car. I speeded along behind the ambulance through the Asheville traffic, skidding into the Emergency Room parking lot on the ambulance's tail.

By the time I parked, Colton had already been rushed into ER, Ethan by his side. I followed the signs to the waiting room with Brit and Kristen trotting along. As a trio, in tandem, we plopped heavily into chairs. "I've never been so physically and emotionally drained."

"Uh-oh," Kristen said, glancing at the big wall clock. "I got to call my mom." She ducked outside so as not to disturb the other waiting families. Brit and I followed. Each of us called home, keeping our explanations brief.

"Hi, Mom, I'm at the hospital with a friend who's seriously ill." She asked who it was. "Someone new in town who doesn't have many friends yet. Brit and Kristen are with me." The siren of an arriving ambulance overcame my voice and verified I really was at the hospital. I added that we might need to stay all night.

Mom trusted me and my judgment. I'd never been a problem kid and usually acted responsibly and rationally. She reminded me of the usual precautions about being out late at night. I promised to keep in touch and let her know how things went.

We got free coffee from a large automatic machine in the waiting room and packs of cookies from a vending machine. I hadn't had anything to eat since breakfast, so the caffeine and sugar hit the spot. We didn't have much to say though.

The scene at the warehouse wiped us out. Brit and Kristen sat beside me, coffee cups in hand, eyes closed but not sleeping. Like me they were probably reliving our chaotic day. Right now, sitting in a soft chair in a cool space with endless cups of steaming coffee was luxurious.

If only Colton survived ...

Chapter Twenty-One

Ethan burst through the swinging double doors from the ER, his broad smile heralding good news. A bugle corps couldn't have announced it better. "Colton's going to make it. He's regained consciousness. Kind of in and out of it, but the doc said that's expected."

"I'm so relieved. I honestly thought he was dead," I admitted to Ethan. Tears formed in his eyes. Brit and Kristen patted his shoulders. I held his hands gently.

Regaining control of his emotions, Ethan spotted my coffee cup and smiled. "Say, where'd you get that coffee? Man, I could use a cup." I escorted him to my new best friend, a coffee maker with a never-ending supply of free coffee. Brit and Kristen jockeyed to help Ethan put cream and sugar in his coffee. I offered him my remaining chocolate chip cookies. He devoured those in a few bites.

Brit said, "I'll make another vending machine run."

With hands full of munchies, I led our little group to a small alcove where we could sit comfortably and talk freely, if and when Ethan was ready. For the moment, he seemed content to slouch in a chair with his long legs stretched in front of him, a grateful smile on his handsome face. He was so unlike the withdrawn, unfriendly man Mr. Clyde and Rhonda described. His resemblance to adorable Colton in looks, personality, facial expressions and mannerisms was striking.

Sometimes, life totally sucks. Only two Matos brothers, and both of them too old for the three of us.

Ethan seemed comfortable in our company and laughed at Brit's random off-the-wall comments. He said, "Thanks for the cookies. I'll buy our future rounds of snacks." Since he hadn't eaten since breakfast either, we pieced together a late night eclectic feast based on the sweet or salty taste of whoever was pushing the buttons on the vending machines. Our motley assortment ranged from Oreos to pretzels to Hershey bars to peanut butter crackers.

Our mood was casual and relaxed as the caffeine and sugar kicked in to boost our spirits. What a day. Justin was in custody. Colton was alive and being treated. We had unlimited coffee and plenty of snacks. We had Ethan to look at for entertainment. How good was that? And since the three of us had reported to our parents we were with a friend at the hospital, we were free to sit here and gaze at Ethan the rest of the night.

Unanswered questions plagued me. Ethan's congenial mood encouraged me to fish for some answers. "If you and Eric are FBI agents, is Colton one too?"

"No way. He's a pharmacist," Eric said laughing. "I think it's safe to say Colton found a way to put adventure into what I consider a dull and dreary profession." From what I'd seen through Vikki's window, Colton's natural knack for having fun hadn't diminished by counting pills.

"One thing I don't get, Ethan, since you and Colton are in different professions, how did you both end up in the same little town in the North Carolina mountains?" Kristen asked.

"That's easy. Eric and I work as partners and were sent here to infiltrate a high stakes gambling ring operating in a four-state area. Shortly after I moved here, Colton finished his pharmacy degree. I mentioned to him how beautiful the North Carolina mountains are and the next thing I knew, he landed a job and moved here.

"I was excited for us to be together again. He'd been away at school and I get transferred all over the place so we hadn't seen much of each other for a while. I'd only be here for a matter of months but it would be fun while it lasted.

"He lived with me while he was looking for a condo, and everything was going great until he got involved with a certain upstairs neighbor. I tried my damnedest to turn him off Vikki but it didn't work. Colton knew Eric and I were working undercover, but he had no idea our assignment focused on Justin."

"How did you get buddy-buddy with Justin so quickly?"

"The FBI decided Justin was the most likely candidate to accept Eric and me as co-conspirators and get us into the gang. Justin's friendly, approachable, trusted by his fellow hoods and easily duped.

"I lucked out renting an apartment in Justin's building which made it easy to get chummy with him. I let it slip in bits and pieces that Eric and I'd been big shots in a major gambling ring in Chicago, bragged we got out of town when things started getting hot and were looking for some new action. It didn't take long before Justin introduced us to the local kingpins and Eric and I were in. We did as we were told, offered small doses of strategic advice from our previous experience as *mobsters* in Chicago and moved into trusted positions.

"Eric and I are tight-lipped when we're working. We don't make friends and we only get friendly with our suspects if the assignment dictates. Believe me, we self-monitor every word we say. The less we talk, the less likely we are to reveal some little detail that doesn't fit our cover story. We stick to sports and the weather," he said.

"One slip-up with this bunch of jokers and Eric and I would've ended up at the bottom of the French Broad River." Ethan didn't laugh when he said that. It was a chilling reality of the work he and Eric did. It took smart guys to pull off this kind of investigation. In spite of my earlier doubts about Ethan and Eric, they were living up to that first class education they got at Northwestern University.

Since we were talking openly and frankly, I asked Ethan if he knew Vikki took cash and a gun from his apartment. "Oh yeah, after I caught her snooping, I checked my stash."

"But Justin told us you didn't know she stole it," Brit interjected.

"I didn't tell him about it. He would've freaked

out. At the first of each month, Justin was entrusted with a large sum of cash. A portion of it came to Eric and me to distribute to out-of-state operatives, but the responsibility was on Justin's head not to mishandle or lose it. No way would I have told him Vikki helped herself to any of it."

"When you heard Vikki was dead," I asked, "did you think Justin did it?"

"Yeah. It's a local police investigation and I wasn't involved, but I felt sure it was Justin."

"Not only would Vikki not tell him where she'd hidden the cash from your apartment but she'd taken money from Justin's duffel bag hidden in his closet. When he wouldn't agree to share with her, she threatened to take everything to the police as evidence against you and him and the gambling ring," I said.

"Did he get the duffel bag money back?" he asked.

"Nope. He tried to talk her into returning it but she wouldn't tell him where it was. That's why he killed her. He didn't find a penny of it. Do you think you'll find it?"

Ethan shook his head. "Not unless Vikki trusted somebody who'll some forward with information, but I wouldn't count on it. We'll search the logical places, but it probably won't turn up. My guess is Vikki hid it in some unimaginable place. I didn't like her but I'm sorry about what happened to her." I understood. I felt the same way.

"Colton called me last night. He had no idea what was going on, but he figured I ought to know what the three of you've been doing. He was supposed to come by my place today and give me the details, but he didn't show up."

"Actually, he was at your building today. I saw him. Your car wasn't in the lot but Justin's pick-up was. He must've lured or forced Colton to go to the warehouse, tied him up and left him to die. He swung back by the warehouse just in case."

Ethan flinched. "Was he mad at Colton because of Vikki?"

"No. Tying Colton up in that stifling room had revenge written all over it, but more importantly, he may have been worried Colton knew too much, maybe even knew where the money was hidden."

Ethan listened thoughtfully. "Hold on a minute. Justin stopped by my apartment last night to talk about making our pay-offs today and had just gone out the door when Colton called. I have a new cellphone and accidentally hit the speaker button when I answered. Justin was bound to still be in the hallway. Before I got the speaker turned off he could've heard Colton mention Vikki, money and guns.

"Lucky for you, Amy, Colton didn't mention your name. You can bet Justin would've come to your house." I had a frightening vision of Justin trashing my beloved *Hello Kitty* hide-away and then trashing me.

A nurse came out to the waiting room. "Y'all can see Colton now," she announced, apparently assuming we were all family members.

"Hey, let's go see the patient," Ethan said, leading us toward Colton's cubicle. I thought Colton looked pretty good considering what he'd been through. He was pale and wilted, eyes closed, lips cracked but better than when we found him in the warehouse.

A doctor joined us at Colton's bedside with an

update. "I don't think the whack on the back of the head is going to give you any problems but we'll watch it. It's a good thing these young ladies got you out of that room," the doctor said. "Your body couldn't have lasted much longer."

Colton nodded at us. "I remember the drips of water and I think they gave me some pills," he said in a hoarse, barely audible voice. We barely kept from laughing and hoped he didn't remember the Midols.

"My head throbbed but they kept dragging and pulling me out of that building." With tears in his swollen eyes, he said to me and Brit and Kristen. "Thank you for saving my life."

"I can't believe you remember any of that," I said. "Why did you go to the warehouse? How did you get there?"

"Justin met me at Ethan's door and said Ethan wanted me to meet him at the warehouse office instead. The back room was stifling and I was trying to turn the AC on. Justin must've followed me and hit me while my back was to the door. It's a blank from then until you three tried to carry me out.

"It's fuzzy but I heard Justin threaten the three of you. Didn't he have a gun? When I woke up in the ER, I thought Justin shot me. I asked if he shot you girls too."

The doctor interrupted to say he was having Colton moved to a room shortly and we should leave so he could sleep. We waited with Colton until an attendant arrived to take him upstairs. "Sorry I messed up your case by hooking up with Vikki," Colton said to Ethan. "If you could've just told me."

Ethan touched Colton's shoulder gently. "Forget it. But this is the last time I tell you where my assignments are, little brother. The last thing I need is Romeo showing up and romancing himself into the middle of one of my investigations."

Colton cranked out a half-smile, the first since we found him. "You don't have to worry. I've learned to be more careful about choosing my girlfriends. But," he added seriously, "if I'd known Vikki was in danger, I would've done anything to save her."

We nodded in agreement. We all would've helped her.

The attendant came for Colton and Ethan hugged him good-night. We waited while he was wheeled into the elevator and the doors closed.

We emerged from the ER into the cool mountain night. Elated that Colton was safe and on the mend, it was one of those dancing in the street, or even in a parking lot, moments. We waited with Ethan for an FBI car that was on its way to pick him up.

Suddenly, from behind me, I heard, "Good Evening, Agent Matos. What do we have here? Sugar Liquor's intrepid crime busters." The voice of doom. Mike.

"Hello, Chief Kilpatrick," Ethan said. "I owe these girls a debt of gratitude. They discovered my brother was missing and got worried enough to track him down. When they found him tied up in a warehouse, he was nearly dead. Our agents tailed Justin to the warehouse to arrest him, but the girls had overpowered him, called 911 for police and an ambulance for my brother. Your niece was holding Justin's gun on him. They did a damn fine job." Mike scowled at us. The FBI was singing our praises.

Ethan turned to me, looking puzzled. "Question, Amy. What made you go to the warehouse looking for Colton? And how did you even know about it?"

I started with Colton mentioning the warehouse as Ethan's place of business, Colton not showing up for work, looking all over town for him and going to the warehouse as a last resort. "Kristen got the warehouse address off the internet."

"Resourceful," Ethan said. "I would never have thought to look at the warehouse for Colton even if I'd known he was missing. I was surprised when the agent tailing Justin reported he'd gone there. I pointed it out once when Justin and I were passing on the interstate, but I had no idea he'd remember it. It was a front so Eric and I looked like legit businessmen."

"Not a very good one," Brit replied. "Your merchandise boxes are empty."

"You cut me to the bone. I thought they looked authentic," Ethan said and laughed.

"Yeah, until you pick one up," Kristen came back at him.

Ethan turned to Mike. "I put a tail on Amy earlier in the day. She was so friendly with Justin, I thought she and Brit and Kristen might be involved in some shady deal with him. In fact, I thought he had them looking for the missing money." I was incensed that Ethan thought I'd be tied up with anybody's shady deal.

"What?" Mike asked. Ethan said it was a long story and they'd discuss it tomorrow.

"The less said, the better," I mumbled to Ethan. "What did you say about the FBI agent following us?

"Oh," Ethan said. "She tailed you while you were running all over Sugar Liquor. She called in and reported that you seemed to be driving around in circles so I told her to drop the tail. Of course, now I know you were looking for Colton."

Mike said, "I'm on my way to the warehouse since this involves a murder committed in Sugar Liquor. I wanted to make sure your brother was okay." That was the kindest thing I'd ever heard Mike say. Was he sucking up because Ethan was FBI?

As Mike walked away, Ethan said, "Nice fellow. That was thoughtful of him." Brit, Kristen and I looked at each other, engaging in a three-way prolonged eye rolling episode.

Ethan asked me about the missing money and guns we took, and I explained I'd retrieve them from their hiding place in Pisgah Forest in the morning. "I'd like to go with you to take possession and partly out of curiosity at where and how you hid them." We agreed to meet in front of Gene's Diner at ten.

Mike would be furious when the extent of my, Kristen's and Brit's involvement came to light. He would never admit it but things had turned out well. The FBI had broken up a big time gambling ring. I found and saved the missing pharmacist, and I figured out Justin was Vikki's killer. Justin was in custody and I was turning ten thousand dollars and two guns over to the FBI. Not a bad couple days' work for a budding news reporter.

Chapter Twenty-Two

It was early dawn when Brit, Kristen and I finally got to my house. I detoured through the kitchen and propped a note against the coffee-pot telling Mom that my friend in the hospital was doing well and that Brit, Kristen and I were catching a little sleep. Wearily, we climbed the steps to the cupola. Hildy was asleep on my bed, but she jumped up to rub around my legs and purr loudly. She and *Hello Kitty* had never looked more welcoming.

Pretty soon the whole town would know what had happened. The three of us would have a lot of explaining to do. Mike would probably stay up the rest of the night composing a list of things to bellow at us, none of them complimentary, congratulatory, nor involving awards, rewards or plaques. That didn't matter though. "I feel good about what we did," I said to my fellow sleuths.

"Me too," Brit said. "Imagine us helping the FBI."

"Hey, I got big news for y'all," I said to Brit and

Kristen. "I've been holding it for days. I thought I was going to explode but I wanted to tell y'all together. Guess who has a date with Cody Evans tomorrow night."

"Not you?" Brit asked skeptically.

"You didn't ask him for a date, did you?" Kristen asked, narrowing her disapproving eyes.

"Of course not, you idiot. He asked *me* to go to the movie." I hoped I sounded as smug as I felt. I didn't add that I wasn't sure if it was a date-date or just two friends going to a movie. I could hear their wheels turning trying to figure out how I'd pulled this off. Good luck to them. I wasn't even sure myself.

"And ladies, I have another surprise for you. This one is awesome."

Kristen said, "You can't top having a date with Cody."

"Oh, but I can," I replied. "Y'all close your eyes. This is going to take a few minutes." I made several trips back and forth to my bedroom on the second floor, carrying boxes up to the cupola. Brit and Kristen took turns complaining for me to hurry up.

"Okay, open your eyes," I told them as I unfolded the box flaps. "Surprise. Justin gave me Vikki's lights. Like for when we have a party or something."

Kristen and Brit stared at the boxes like they were twinkling sticks of dynamite. "These were Vikki's?" Kristen asked.

"Yeah. Isn't it neat I got them?"

"Amy, I swear it's dangerous for you to be left on your own. When on earth did Justin give these to you?" Brit asked.

"The day he caught me snooping in his

apartment and I told him I was cleaning up the mess from the break-in. Anyway, he offered me the lights. I started to decline but decided they'd be a fun memory of all the times Vikki entertained us. I'm glad I took them."

"Vikki was something else all right. She was her own unique mixed bag. Take her or leave her. No pretense. Justin, on the other hand, was sweetness and goodness on the surface but full of greed and evil underneath," Brit said.

I started unpacking the lights. "I say we hook up these lights right now in a farewell show for Vikki." Brit and Kristen struggled to get up from their cots and, in a few minutes, my cupola was ablaze with flashing, glittering, twinkling, revolving lights. We danced until we collapsed which didn't take long in our exhausted state. Brit unplugged the lights. I took one last, sad look at Vikki's dark apartment window.

Tired as I was, I couldn't go to sleep. I was too excited. I couldn't wait until tomorrow. After Ethan and I went to the forest and got the money and guns, I was writing my first-hand account about the gambling ring and Vikki's murder. I was going to call the *Charlotte Observer* or even the *Atlanta Journal-Constitution* and ask to submit my story, complete with a by-line, of course.

I'd show that stupid-ass *Sugar Liquor Times* that Amy Jackson was a real investigative reporter who knew how to track down a story and write it.

Maybe, on my next case, I'd be telling the story in front of a TV camera.

About the Author

Pat Meece Davis

Although she is a seventh generation native of North Carolina's Blue Ridge Mountains, Pat has spent most of her adult life in State College, Pennsylvania, except for stints living in the Netherlands and Australia.

A graduate of Western Carolina University, she attended graduate school at Penn State University, receiving Master's and Ph.D. degrees. Because of her lifelong love of words, she turned to full-time fiction writing a few years ago.

The Night the Dancing Stopped for young adults is the debut novel in *The Nosy Chicks Mysteries* series. In addition, two adult mysteries are in the editing process. *Deadly Delivery to Amsterdam,* a romantic mystery, is partially completed and is her first book to combine her love of writing with international travel. With her six children as adventurous traveling companions, they have visited many stunning locales on this beautiful planet.

Pat is an active member of the North Carolina Writers' Network (NCWN), Net-West division-NCWN, and the Writers' Guild of Western North Carolina (WGWNC).

E-mail her at patmeecedavis.author@gmail.com
Visit her at website http://patmeecedavis.com